A Most Curious Murder

A Most Curious Murder

A Little Library Mystery

Elizabeth Kane Buzzelli

CROOKED
LANE

NEW YORK

Copyright © 2015 by Elizabeth Kane Buzzelli

Published in the United States by Crooked Lane Books, an imprint of The Quick Brown Fox & Company LLC.

Crooked Lane Books and its logo are trademarks of The Quick Brown Fox & Company LLC.

Library of Congress Catalog-in-Publication data available upon request.

ISBN (hardcover): 978-1-62953-606-4
ISBN (ePub): 978-1-62953-607-1
ISBN (Kindle): 978-1-62953-666-8
ISBN (ePDF): 978-1-62953-677-4

Cover design by Matthew Kalamidas/StoneHouse Creative
Book design by Jennifer Canzone

Printed in the United States.

www.crookedlanebooks.com

Crooked Lane Books
2 Park Avenue, 10th Floor
New York, NY 10016

First Edition: July 2016

10 9 8 7 6 5 4 3 2 1

Child of the pure unclouded brow
And dreaming eyes of wonder!
Though time be fleet, and I and thou
Are half a life asunder,
Thy loving smile will surely hail
The love-gift of a fairy-tale.

Lewis Carroll
Through the Looking Glass

Chapter 1

"Oh dear," said a little voice from behind Jenny Weston, who knelt in the wet grass, in drizzling rain, early morning light making long shadows of the destruction around her.

"'Like jars of strawberry jam.' That's from *Alice in Wonderland*, you know. But everyone knows that," the voice, belonging to a little girl, said.

"Go away," Jenny mumbled. She wished the kid would leave her alone to face the ruin of her mother's Little Library by herself.

All the books her mom loved were scattered over the grass, each soaked and swollen, some covers empty, pages torn and tossed everywhere, now giving the weak rustle of dying weeds when the chilly wind blew in off Lake Michigan.

And the library box that held the books—special to so many in Bear Falls, Michigan, especially to her mother, Dora—smashed and splintered into jagged red, green, and white shards. The post it once stood on was split in two. Jenny squeezed down her feelings—all the hurt and anger and outrage.

She knew immediately when she drove in after her all-night ride that there wouldn't be any happier or sunnier days back here in Michigan than there'd been in Chicago. This wasn't a return to Eden, after all, only another war zone.

She reached out to retrieve a large, wooden splinter near one knee. Red—part of a chimney. And another piece—a green step to the screened porch. Her father had built the Little Library, an exact replica of the house they lived in. All of it gone.

"What I mean to say is," the squeaky voice came again, "'The day was wet, the rain fell souse, like jars of strawberry jam.'"

"Go home. It's too early for you to be out," Jenny said without turning. "You should be in bed. And anyway, I'm busy here."

She sniffed to emphasize the *busy* and then wrapped her arms around herself, shivering in her wrinkled shorts and yellow shirt. Although it was June, it was a damp and gloomy morning, with rolling dark clouds overhead and a fine drizzle among the pines separating the houses along Elderberry Street.

Jenny moved from one knee to the other, reaching out to touch remnants of the little house. A last gift for mom before dad was killed out on US 31, his car struck and sent into a ditch, then into a tree. Dad was left to die by the faceless, nameless driver who hit him. The Little Library had been an anniversary gift for Dora, his wife—a one-time librarian who followed her husband to this disappointing place, a Northern Michigan town without a library.

"Awful that the house is nothing but splinters," the voice talked on. "I liked it just the way it was. Looked like Dora's, with the red chimney and the dormers and all. And such fun that the roof opened the way it did and books were tucked inside like little soldiers in their cots."

Jenny squeezed her eyes tight enough to hurt. She wiped rain from her face. *Maybe,* she thought, *if I keep my eyes closed and click my heels, this smart-aleck kid will disappear.*

So many memories bubbled up. Good memories and bad memories. Her life mixing in sudden, independent scenes: running through the sprinkler under a hot July sun; barely escaping when she and her older sister, Lisa, stole kohlrabi from Adam Cane's garden; Dad calling her mom out to see the surprise he'd built for their anniversary . . .

"Come out, dear Dora, and see what your man has wrought." Jim Weston, a large and powerful man, stood at the curb so proudly six months before he died. A flourish of the cloth he'd laid over the Little Library, and then his carefully rehearsed speech: "Because Bear Falls has no library for my own beautiful librarian, never had a library, will never have a library, and you, dear Dora, are a reader to be reckoned with . . ."

Dad was the perfect traveling salesman—in death too: he was found by a passing motorist, dead behind the wheel.

Terrible what someone had done to the Little Library. And even worse, now Jenny had to go into the house and break the awful news to her mom, and on her first morning home.

"If you ask me . . ." the voice went on.

"Listen, kid, go away, okay? It's barely daylight. You should be in bed."

She turned to find not a child but a Little Person standing behind her, a very small woman in tiny, green-smudged sneakers; her faded jeans rolled so a bit of flesh showed above her ankles. The sturdy body was wrapped in a child's plastic raincoat, the flowered hood tied tight around a small, pretty face—eye-level with a kneeling Jenny—topped by tendrils of wildly curly blonde hair.

"Well, I'm certainly not a kid." The indignant woman shot her pale eyebrows high. "Thirty-three years old. Don't look it, do I? Not a day over twelve, I'll bet you'd say."

"Maybe ten," Jenny growled, not in the mood to play games.

"Hmm. Don't worry your head over hurting *my* feelings." Her round, blue eyes narrowed with sarcasm.

"Sorry." Jenny wiped her wet hands along the sides of her shorts. "You're not what I expected."

"That's okay. You're not what I expected either. You don't look like your mother at all. Much taller than I imagined."

"I'm on my knees. How can you tell how tall I am?"

"One learns to gauge a person's height. Your body's long. Your legs are long. Put them together and you get a tall person. Maybe a gigantic person." The woman rubbed her hands, gave them a shake, and nodded to emphasize the rightness of her equation.

Jenny wiped her eyes while checking out the odd creature standing behind her with legs apart and fists wedged at her waist.

"You *are* Jenny, Dora's Chicago daughter, aren't you?"

Jenny nodded.

"Your mom told me you were coming. I was glad to hear it. Your sister, Lisa, has been here before, but never you." She raised her eyebrows as if in judgment.

Jenny bristled but said nothing.

"Well, anyway, I haven't said a word to Dora, but I've had this terrible feeling." She leaned in closer, finger at her nose. "Something's coming. Something's certainly coming. It's been in the air."

Her hand circled the ruin in front of her. "I never imagined this."

The woman shrugged after a strained minute and stuck a soft hand out for Jenny to shake. "Welcome home. Sorry it's to this mess. I'm Zoe Zola. Next-door neighbor." She pointed toward the house to the south. "Been here a year. Your mom and I are good friends."

"Did Mrs. Ford move?" Jenny wracked her brain. Five years since she'd been home. A lot could have happened in that time.

"Died. Poor Granny." The little woman drooped with sadness.

"Sorry about your grandmother, but I've never seen you before either."

"Would've remembered, eh? 'Smaller than a tadpole.' No. 'Smaller than a minute.' Heard that one a lot. How about 'Smaller than a bumblebee'? You ever hear of a pygmy shrew? One man told me I was smaller than that." Zoe's eyes weren't laughing.

Jenny wondered how to escape from this odd person. Could be a mad killer. Maybe a religious nut. Jenny entertained herself with wild possibilities.

Zoe Zola talked on. "Granny left me the house, though I barely knew her. My mother's side of the family. They didn't like me much. Surprised me when I got the news. But it was welcome. You can just imagine. A home of my own. In a little town. Quiet enough to think for long stretches of time. Quiet enough to take my mind off . . ." She glanced the short distance down to the ground. "Well, enough to take my mind off other things, survival being one of them. I write books, you see, and writers always expect to exist in someone else's garret. Not our own garret, you understand, because we're never rich enough to own one." She puzzled, with a finger at her chin. "What's the name of the bird that crawls into other people's nests?"

She ruminated a while. "Cuckoo!" she squawked, giving Jenny a satisfied smile.

"Why are you out so early? It's raining."

"Really?" She put her hand out. "It's my dog. She's old and has to pee a lot."

As if she'd been waiting for an introduction, a shiny black nose lost in dirty white fur nudged out from behind Zoe Zola's legs. The nose belonged to a small, shaggy dog with drooping ears and a quiver running from her nose to the end of her tail. The only bit of color on the little thing, other than mud, was a red collar peeking out around her neck. The dog snuffled back and forth, nose to ground, then looked up at Jenny, who stared down into an opal of an eye—a half-blind little dog. The other eye was happy to see her, deep brown and wet. The dog gave the smallest of necessary yips.

"Her name is Fida. She doesn't mean you any harm," Zoe said. "She's just upset at this awful mess. And it wasn't Fida who made the comment about the strawberry jam, which, if I may say so, was apropos at the moment."

Jenny took a deep breath. *Oz. No. One of the Lollipop Guild. And Toto, too.*

The little dog gave another sharp yip. Zoe cautioned, "Quiet." Then her face lighted with playfulness. "Fida is a feminist because we agreed to it being so. Her name would have been Fido if she'd been born of the other persuasion. Instead, she calls herself Fida." The dog, happy now, wiggled forward until her head lay on Jenny's knees, her one good eye turned up in adoration.

"None of this is what it seems to be, you know."

Jenny muttered, "You can say that again."

"And not what you're thinking at all." Zoe grabbed Fida by the collar, pulling her away from nuzzling Jenny to death.

"And it's not about strawberry jam," Jenny came back.

"Oh, that." Zoe flipped a hand to blow away the thought. "I write books about fairy tales and magic people. *The* Wizard of Oz *as Dream* came out a couple of years ago and is still doing very well with certain factions of people. You know, those who think all day and truly worry if Dorothy dreamed all of that nonsense or if Oz really exists. I'm of the latter ilk. But then, I have first-hand information.

"Currently I'm working on *Lewis Carroll and the Two Alices: A Study in Madness and Murder.* 'Off with her head.' 'We're all mad here. I'm mad. You're mad.' The Hatter, well, of course he's mad. And the dormouse into the teapot. An amazing human being, Mr. Carroll. Or Charles Dodgson, as he thought he was called. In his personal notes alone, there must be at least a dozen or two ideas to fit each and every happenstance of life."

"Including broken libraries?" Jenny felt annoyance settling in.

Zoe was about to answer when her body froze. Her hand shot into the air.

"What?"

"I smell it coming!" Zoe said and then slowly lowered her hand.

"I think I'd better go inside . . ." Jenny started to get up, gauging—if she ran very fast—how long it would take to get up to the house.

Zoe shook her head. "I don't mean to spook you."

"You are."

"It's just . . ." She put a pudgy finger to her lips. "I can smell things. An amazing nose, though sometimes awkward to deal with. I smell when storms are born. I smell the least bit of tumult in the air."

"Really? And what do you smell now?" Jenny stood and brushed wet grass from her hands and knees.

Zoe looked left and then right from the corners of her eyes. "I don't know," she whispered.

"There's nothing . . ."

Zoe frowned and nodded hard.

"Yes, there is, Jenny Weston. There's something coming at us. If you ask me, I'd have to say maybe you should turn around and go right back to Chicago."

Chapter 2

Jenny put fingers to her forehead, rubbing hard to make the fog in her brain go away. She was exhausted, and none of this was what she expected—coming home. She'd expected Mom, welcoming and smiling as she had been before Jim Weston died. Mom with her arms out. And that soft place on her shoulder where Jenny's face could nuzzle.

She'd come home to forget Chicago and the divorce her now ex-husband Ronald Korman had forced on her, to forget she had no job since she had worked in Ronald's law office, which was no more. She had no apartment, no friends, since they'd all been *their* friends and were too nervous around her or embarrassed for her since Ronald ran off with Suzy or Wendy or whatever the client's name was—off to Guatemala but, super courteous as Ronald was, not without one last call to wish her a "good life."

The weird little person beside her now said, "Humph," making Fida growl. "I'll bet you're thinking it had to be a car that jumped the curb and took out the library, right?"

"Please . . ."

"Do you see any tire marks in the grass? Do you see where the pole is broken? A car would have knocked it over, but much

8

lower down. See those long slits in what's left? Well, *I* see them fine from my vantage point. There are advantages, you know, Miss . . . eh . . . Jenny, to my . . . situation. Those are axe slits. Bet you anything." She nodded hard, spraying Jenny with raindrops from her hood. "And just look at the books. Thrown all over the place. Flattened like a herd of dead possums. Wouldn't have been lying around like that if a car hit the post. They would've fallen closer. Some would've been left inside the little house. And can you imagine *all* the books being shredded to smithereens by a slipping and sliding car?"

"I'm going in the house now . . ."

Zoe ignored her. "And see how someone stomped a few?" She pointed to the clear print of a shoe on the back of *The Adventures of Tom Sawyer*. "Look at the pages. Torn out. Thrown about. The rain got 'em or they'd be blowing to the four winds. Or even one wind, which we have today—out of the west. I like a west wind personally because it comes from where the sun goes down and means a time of rest."

She stopped to look around. "I don't see the sign-out sheets." She frowned at Jenny, then pointed to a soggy mess of papers in the street. "Oh dear, there they are. Soaked. The names will be gone. Wiped away. I don't, personally, like to see names wiped away like that—as if they'd never been. It makes me sad."

"Sign-out sheets for the books?"

Zoe nodded. "People take a book, leave a book, and sometimes leave a date they'll bring the book back."

Jenny listened.

"Some leave requests for a certain book, and your mother calls around until she finds it. That's what I mean—the sign-out sheets. Too bad. Lost to the world forever. Something to think about."

"I don't understand what you're getting at." Jenny meant it with all her heart.

"Sorry. It takes a little magic to figure out the world." Zoe flipped a hand at her. "You don't seem to have any in you. Too bad. A thing to fix while you're here."

"You make no sense."

"I know, but Mr. Carroll taught me to keep talking—words and words and words—until the words sort themselves out and everything is clear, or becomes completely unclear and it doesn't matter anymore. I hope that doesn't bother you."

Jenny shook her head. Bothered or not, she was far behind this Zoe Zola, with her hands twitching, mind flitting, eyes blinking. Far behind this little Sherlock Holmes who smelled trouble coming at her.

"Take that," the woman said.

Jenny followed a stubby finger pointing toward crumpled and twisted book pages. "I see manic glee here. I see retribution. I see—well, what else could there be? Maybe a teenager who hates school and books and anything that reminds her of learning. Or a man who flunked out of college because of a terrible paper on Coleridge. You know, of course, that Charlotte Brontë thought Coleridge an exceedingly ugly man. Anyway, to me, this looks very much as if somebody wanted to get even for a thing no one else remembers."

Curiouser and curiouser, Jenny couldn't help but think. She wished her sister, Lisa the Good, wasn't filming a documentary in Montana and had come home, too—a grand family reunion to discuss Jenny's recent divorce and make plans for her amazing future.

And by the way, Lisa, would you please deal with this odd little lady who lives next door to us?

"I know what you're thinking." The round, blue eyes opened very wide again. "And I am not a crazy person. I smell things. I know things. Personally, I think I have a rare gift."

"I wasn't thinking crazy."

"Yes you were, but I'm not crazy at all. I am unique, you might say. I am . . . well . . . different from others, but then that's what I've always been, and, if *I* may say so, if you come into the world a certain way, you might as well take advantage of it and surprise people." She narrowed her eyes and studied Jenny.

"Like you, I imagine. Home because you're freshly divorced. Or did I make that up? Home because you don't know what to do with your life. Home because you've had no training in disappointment. Though I did hear you were badly dumped before you left Bear Falls."

"Really?" Jenny was beyond being mad.

"That's why we'll be friends."

Friends? Jenny didn't even like her. Nosy. Obnoxious. She opened her mouth to tell her to mind her own business, then snapped it shut. "I don't think . . ."

"I can teach you how to take *alone* and turn it into exactly what you want it to be," Zoe went on.

And there it was—the all of it laid out like salami on a plate. *Alone* because she wasn't lovable. *Alone* because only her mother would want her. *Alone* because the divorce was new and painful. *Alone* because she didn't have a job. *Alone* because she had no friends.

But there was nothing new about dealing with rejection. She was a pro at that. Right back to Bear Falls, where she got her first lesson in disappointment.

"I'll tell Dora with you." The offer was sincere, punctuated by a small bark from Fida.

On the march to the screened porch, Fida, in a hurry to keep up, ran between and around Jenny's legs while Zoe turned again and again to chastise her.

Certainly down the rabbit hole, Jenny thought as she clumped up the steps. When she saw her mother, hair in paper curlers, clutching a robe around her, and bending to peer through the screen, her stomach dropped to basement level. As Jenny pulled the door open, Dora Weston stretched her neck to look beyond her visitors, out to where her Little Library used to stand. She choked back a strangled, "Oh dear!" but opened her arms to Jenny.

Chapter 3

It was a sad tea party, three women around the kitchen table, Fida at their feet, and Ed Warner, chief of police of Bear Falls, sitting uncomfortably on a rush-bottom chair off to one side. Everyone had a flowered cup of steaming tea in front of them. Ed Warner's cup sat next to a piece of apple pie, untouched as he filled out his incident report.

"How you doin'? Didn't know you were back in town," was the first thing he'd said to Jenny. "Thought you'd gone off to make good in the big world. Doesn't always turn out, does it?"

Same humorless, dour boy Jenny remembered from high school. Even then he'd had the personality of a disgruntled beaver.

"You know we've got our eighteenth high school reunion coming up? Case you're interested. Me and the wife are going."

Jenny scowled at the thought of a high school reunion; she'd rather be embalmed than attend.

"I'll keep it in mind." Jenny smiled at the man. "Right now, I'm really worried about that disaster out front. My mom's upset, I can tell you."

Dora Weston nodded and took a sip of her tea. She pulled her light-blue robe, with satin tie at the neck, around her, then patted self-consciously at the toilet paper curlers in her hair.

"Bet she is. Terrible accident."

Zoe made a noise.

"Hit-and-run," he said, and then he remembered the words weren't the best to use around Dora. He'd been too young to be a cop when Jim Weston was killed, but there wasn't a soul in town that didn't remember the day. "Probably a car slid off the street in the rain."

Zoe snorted and rolled her eyes at Jenny, who ignored her, thinking hard about mosquitoes and gnats and other little pests.

"You know Zoe Zola? Mom's neighbor."

Jenny remembered Ed as the kid with ears big enough to lift him off the ground and a long body skinny enough to slip through a keyhole. The kids called him Bobblehead because he couldn't keep his head straight on his shoulders. The thought made Jenny smile until she remembered they had called her Morticia because of her long, black hair and pale skin that no amount of sun could darken.

Ed tipped his head, wobbling just a little. "Good to see you, Ms. Zola."

"I've got some ideas about what really happened here, Chief." Zoe sat up as tall as she could get, mustering authority. "Solid ideas. Good ideas. Ideas to bring an end to such tomfoolery once and for all."

"Really?" Ed chuckled, giving her a bemused look. "Well, we'll just have to hear your ideas, won't we?"

"Malicious destruction of property," Zoe muttered at the chief. "That's the first of it. But not the worst of it."

He gave her a dubious look. "Terrible thing. As I said, probably a car, sliding off the road."

Zoe sighed. "And how could anyone do that and leave no tire tracks behind?"

He tipped his head and half closed his dark eyes. For a while, he only thought. When he'd decided something, he said to Zoe, "Seem to know a lot about a lot of things, Ms. Zola."

"I have some ideas that will help. And some that will hinder. I'd like to share them all with you, Chief."

"Let me get the facts down first, if you don't mind. Need to have a little talk with Mrs. Weston here."

"Did you rope the area off so gawkers won't spoil the crime scene?" Zoe charged ahead. "There are book thieves and book burners and book runner-overs everywhere in the world, you know."

Ed took a deep breath and shook his head. "Not what you'd call a major crime scene, Ms. Zola."

Zoe's eyebrows rose. "On the contrary, you realize that the people of Bear Falls have been attacked? Their books stolen from them."

Ed eyed her, then turned back to Jenny. "Your mom get any threats? Got any enemies?"

Jenny opened her mouth to answer but was interrupted.

"I'm sitting right here, Ed Warner. And I have a brain," an indignant Dora piped up, her back straightening, her curlers jiggling. "If you have questions, please address me directly." She licked her lips and pushed her chin higher. "I may be getting old, but years haven't made me stupid, nor dead, for that matter. And no, nobody's threatened me."

The chief looked apologetic. "Sorry, Mrs. Weston—I hate to bother you with some of this."

"Talking about it won't hurt me any more than looking at my murdered books."

Zoe jigged her head from side to side. "We've got malicious destruction of property going on. We've got ruination of a dream, a greater offense. We've got tampering with great minds. We can't let him get away with it."

"Who?" Ed Warner demanded.

"I don't like to name names, but since you're demanding the way you are—"

"I haven't demanded a thing, ma'am."

Zoe's small face clamped shut. She folded her arms across her chest and stared at him.

"This is totally impossible." Jenny threw her hands up.

"So what?" Zoe turned to her. "'Sometimes I've believed as many as six impossible things before breakfast.'"

"Stop it! Don't quote quotes at us! If you know who destroyed Mom's library, tell us." Jenny was ready to shake the little woman.

Zoe squinted at her—one eye half open, the other closed. "All right then. It was Adam Cane."

"Adam Cane? The old man who lives on the other side of you? The Adam Cane of the Cane family in that mansion over on Oak? I've known him since I was a kid."

"That's the one."

"Oh, Zoe." Dora shook her head. "Maybe Adam's a little cranky, but he's not a hooligan."

"Then why'd he threaten to kill Fida, I'd like to know?" Zoe folded her arms across her chest and stared at them—one by one.

"Your dog?" Jenny asked.

"You know her name well enough."

"He did that?"

"For peeing on his front lawn, which, if you ask me, is nothing but a field of weeds anyway. And—also if you ask me, but I don't suppose you will—a little dog pee is the best thing to ever grace those soulless sods of his."

"But Fida's not my mother's responsibility." Jenny couldn't help herself. "Why didn't he knock over some of those little statues in your front yard if he wanted to get even with you?"

The chief sat back and let the two go at it.

"So you've noticed my gardens." Zoe looked pleased.

"Just getting out of my car this morning. Couldn't help but notice. Come on! Lighted houses!"

"Of course. I have a fairy garden par excellence, if you ask me, and you haven't. You must come see what I've done, and in the back of the house, too. I'll walk you around one day, explain the little houses and introduce you to the fairies who live in them."

She clapped her hands, then thought hard, setting her chin on one small fist. "Now what were we saying?"

"If you don't mind . . ." The chief held a pencil over his notebook.

"Oh, yes," Zoe said. "Did you think Fida's the only thing Adam Cane objects to? When I first moved here, he came to my front door. I thought he was the welcome wagon, but all he wanted was my signature on a petition calling for your mother to take down her library. He said it brought too many cars along our street. Twenty books are all she had in there at any one time. As if so few books would cause a traffic jam. The petition said zoning rules dictated there are to be no unattached buildings in Bear Falls. I asked him what about my shed, and he changed the subject, since he has an old shed as big as mine in his backyard. Adam Cane doesn't like people to be happy. Seems to swipe against his grain."

"There are good reasons, Zoe," Dora said. "Adam's family did terrible things to him."

Chief Warner broke in. "It wasn't you, by any chance, Ms. Zoe? I mean, you didn't destroy the Little Library 'cause you're mad at Mr. Cane? I hear you were on the spot this morning."

Zoe's eyebrows shot up. "I think I better nip things right here in the bud—a garden metaphor, if you get my drift."

Jenny let her exasperation fly. "We not only don't get your drift, we don't understand a thing you say."

"You know what that means?"

Jenny didn't bother answering.

"It means you're not a deep thinker. I do so hope we can fix that while you're here."

Ed snapped his notebook shut and stood. He looked oddly pleased to be on his way.

"I hope you talk to Mr. Cane." Zoe spoke to the man's belt buckle.

Ed smiled a fatherly smile. He might have patted Zoe on the head—which Jenny was certain he'd live to regret.

"You want me to talk to Adam, Mrs. Weston?" he asked.

"I don't know, Ed." Dora turned to Jenny. "You decide, Jen. I don't want trouble."

Jenny hesitated. "Of course, go talk to Adam Cane. Mention that the library and the books have to be replaced. We can get him an estimate of what it will cost."

"How can my book box ever be replaced?" Dora hugged herself. "Jim was so careful to copy our house exactly. Anything else will be too sad to look at."

Ed set one foot on the creaky dining room floor, heading out toward the front of the house. "I'll talk to Adam. I know how to handle him. Oh, and we'll be taking pictures, looking around to see what else we can find. I'm taking some of that wood from the library box and a couple of your books. One's got a footprint on it. Muddy. Won't get much in fingerprints, though, I imagine, not with the rain. You can clean up after we're gone."

The last was for Jenny, who thanked him and smiled, happy to see him go.

Halfway across the living room, Ed turned to assure Dora he'd be working hard on this and that he'd be in touch, soon as he found out anything.

"Hope you build it right back up, Mrs. Weston." He called over his shoulder, "People in town will miss that Little Library of yours."

Dora shook her head at the man and fought tears.

Zoe, following close behind, stopped him before he reached the door. "Chief, maybe you want to talk to the other neighbors. Somebody might've seen something, or at least heard the sound of chopping in the middle of the night."

He turned less-than-friendly eyes down at her. "I know how to do my job, ma'am. Hope you'll let me get to it."

He was gone, the stomp out to the porch a little harder than when he'd come in.

Zoe sighed, coming back into the kitchen. "Oh my. 'It's exactly like a riddle with no answer.' Poor man," she said, half to herself. "He doesn't like me at all. I don't understand. I tried to be so helpful."

She put fingers to her nose. "Oh dear. I wish people would listen."

Instead of hooting as Jenny wanted to, she said, "You know what, Zoe? Sometimes you don't make any sense at all."

"Maybe not to you, Jenny Weston. As I said before, no magic."

Chapter 4

"Anything left?" Dora cleared her throat and took up a paper napkin to swipe hard at her nose once Ed Warner was gone. "Any of the books survive?"

"*War and Peace*," Jenny said. "It got buried under *Fifty Shades of Grey.*"

"Ah, at last, a use for that particular book."

"I thought you didn't allow porn," Jenny teased.

Dora colored up. "Ladies asked for it. Curious, you know."

"Did you read the book?" Zoe asked.

"Well, I had to, didn't I?"

Dora tipped her head and stuck out her bottom lip, daring either of them to smile.

"I'm taking this one home." Zoe held up the copy of *The Complete Poems of Emily Dickinson* she'd put on the chair, tucked under her. "I'll dry her out."

"I think *A Full and Complete History of Bear Falls, Michigan* looked kind of okay." Jenny searched her brain for something more to offer.

"Wouldn't you know it?" Dora snorted and threw up her hands. "Priscilla Manus, president of the Bear Falls Historical

Society, wrote it. She's over here every week checking to make sure somebody takes out her book. She'll probably donate another one, or two, or three, even if we don't need them. She's been bedeviling Zoe ever since she moved here to help with a reissue of the book. Probably be after you, too. If you stay long. And I hope you will."

Dora drew a cautious breath. "I don't suppose my mother's *Hans Christian Andersen's Fairy Tales* made it? It was out there yesterday morning. So it's probably gone."

Jenny looked to Zoe for support, then shook her head. She didn't tell her it was one of the worst off of the books, every page ripped out, only the stained board covers left.

"How your grandmother loved those stories. I read them to you when you were little, remember? You and Lisa? You hated the stag beetle for betraying Thumbelina. And how Lisa loved the old field mouse. I'd hoped to pass that book down to a grandchild." She sighed. "If one of you girls ever felt like having a baby, that is."

She shook her head vigorously. "All my fault. I shouldn't have given that book to anyone. Millie Sheraton's girl came to the door and asked if I had a fairy tale book and I couldn't bear to say no. After that, I put the book in the box just in case another child needed a dose of fairy tales."

"Nobody's fault, Mom. Unless you count the person who took an axe to the box."

"Oh, yes it is. Look what I've done. Think of my poor future grandchildren. Oh my."

Jenny smiled and didn't think of her poor babies since there weren't going to be any.

Dora put a hand up to finger her toilet paper curlers. "And the others . . . Oh dear, let me think. People have been so generous, leaving their books in my care, and look what's happened! No one will ever trust me again!"

Dora wiped at her eyes. "Ed said a hit-and-run, didn't he? I saw him backpedal, but that's what he said. Just the way Jim died. Terrible to think about. Like having a curse on us. Oh dear, oh dear. If Jim knew about this, he'd be so disappointed."

Jenny took her mother's hand in hers. It was a nervous, flighty hand that couldn't stay still until the teakettle whistled. Dora made a move to get up to make a fresh pot of tea, but Jenny stopped her.

"I'll get it," Jenny said, hoping to show she could take over a lot of things now that she was home. Maybe she could even find a way back to who she once was in this house, where she didn't seem to fit now and where a tiny neighbor was more at home than she.

Sipping her fresh tea, Dora leaned back and sighed. With the morning light behind her, Jenny couldn't help but think what a pretty woman her mom still was at sixty-three. Lisa looked a lot like her, but on Mom the blonde was going to gray. The bright-blue eyes were fading, wrinkling only enough to make her interesting. Dora was aging, but in a kind way. Her half smile was still enchanting. A sturdy-bodied woman, not fat, not thin. *Motherly*, Jenny thought, and laughed at herself. That word had so many meanings. Not endearing when Jenny was a teenager and Dora had put her foot down about slipping grades. Not endearing when the principal called, reporting that Jenny was in another fight. But charming again, yes—Jenny had to smile. She thought of how Dora had bit her lip and said nothing all through Jenny's pretentious wedding to Ronald Korman.

Warm and kind and welcoming when Jenny needed her now.

"I hope Adam didn't do it, Zoe. Truly," Dora said. "Man's had so much of his own trouble, seems he'd think twice before making trouble for somebody else. That father, Joshua Cane.

Awful man. Jim and I heard about him from the first moment we moved to Bear Falls."

She shook her head. "We saw him from time to time. Never spoke to him. People warned us not to. A big man. He had one of those plastered-down comb-overs, looked like a small plowed field on his head. And what a strut! That strut alone, fancy cane swinging beside him, was enough to keep people out of his way. I don't think he forgot, not even for a second, that he was worth millions. From what I heard, he left all of it to Abigail. Nothing to the boys."

Dora was unhappy. "I don't really like talking about the dead. They can't defend themselves—but dead or alive, Joshua Cane was a terrible person."

Dora looked as if she was trapped someplace in her memory. "And what a funeral. That was in 2006."

She put her teacup to her lips and held it there. "Big affair. Lots of dignitaries came to town. I think the governor was here. The police chief we had then called in other police from Traverse City to help with crowd control. He's got a big monument in the cemetery in Acme—too important for Bear Falls, you understand. You know how rich people get lauded, at least until the grave is closed."

"Poor Adam Cane," Zoe sighed. "Just another 'wasp in a wig,' in my opinion."

"Geez, Zoe." Jenny gritted her teeth. "Not now."

"Well, it's true. *Alice Through the Looking Glass*. You won't remember because the illustrator took the wasp right out of the book. Poor man didn't know how to draw a wasp in a wig. The manuscript was only recently found so, of course, I'm featuring it in my new book. The story went that the poor wasp was bedeviled into shaving the beautiful ringlets from his head and wearing an awful yellow wig. Now that's just the way Adam and Aaron listened to their friends and became hippies, is what I heard."

"I'm not sure that's the way it went." Dora looked disturbed. "They looked down on money. Scourge of the earth to them. That's what hippies thought." Zoe lifted her chin higher to better see their faces. "But then the wasp's friends didn't like him anymore. He couldn't grow back his ringlets and had to wear the yellow wig, which cost him everything and left him a disgruntled old 'wasp in a wig.' Just like Adam Cane."

"I don't quite see what you mean." Dora looked puzzled.

"Oh, Mom. Why bother to . . ." Jenny groaned. "This is the one who smells trouble coming. Literally."

Zoe looked off, ignoring Jenny. "You see, when the brothers could've used the money to take them into their old age, they didn't have it. Lost it all because of what they'd become. They followed their friends. Isn't that right, Dora?"

Dora nodded slowly.

"Anyway, with no money, they were forced to work at menial jobs around town. That's what I heard. People didn't respect them. All those hippie friends were gone."

Dora turned abruptly to Zoe. "I see what you're saying now, about 'The Wasp in the Wig.'"

Zoe nodded gravely and intoned,

So now that I am old and grey,
And all my hair is nearly gone,
They take my wig from me and say
"How can you put such rubbish on?"

And still, whenever I appear,
They hoot at me and call me "Pig!"
And that is why they do it, dear,
Because I wear a yellow wig.

"You're a piece of work, Zoe." Jenny was so flummoxed by the woman at this point, she didn't know up from down.

This certainly wasn't the homecoming she'd expected. Certainly not this Zoe Zola, puffed up and drinking her tea with a tiny pinky stuck up in the air. A woman who sniffed the air and made predictions. Nor a sleeping one-eyed dog under the chair, snorting from time to time and pedaling her paws as fast as she could go.

If the Hatter leaped through the window yelling, "Clean cup," she would simply get up and move.

Chapter 5

Jenny bent to pick up a slippery book and stuff it into the black garbage bag she dragged behind her. Zoe and Fida started at the street and came up the lawn, working toward her, dragging their own garbage bag.

When they met in the middle, Zoe hummed, "Taps," then drew the blue strings on her bag, closing in the books and pages along with grass and twigs and an old newspaper or two from the street.

"Ready for cremation," she announced and kicked the bag from one side to the other. "I'll stick them in the burning barrel, out behind my garden shed, unless you want to do it."

"No, no." Jenny's blood ran cold. "We can't burn them!"

She was her mother's daughter, after all.

"What then? Burial at sea?" Zoe asked.

"I'll dig a hole. We'll have a proper burial for all those fine minds." Jenny fell into the mood.

"Dead minds. Living minds. Words, words, words. Sentences. Ideas. Wisdom. Unhappy birds—all of them—never to fly the same way again." Zoe gestured toward the place where wisdom went.

"We'll get new copies. Nothing's really lost," Jenny said.

The ground at the back of Dora's yard was soft and easy to dig. Before long, the hole was deep. The loose pages didn't look like much thrown down to the bottom of the pit, on top of the dozen or more books. It took only a little while to shovel dirt in over all of it and then pat it down. With the job done, Zoe suggested the proper flowers to plant over dead books.

"Bleeding heart. Maybe that one for the Victorians in the bunch. For *Tess of the d'Urbervilles*," she said.

"Why can't we keep it simple? I'll plant a rosebush."

Zoe's look could have frozen the devil's tail.

She went on. "Gas plants. For long-winded writers. Henry James comes to mind."

"Hmmm," Jenny thought hard. "Loosestrife for all those shades of grey."

"Or passion flower," Zoe said. "I didn't read the book, but I think that one would work well."

"Snapdragon for Gertrude Stein."

"That's mean," said Zoe.

"As if you aren't."

By the time they got back to the house, they were almost friends.

* * *

Dora, who'd declined to take part in the burial, waited, rocking fast on the porch.

"I think I'd like an annex," she said as they fell into rockers beside her.

"An annex to what?"

"To the library, of course."

"What kind of annex?"

"For children's books. Another whole house, but like the first one Jim built."

"So you've changed your mind?"

"I think I have."

"I've got the perfect carpenter for you." Zoe clapped her hands. "Tony Ralenti. He used to be a detective in Detroit, but he was shot in the knee and decided to look for a quieter place to live. He lowered the cupboards in my house. Cut off some furniture legs—like on my bed—so I don't have to take a flying leap to get in. Built me folding stools that make me taller than anyone I know. Bet you anything he can make that library house look just the way it used to look."

"Two houses," Dora insisted. "Identical. One for children's books."

"Children won't know which is theirs," Jenny complained. "You'll confuse them."

Dora *tsk*ed at her. "We'll attach flags. One will say 'Big People' and one will say 'Little People.'"

Zoe took exception to that, and all talk of rebuilding stopped.

* * *

There wasn't much to do the rest of the day. Jenny knew she should drive over to the grocery store; Mom's refrigerator was empty. But she didn't feel like going anywhere. There would be too many people at Draper's Superette. They'd all want to know about her life, brag about their kids, and probably comment on Mom's library—aflutter with sympathy and offers of help.

She knew Bear Falls people. Along with the bad ones who had driven her from town to begin with, there were plenty of good people. It wasn't that she didn't want to see them; it was just that she was tired and needed time to come to terms with at least one or two of the things that had happened to her before and after coming home.

Zoe went back to her house to write the next chapter of *Lewis Carroll and the Two Alices*. Jenny found cheese and ham slices for sandwiches. She toasted the bread and put a round of pineapple from a can on each plate. *Best I can do*, she told herself, thinking pineapple always went with ham and made for a festive touch.

She made a list of things they needed from Draper's and then set it aside.

After lunch, Dora remembered the toilet paper curlers in her hair. Jenny took them out and combed the soft blonde-and-white-streaked hair so it curled softly around Dora's ears. Looking in the mirror, Dora smiled. "Funny. I look like my mother. Only older than I remember her. I like that. Too bad you don't look a thing like me. You are all your father." She reached out to run her hand softly over Jenny's long, dark hair. "You've got his nose—so strong. And his body—agile, lean. And his hazel eyes—sometimes I see him in there with you."

"Dad always said I looked like the mailman."

Dora dismissed her nonsense with a wave of her hand and suggested they do a picture puzzle together. She brought out a box with the Leaning Tower of Pisa on the front. They sat down to worry pieces of the puzzle into place and argue over pieces that didn't seem to belong anywhere. Jenny, getting bored, finally made pieces fit whether they belonged or not and put the puzzle away.

Dora yawned. "I'm a little tired," she apologized as she got up and walked toward her bedroom.

Jenny followed down the hall to cover her with a light blanket and open a window in the stuffy room because the rain had stopped, the day was warming, and the lake air smelled like freshly turned earth. Dora thanked her and said she didn't like being closed in.

"Winter's too long up here." Dora yawned and drew the blanket to her chin. "Can't have a window open then."

Jenny shut the door softly behind her and went to the back-yard to sit under the black walnut tree and read. Early summer bees swarmed and buzzed around her head, chasing her back into the house where she settled into a white wicker chair on the porch. She listened to car motors and children's voices along Elderberry Street. Every once in a while, a teenager would drive by with his radio on full blast. "Va Va Voom" got stuck in her head. She gave up trying to read and closed her eyes to soak it all in—all of home.

Two days ago she'd been in a Chicago courtroom, preparing to see Ronald Korman again after eight months.

She'd tailored the scene in her head to fit her depression: Ronald, in an ill-fitting summer jacket, would be sitting in the front row when she walked in . . . No, when she *strutted* in, look-ing beautiful, of course. Her long, black hair would glisten and flow. Her pouting lips would be wet and lustrous. A gauzy dress would swirl about her stunning body. She would nod left and right and raise a hand in a Queen Elizabeth wave.

And Ronald, on seeing her, would fall to his knees, beg her to come back to him, and swear he'd given up Tiffany or Chas-tity or whatever that client's name was. His arms would lock around her. His tears would flow until there were two wet paths running down his cheap summer jacket. But she . . . oh she, cool and vengeful, she would brush him aside, stride to the judge's bench, grab the divorce papers, and wave them in Ronald's face.

Ronald didn't show up in court. His attorney said he was out of the country but was amenable to the settlement they'd worked out ahead of time.

Jenny decided she wasn't going to be "amenable" to anything. The bored attorneys, standing in a little clique on one side of the judge's bench, shot their eyebrows high as she stood to say she'd like twenty dollars more a month in alimony.

Twenty dollars! She could hear them scoffing and muttering as she stuck to her guns and his attorney went out to call Ronald, wherever he'd finally settled, to get the okay. And then the man returned to the bench to say sarcastically, loud enough for everyone to hear, "Mr. Korman said he was fine with the twenty dollars more a month and wants to know if Mrs. Korman would also like the, I quote, 'crummy can of cleanser from under the sink.'"

The judge shut him up and it was over. A monthly dollar amount settled on the last eight years of her life. No place to go—the lease on their apartment was up. That was when Lisa called to see how she was doing and suggested she go home awhile. She was worried about Dora, she said. Mom seemed tired when she called.

If Lisa had asked a few more questions, she would have learned that Jenny didn't have anywhere else to go anyway—not at the moment—and home to Bear Falls was as good a place as any.

Jenny fell asleep until the door to the house creaked open and Mom joined her on the porch. They talked about supper—and what was in the house, which turned out to be eggs and bread. Jenny knew she could at least cook eggs and did, though the scrambled eggs were dry and the toast a little beyond brown.

After supper they shared a couple of hours of television in the living room and then Dora was tired again. She yawned through the evening news and was getting up from her recliner when there was a pounding at the front door.

"Who could that be at this hour?" Dora turned startled eyes to Jenny. "Somebody must be in trouble. You'd better answer."

Jenny, after living in Chicago for so many years, wasn't in a big hurry to answer loud noises at the front door. She looked through the glass at the man staring back at her: long and wild gray hair held back by a blue headband, an ugly, angry face twisting as the old man yelled.

Dora, behind her, said, "For heaven's sakes, that's Adam Cane. He hasn't talked to me in—Why, open the door, Jenny."

She did, reluctantly.

His first words were a snarl. "Who do you people think you are?" He leaned in the open doorway, chicken neck sticking out of a faded undershirt. A hand, holding a blackthorn walking stick, was raised enough to be a menace.

"I'm sorry. You are?" Jenny feigned ignorance, buying time to think how to get rid of the man.

"You know damn well who I am, Jennifer Weston, or whatever your name is now. And I know you well enough. Always was trouble—stealing the kohlrabi out of my garden. Trouble as soon as you came back to town. You and your mom callin' the police on me! That's a laugh. I should've called them when you and your friends kept ringing my doorbell, the way you did, leaving a burning bag of crap behind for me to stomp on."

"Mr. Cane?" Jenny smiled and stepped fully into the doorway, blocking his entry to the house.

"You're damned right it's me. Had a visit from the chief of police today. Seems somebody broke up that box of books your mother keeps out there." He turned to flail a hand toward the street. "Somebody did away with it, and I say that's a good thing. Too many people hanging around. Too many cars. And I don't like people breaking the law the way your mother does. We've got zoning here in Bear Falls, ya know."

"Adam?" Dora said from behind Jenny, then pushed her daughter aside.

"Whatever are you talking about? It *was* a terrible thing. If you've got nothing to be ashamed of, talking to the police was the right thing to do. And if you didn't go yelling like a madman about our neighbor's little dog, why, nobody would have connected you to the destruction out front."

"Street's so bad, I hardly want to live here anymore," he mumbled, calming a little. "Should be a hermit, like Aaron. Tried being a good neighbor."

"Threatening a dog? Shame on you."

"I knew it was you sent Ed Warner down. Had to be. You or that shrimp that lives next to me. Her and that damned dog—pees on my grass every chance she gets."

"Zoe does that?" Jenny pretended to be shocked.

Which only made him madder. "You know what I'm talking about, Jenny Weston. Wasn't me broke up that damned thing you people keep your books in. You send the chief to somebody else's house next time, Dora. Not mine." The man, in his dirty blue pants and down-at-the-heels sandals, was too pathetic to be a threat. Jenny started to close the door in his face. Dora stopped her.

"I'm so sorry if you were troubled." Dora put a hand out to Adam, which he pushed away.

"Only trouble is you and this daughter of yours. And don't think you're going to blackmail me for new books—like the police chief said. You find some other old fool to prey on. It's not gonna be me."

Now Jenny put a hand on the old man's chest and gave him a shove out of the doorway and across the porch. His ankles turned in his ancient sandals.

Adam caught himself with his walking stick and righted his body. He held himself firmly in place, half bent over, staring directly at Jenny.

"You turned sour, Jenny Weston," he growled. "All because of that Arlen boy. Used to feel sorry for you, but now I see why Johnny hightailed it to another girl."

"Go back to your own house," Jenny snapped and closed the door in his face. She leaned against the door and pulled in a couple of quick breaths. Mention of Jenny's good-for-nothing high school boyfriend had her bristling.

"He didn't mean that," Dora said. "He's such an unhappy man. A 'wasp in a wig,' as Zoe says. She's got that one right."

Chapter 6

The dark beyond her window moved, long shadows reaching across the lawn. There were no streetlights here at the back of the house, only starlight and moonlight filtering through the pines. The smell of pine pitch feathered the edge of a warm breeze. Jenny sat on the wide window seat in her old bedroom and thought about the last eight years of her life—all of it destroyed, like one of the ruined books, by Ronald Korman.

There were good things to show for the Chicago years: training as a paralegal in Ronald's law office, living a different life from anything she'd known in Bear Falls, and now money from Ronald to keep her for a while, until she figured out where and how she wanted to live next.

And the down side? There were plenty of those: The cheating, low-down creep made her feel as loveable as a tick attack; she no longer had a home of her own; and she was left with one more crappy life experience with a man, a man like her first love, Johnny Arlen, who left her for a bimbo named Angel.

She sure knew how to pick 'em.

She leaned against the wall, hoping she didn't have to tell Mom about the divorce—at least not until Mom noticed that

Ronald never called and never visited and that she never talked about him. She'd told her this was a vacation. That she was tired. That she wanted to spend some time with her.

Maybe Mom was just too polite to ask.

Maybe Lisa'd already spilled the beans and Mom was pretending.

"The man's a turd." Lisa, older by two years and by a hundred years in wisdom, had been sympathetic.

From there her suggestion had been to get out of Chicago. Then she played on Jenny's guilt for not going home in five years.

So it was Lisa's fault that she was here in Bear Falls, in the old house, trying to fall asleep in her old bed under the polyester quilt she'd picked out when she was nine. Sleep eluded her, and she turned on the bedside lamp covered by a frilly yellow lampshade that was dried and cracked. Everything in the room was so . . . used.

She lay under her Bon Jovi poster and felt the same life-ending gloom she'd known when Johnny had married pregnant Angel Cornish and the town's unctuous sympathy poured over her, his leftover, like thick molasses. She had left for college—a little early—and then went to Chicago with only a few days at home in between. She always invited her mother and sister to come visit her in Chicago and loved when they agreed.

Now Jenny was home—full circle.

That was the thought that drove her to the window seat to pass the night, where she could jump out and run if she couldn't stand another minute in the house.

She was half awake at a little before four when she heard Zoe's voice calling softly between their houses. "Fida." And then again, more demanding: "Fida, where are you?"

When she next heard Zoe calling her dog, it was farther away—toward her backyard. "Fida. You come here, you hear me?"

The voice faded. Jenny spent the rest of the night nodding on the window seat, sleeping from time to time, jerking awake only when morning sun lit the dark places behind her eyes.

Chapter 7

"Did you hear Zoe calling Fida in the middle of the night?" Dora came from her bedroom, yawning and stretching, pulling her robe tight around her body.

"Uh-huh."

"Seemed like it was about three or four. What was the dog doing out at that hour?"

"I don't know. Had to pee, I suppose." Jenny set the table for breakfast while her mother brought eggs from the refrigerator and pointedly held on to the carton.

"How about a poached egg?" Mom asked.

Jenny gave a slight laugh. "Guess you didn't like how I scrambled them last night."

"A little dry, dear."

"I swear I'll go to the market today, soon as I can."

"That would be nice." Dora smiled. "You've got the list. Maybe add some bagels. I've been longing for a good bagel."

"You won't get one in Bear Falls."

"Oh, I know. But even a pack of frozen would do. Just something different for a change."

Jenny toasted the hard bread while her mother put a pan on the stove to poach the eggs.

"You think she found her?" Dora asked as she set the table with bright-yellow dishes.

"You mean Fida?"

Dora nodded.

"No idea."

"I'll call and ask," Dora said. "Zoe is such a fun person—all that fairy tale business of hers. She really is a dear. I feel so lucky to have her as a neighbor. After all, she's a lot like me, loves books of all kinds. Though she won't read Priscilla's town history. I suppose I can't fault her. Priscilla still tries to corner her, holding out the book as if it was a French postcard or something."

Dora innocently kept cracking eggs on the side of the pan to drop them in the boiling water. "I just thought it would be nice for her to be up on what the people of Bear Falls have done in the past." Dora sighed. "Guess you can lead a horse to water, you know, Jenny? But you can't make her read."

Dora went to the wall phone when the table was set to her satisfaction. She dialed, then talked a while. After she hung up, she turned worried eyes to her daughter.

"Fida's gone."

"Gone? Gone where?" Jenny stuck the butter back in the refrigerator.

"Said she didn't know. Oh dear, Jenny. She sounds awful. Said she's been surrounded by awful smells all night. I think she's afraid something's happened to the poor dog. She has that handicap, you know."

"Zoe?" Jenny shrugged. "Doesn't seem like a handicap to me. Just a little shorter than the rest of us."

"Not Zoe. I meant Fida. Got that one blind eye."

"You think I should go over and see if there's anything I can do?"

Dora's face relaxed. "That would be nice. She helped us almost all day yesterday. It seems the least *we* can do."

We turned out to be *Jenny*, alone, making her way through the pines into Zoe's backyard after breakfast and into a garden like none Jenny had visited before and wasn't sure she ever would again.

She knocked at the back door, then turned to look at Zoe's garden.

It was huge, stretching from beds at the back of the house to rows of dying tulips and daffodils. Flowering vines grew thick on Zoe's side of a tall fence hiding Adam Cane's yard from view. There were long beds of near-blooming peonies in all colors running down the center of the yard, running toward what Jenny imagined was the back of the yard, up a slight hill and out of sight. Jenny couldn't see all of the garden because of tall rhododendrons in bud. The rhodos curved into lilac bushes in full blooms of deep purple, white, pink, and pale blue stretching around, and almost completely hiding, a yellow shed. Through all the color and all the green, a flagstone walk meandered from bed to bed.

Jenny knocked again and waited, turning back to look hard at what she recalled Zoe calling fairy houses standing in every flowerbed.

Some, she could make out, were made of wood, painted with flowers. Some were made of tiny stones. A few of tiny bricks. The houses stood between dying tulips or were hidden behind budding roses. In one bed there was a two-foot-tall castle, complete with turret. In another daffodils bobbed around a miniature opening to a cave. There were other houses hidden under tall plants and what looked like tiny statues throughout the gardens.

Jenny pulled away from the astonishing sight to knock again—hard this time.

Zoe's pretty face, when the door opened, was almost unrecognizable—her skin mottled, eyes nearly swollen shut. Her hair was uncombed and stood up like a fright wig.

"She didn't come back?"

Zoe shook her head. "I looked most of the night. I put her out about three thirty because she had to pee, but when I called her back in, she didn't come."

Zoe wore a pair of mismatched pajamas with tin soldiers printed on the top and Humpty Dumptys patterned on the bottoms. She looked like an ad for a mixed-up cartoon.

"Get dressed and we'll go looking," Jenny said. "I'm sure she's somewhere nearby. With one eye—well, I can only imagine the poor thing trying to find her way home last night."

"I'll bet anything he did something to her." Zoe gave a quick nod of her head and a sniff of her nose toward Adam Cane's yard.

Jenny thought a minute. *What would Lisa the Good say in this predicament? Something soothing.*

"I don't think he'd ever really . . ."

Zoe narrowed her eyes. "Don't treat me like a child. We both know what the man's capable of doing. You saw what he did to something your mother loved."

"Why don't we go ask him?"

"He'd never tell the truth."

"What about going to the police?"

"How would that get me Fida back? Adam would lie, and you could see the chief doesn't like me much. Not about to set his pants on fire looking for my dog."

Jenny was out of ideas with nothing more to offer. "Get dressed." She couldn't help the impatience in her voice. "We'll keep looking until we find her."

"You want to come in?" Zoe pushed the door wider but with little enthusiasm.

"No. I'll walk around your yard."

Zoe didn't perk up. "Suit yourself," she said, closed the door, then opened it again to call after Jenny. "It's a fairy garden. They might be sleeping. Don't bother 'em."

With a roll of her eyes, Jenny walked down the steps to take a tour.

Between two pumpkin-shaped houses, she found a tutued fairy standing on one toe. Jenny smiled and fought the urge to yell "Boo" at the tour jeté-ing statue.

From inside a building with a waterwheel on one side, a fairy with pointed ears peeped out.

Jenny laughed as she made her way past the beds—as creative as any garden she'd ever visited.

A worried fairy face peeked out one small, four-paned window. At the castle, a tiny Rapunzel sat in the tower, her long, blonde hair hanging out a narrow window. One house after another, fairies old and young watched her. What fun! In this garden she could be a carefree little girl again, the way she and Lisa once pretended that they would grow up to be princesses and live in faraway castles and marry doting princes and have nothing but beautiful children.

She worked her way past the rhodos, searching out the scent of lilacs over by the yellow shed.

At first she mistook the pile of rags, lying on the stone walk between the lilac bushes and the shed, as part of a construction site—a new fairy bed in progress. Or clothes for a scarecrow Zoe was putting together. She smiled as she got closer, wondering what would come next in this enchanted garden, then was struck by an awful thought—that the discarded bundle could be Fida, dead and wrapped in an old quilt and dropped there for Zoe to find.

She stopped, took another step, and almost tripped on pieces of ceramic scattered over the walk. She bent to see what she could see. Much too large a bundle to be a little dog.

Blue. And red plaid. And colorless sandals on a pair of dirty feet sticking out from beneath the ragged bundle. A blackthorn stick lay near the shed.

She pulled the rags away and stared down into the face of a dead man.

"Mr. Cane!" Jenny yelled at the sprawled figure. "Mr. Cane!"

She bent over the man, shaking him until she saw the pool of blood beneath his head. She fell to her knees and caught her breath. Not only a pool of blood, but a deep gash in the long, gray hair wrapped by a blue headband. She waved a hand at the gathering flies and then laid a hand on his chest, feeling for movement, for breath going in and out.

Nothing.

She felt for a pulse at his wrist.

Again nothing. She called his name then held her breath, hoping for the slightest sound.

Adam Cane was dead. A broken fairy house lay in pieces beside his head. In the first minutes of her confusion, she told herself he'd had an accident. It appeared that he'd fallen over the fairy house, or maybe he'd tripped on his cane and fell.

She looked beyond the body to where a pointed hoe lay tangled among the branches of a broken lilac bush. Without understanding why, Jenny got up to move the hoe as if that lethal point, so close to his head, could do more damage.

She touched the wooden handle, meaning to push the hoe off to one side. It seemed important to make things better. Caught in the broken bush, the hoe didn't move when she pushed it. She pulled at the handle and then, when it caught, she pulled again. She put both hands on the metal end itself and pulled.

When it wouldn't budge, snagged too deeply in broken branches, she decided to leave it where it was and go for help. As she got up, she noticed that she'd left behind a shiny handprint on the stone where she'd been leaning.

She turned her hand up to check it. Her palm and fingers were stained red. No cuts. Nothing hurt. She looked at her other hand. More dark red stains.

Horror struck her hard when she glanced at the pointed head of the hoe. A single drop of viscous liquid dripped. The drop fell slowly to the dark stone beneath. On the stone, a puddle of coagulating blood spread out to blackened edges.

Chapter 8

"You see?" Zoe said, in a hushed voice. "You still don't smell the trouble all around us?"

Jenny and Zoe stood over the body.

Jenny held herself still. The dead man lay as if sleeping—except for the blood. She wondered if she was in shock. She didn't feel that any of this was real.

She'd run back to the house to get Zoe, dressed and ready for the Fida hunt. Zoe'd called the police and then they'd come out together to watch over Adam's body. Something they had to do for the man, whether they liked him or not.

Zoe's hands covered her mouth. Her eyes were huge.

"I can't believe he died here," she whispered from behind protective hands.

"Somebody killed him." Jenny pointed toward the hoe.

Zoe shuddered and mumbled, "Do you think he took Fida?"

"Why would he do that? And where did he put her?"

"He could've killed her. Maybe buried her."

"Oh, Zoe. Don't we have enough misery for one day without imagining more?"

Ed Warner, head bobbing nervously, with a deputy trailing in his wake, finally arrived. The deputy herded them back up the lawn to Zoe's house, leaving them there with the stricture to stay put. "I'll be back to talk to you both as soon as I can."

"Could you check inside Adam's house for me?" Zoe put a tentative hand on the deputy's arm.

The deputy frowned down at the hand. "What for? The man's dead in your yard, Ms. Zola, not at his house."

"My dog is gone. I think he took her . . ."

He leaned away from Zoe. "If I were you, I'd worry more about the man murdered in your yard than about your dog."

"Of course. It's just that . . ." Her eyes blurred with tears.

He saw the sheen in her eyes. "I'll talk to the chief. Figure that dog's pretty important to you."

The young deputy was gone before Zoe could thank him.

They sat in Zoe's living room and listened to the voices outside—in the garden and then between the houses. They didn't say a word until Jenny's cell rang.

Dora was on the other end. "What on earth's going on over there? I just got home and there are police cars everywhere. I thought something happened to one of you. Can't be the dog. It isn't, is it? Anything happen to Fida?"

Jenny broke the news as easily as she could, saving some of the more lurid details for when she saw her face to face.

"Oh no. Poor man," Dora said. "That family's cursed, Jenny. Someday I'll tell you."

Dora wished them luck and hung up. Jenny tried to make small talk with Zoe to ease their tension, but nothing helped as they waited for one of the policemen to tell them what happened.

From time to time, they talked about the shock of Adam's death and then worried about Fida. After that, there was little to say. They sat on Zoe's low, curved sofa and waited.

* * *

Zoe's house wasn't at all what Jenny expected. No fairies or trolls or magic dolls. The living room was neat and orderly. Maybe more flowers—on the drapes and cushions and set about in vases—than Jenny would have liked. Everything else was low key and functional: two small chairs done in a soft green, end tables low to the floor, lamps much too short for a full-grown person to read by. All very nice except for Jenny's bizarre feeling that she'd nibbled one of Alice's cookies and grown way too large.

Zoe paced from time to time, stopping at the front window to pull the gauzy sheers aside. "Oh my," she said. "People are gathering. Maybe I should go out and talk to them. I mean, it was only yesterday the police were at your mom's house. They're going to think there's a crime wave in Bear Falls, all centered around us. Drawing a crowd is never a good thing."

"Stay where you are. You don't want more trouble with Ed."

The room was quiet again. The women stared at the floor for the next hour. When the phone rang this time, Zoe ran to get it.

"My editor, Christopher Morley," Zoe said, disgruntled, when she came back a few minutes later. "He's hoping to see the new manuscript soon. As if I can write with everything going on around here. It's Armageddon, I told him. I've landed in the place of bad dreams. I knew it would happen. Walk along happily, mind your own business, then boom, it's the rabbit hole, for sure. And then you're big and then you're small and then you're falling and then you're playing croquet with a mean queen, and your world turns and everything's different. And then you're doomed. That's what I told Christopher Morley. I'm doomed. Now he's worried about me."

"Doomed for what, Zoe? What are you talking about?"

"I see it now." Her hand went to her forehead. "There I am, stuck in quicksand. Going down and down until no one sees me anymore. And there's Fida. And Mr. Cane. It's only the beginning, Jenny. If I were you, I'd go home, pack your clothes, and head back to Chicago. And, by the way, take your mother with you. Keep Dora safe."

"Crazy talk."

"You don't know as much as I do. There are dark places and dark clouds and dark people. When they settle together, good people are doomed. Absolutely doomed."

"You're full of . . ."

Zoe fell into a chair, little legs stretched straight out in front of her. Her scowl was enormous. Jenny wasn't happy with this trip through Zoe's dark, imaginary cave. Zoe's escape to Wonderland was a little too convenient for her. A lot of what Zoe Zola did seemed a little too convenient.

"I didn't kill him, you know," Zoe said, as if reading Jenny's mind.

"Neither did I," Jenny snapped back.

"Really?" Zoe sniffed. "All I know is that this place was quiet until a certain person moved in next door."

"By that, you must mean me."

"I'm not saying who. It's just odd—you're here barely twenty-four hours and all hell breaks loose."

Jenny's ears turned bright red. *The nerve of the little pest!* "I'll tell you something, Zoe," she said when she could talk again. "I'm no more thrilled with you than you are with me. In fact . . ."

A deputy Jenny vaguely remembered from a lower class in high school walked in to say Ed Warner would talk to them soon.

"Did he send somebody over to Adam's to see if my dog was there?" Zoe begged.

The man nodded. "I think so. I'll find out and let you know."

Another half hour passed until Ed walked in, worked his tall body into one of the small chairs, and tried to settle back. He looked from woman to woman, shook his head, and clasped his hands together.

"You need something to drink?" Zoe offered, half out of her chair, craving something to do.

He shook his head. "Like to get this over with."

"My dog?"

Ed shook his head. "Nothing in there. No sign of a dog. Sorry to tell you that. Maybe she just ran away, ma'am."

Zoe shook her head. "She wouldn't. And she didn't. He did something . . ."

"You were here last night, right?" he interrupted.

"All night. Most of it hunting for my dog."

"Until about what time?"

"I was out until about four thirty."

"In the morning?"

She nodded.

"You didn't see Adam Cane?"

She shook her head.

"You two weren't exactly friends."

"I didn't kill the man," Zoe said. "Look at me, Chief. Do I look like I could hit anybody in the head with a hoe?"

He gave Zoe a long, speculative look. "Thing is," he said, "you wouldn't have to be big to kill him."

"Wield a hoe and crack in his head? You've got to be kidding."

He shook his head. "Found a trip wire. Side to side over your path. Adam Cane was on the ground when somebody struck him. One blow to his head and one to the middle of his chest. Could've been anybody. Somebody set a trap. That makes this a premeditated murder."

"Can't be," Zoe protested. "I saw my fairy house. He fell over that. Very sad . . . but . . . a trip wire?"

He shrugged. "We'll be checking for fingerprints on the stakes that held the wire and on the hoe. Maybe that's all it will take. Sure hope you didn't have anything to do with it."

"It's my hoe," Zoe protested as the chief got out of his chair. "My fingerprints will be all over it."

"And I touched it," Jenny spoke up. "I was trying to move it away from Adam."

Ed Warner stood, hitched up his pants, and scratched at the back of his neck. "We'll see what's what when I get the report back from Traverse City. Know anybody else who might have wanted Adam dead? I mean, besides you, Ms. Zola? Him hating your dog so bad and now your dog's gone . . . seems like a good reason to me."

Zoe said nothing.

Ed had a few questions for Jenny. Not much, and then he was gone.

Chapter 9

In the morning, Jenny drove to Draper's Superette. Dora was at Zoe's. She couldn't stand the thought of Zoe being alone. That left Jenny to play provider and search for provisions.

She drove into the familiar, unpaved parking lot and parked amid a long line of blue, red, and black pickups.

The small market sat away from the commercial parts of town, in the midst of the forest, with Lake Michigan as a backdrop. Today the waterscape, off on the horizon, was a sheet of sun sparks. Her hands cupped above her eyes, it made her smile to watch the lake move in ridges of light. It could have been the backdrop to her life, the one immutable forever. No matter what terrible things happened, she had to admit she was happier here on the side of the lake where she'd grown up, where life didn't whirl past as it did in Chicago.

Jenny took a single, long breath and headed toward the market.

Despite the out-of-town location, Draper's was the town center for neighbor meeting neighbor, for gossip spreading, for reputations ruined, but also for money raised for a family in need, for funeral expenses if a family had no money. Draper's was where clothes and toys and furniture and food were collected, where notices went up for spaghetti suppers in aid of those whose houses burned or were struck by a tornado or crushed in a winter of record snow.

After Johnny Arlen dropped her and married Angel, she'd stopped going to Draper's. The market had blazed with indignation—people on both sides, hers or Johnny's. She even heard of a fistfight or two in the parking lot over who was at fault.

Wind off the lake pushed at her as she headed toward the store, where old, out-of-date posters hung in the large, flyblown windows. A half-torn banner advertising a winter sale on anti-freeze flapped over the automatic front doors. Two ancient benches, touting a defunct auto repair shop, sat out front, while shopping baskets gathered helter-skelter, one—wind behind it— making a wild break for freedom across the gravel lot.

Besides being Bear Falls' idea of a general store, Draper's attracted elderly men who hung out on the hard, red benches in the tiny coffee shop. They noted the coming and going of every customer—with a comment for each. Greek chorus of Bear Falls, Jenny called them.

She grabbed one of the abandoned carts on her way through the automatic door and was immediately hit by familiar smells: lettuces and peaches and cleaning fluids—all lumped together. Bakery scents and fish.

She moved fast, past the coffee shop, waving to the elderly gentlemen sitting in the plastic booths.

"Jenny! Jenny Weston!" she heard as she wheeled by a display of spaghetti sauce.

Cassandra Hatch, an acquaintance from high school, stood in her usual place behind a checkout counter, waving and smiling as wide as a smile could get. "Heard you were back.

Come through my line, okay? I'm dying to find out how you've been doing."

"I sure will," Jenny called back to her.

Cassandra was one of those girls you remember from high school as kind of sweet. Maybe a little sad. Even in high school, Cassandra had an old woman's face: wrinkled forehead, squinty eyes. There'd been talk that her mama ran her father off for taking liberties with Cassandra no father should take. Jenny didn't hear it directly; it came from a neighbor, Minnie Moon. She and Mom had been standing out front, talking. Jenny overheard. It was one of those things a girl knew right away was bad. One of those things you didn't talk about with anyone. It was something that made you know you were growing up and made you realize you didn't want to.

Cassandra was going to ask about the police at Jenny's house. Then she'd apologize for asking and move quickly on to updating Jenny how her kids were doing or how her husband, Dave, got shot outside of Billy's Bar but was doing fine now . . .

Jenny pushed her cart through the produce section, picking up a bundle of fresh asparagus because she loved when things were fresh out of the ground, when she could smell the earth on them.

Early tomatoes were in from the fields. They looked good— maybe a caprese for Mom. She'd liked that when she visited Chicago. A bed of lettuce drizzled with a balsamic vinegar glaze, covered with slices of fresh tomato, fresh mozzarella on top, a leaf of basil, a little salt . . .

She was hungry.

At the cheese counter, she searched for tubs of fresh mozzarella.

Lots of sliced cheese, and hunks of cheese, and strings of cheese. But nothing fresh. That ruled out the caprese. For future reference, she hunted for fresh basil. Only the dried stuff. She looked for the balsamic glaze—nothing even close.

"I'm not in Kansas anymore," she whispered to herself and then went in search of a fresh chicken.

Plenty of chickens—that was a good sign. Lots of root vegetables: celery, carrots, onions . . .

She turned to set a large onion in her basket and ran straight into Angel Arlen, who threw her hands up to stop the charge.

"What do you know?" Angel put a hand at the small of her back and smirked. "Is that really you, Jenny Weston?"

Angel was pregnant again, Jenny saw at once because she couldn't not notice. Angel looked like an upside-down musical note, all puffed in front.

A girl of about ten stood behind Angel. The thin child kept her head down, staring at the floor, lifting and dropping her right shoulder, as if from a nervous tic. Never once did the girl glance up at Jenny.

Angel's tight T-shirt had a big arrow down the front, leading to the word *Baby*. As if anyone wouldn't have guessed.

Jenny choked down surprise and ransacked her brain for something to say to this woman who'd ruined her life.

Angel leaned back on the heels of her old tennis shoes, one hand now atop her swollen belly. She tried to smile, but it fell short—her mouth curving nervously up on one side. "To tell the truth, I heard you was home."

Jenny nodded and forced a smile. "I'll bet you did." She kept her voice warm to hide her inner thoughts.

Eighteen years ago Angel had been the hottest girl in town. Her long, blonde hair—now twisted into a greasy knot at the back of her head—used to hang down past her butt. A sight for the boys to see as she strutted up Oak Street in a T-shirt with no bra, breasts bouncing just enough, hips swaying more than enough to get her message across. In any town, Angel would have been called "easy." In Bear Falls, the word "Angel" didn't come with a kind smile—more with a sniff and a roll of the eyes. Mothers warned mothers. Those mothers warned their boys to keep away. And even Pastor Senise, at the Bear Falls Evangelical Church, was known to whisper to boys he hoped to protect from the rude world, "Angel is no Angel, my son. Best to mind your thoughts around her."

The short shorts were still there, only wrinkled, with a stain just below where her pink top stretched over her belly. Ugly, blue veins ran up her right leg. Wrinkles formed around her narrowed eyes as she spoke. She'd aged badly, but maybe having one daughter who was—Jenny racked her brains—about seventeen by now, and this ten-year-old, all of that plus putting up with Johnny wore her out too soon.

"I hardly recognized you," Angel said after turning to hush her daughter, who whispered that she wanted to go home. The girl's face, when she looked at her mother, was sullen, ruining her slight features. Jenny could see Johnny in the long shape of the girl's head, in the intense blue eyes, in the straight, brown hair. She felt a little sick in the pit of her stomach.

"Me either," Jenny said. "And this is your daughter? Second one, right?"

"Janice." Angel reached out to touch the girl, who ducked away from the hand.

"How nice for you." Jenny swallowed, making herself take a breath. "And I see you're pregnant again."

"What do you mean 'again'? You think I've got too many? This is only my third, Jenny Weston." Angel narrowed her eyes to slits.

"That's not what I meant . . ."

"You ever get married?"

"Yes." She couldn't help adding, "He's an attorney in Chicago."

"You always were going to be a career girl. That's what Johnny said."

"I am."

"Doin' what?"

Jenny smiled, then lied, "I'm in law."

Angel looked away, a blue tinge staining the skin beneath her tired eyes.

They glanced around the store at other shoppers, then back to each other. They each put on forced smiles and looked away again.

Angel tipped her head to one side. "Hear you had trouble over at your house."

Jenny nodded, then shrugged.

"Your mom okay?"

"Sad. A despicable thing to do, ruining her Little Library."

"And Adam Cane dead. People say maybe that little lady did it. They didn't get along, you know."

"People are wrong."

"Oh," Angel said.

They went back to shuffling their buggies back and forth, harsher things they wanted to say prancing between them like angry little horses.

"How's your oldest daughter doing?" Jenny finally asked. "What's she? Seventeen?"

Angel perked up. "Yeah. Margo. Eighteen. She's fine. Got married last year. Got herself pregnant. Didn't want to finish high school anyway. She figured she might as well just go ahead and get married."

"So you're a grandmother."

"Yeah. At thirty-six. Go figure. My kid will be younger than my grandkid." She smirked as if she'd accomplished a mighty deed. "You got any kids?"

Jenny shook her head.

"That's too bad." Angel batted her lashes.

They looked away from each other again.

Angel finally said, "Saw Lisa a couple of times. Never you."

She waited, as everyone seemed to, as if an apology should follow. Jenny felt her face flush. *Okay, lady,* she thought. *If you want to tangle* . . .

"I'm here to help my mom out. She's a little tired. Lisa can't come home. You heard she's in Montana shooting a movie?"

"Yeah, I heard. Your mom sick?"

"No. She's fine."

"How long you plan on staying?"

Jenny shrugged, liking the anxious tone in Angel's voice. "A while, I guess. Kind of a vacation, too."

"What about your husband? He like that you're gone? I'd never leave Johnny all alone like that."

"We're both very busy."

Angel's smile went from anxious to keenly interested. "Bet you don't stay in Bear Falls long. Sure isn't Chicago. Real quiet . . . well, except for over at your place . . . Everybody's talking, you know, like maybe you brought Chicago crime back with you."

"I'll bet." Jenny smiled as if she wasn't being sarcastic. She pushed her buggy back and forth again, eager to get back to shopping—or anywhere else.

"Hope you don't expect to see Johnny." The words came out low, mean, and direct. Angel put one hand on Jenny's cart to hold her in place while reaching out with the other to swat her whining daughter.

"Why on earth would I want to?" Jenny let out the tiniest amount of disgust.

"You know damned well—the way he dumped you and all. I always thought maybe you'd come back and try to get even with me for snatching him away from you."

Jenny gave her a slow once over, dirty feet to greasy hair. She shook her head. "I've got nothing to get even for, Angel."

"Hope you're not taking what I say in a negative way."

"Don't worry." She pushed her buggy hard to dislodge Angel's hand. "Let's just agree to stay away from each other. That all right with you? Makes me feel bad—you embarrassing yourself like this. Honestly, I wouldn't touch Johnny with a ten-foot pole."

"You don't have to get mean about it."

"Bye." Jenny gave a backhanded wave as she hurried off.

"I've been praying for you," Angel called after her.

Jenny kept going, thinking, *And I'm alive anyway.*

The last thing she needed were prayers from this Angel.

Any appetite she had for shopping or cooking or eating or anything else involving staying at Draper's was gone. She picked up two cans of Campbell's Chicken Soup and a box of crackers. Mom wouldn't care. She didn't have much of an appetite anyway. Canned soup might be good for her. Better than petrified eggs.

She made her way to the checkout and waited in Cassandra Hatch's line. The woman, her bundled red hair falling forward over her shoulder, reached across the checkout counter and grabbed Jenny's hand to shake it three times.

"Been ages since you were back. Bet you've got all kinds of stories to tell, living in Chicago this long."

"That's for sure."

"Heard about what happened over at your mom's place. Give her my best and tell her I've got a couple of Nancy Drews I'll pitch in for a new library. Everybody's been saying they've got books for her. And what happened to Adam Cane . . . nobody can believe it. Not in Bear Falls!"

Jenny felt at home for the first time. This was what she remembered: bits of well-meaning gossip, lazy conversations by the falls at the end of Oak, small-town life and small-town people. "Sad, I know," she said and frowned. "And I'll tell Mom about the books. She'll be happy. Thanks."

Cassandra leaned across the counter, motioning Jenny to move in closer.

"Angel's in the store." She gave Jenny a sympathetic smile.

Jenny shrugged. "I saw her. We talked."

Cassandra's watery eyes wrinkled at the corners. "You were the lucky one, you know. Johnny's got a reputation. Drinks bad. I think he runs around on Angel, is what I heard." She gave Jenny a meaningful glance. "Angel did you a favor."

Jenny thanked her and meant it. There were things only women could say to each other. Things that sneaked behind a brave smile.

Cassandra, finished with town gossip, lowered her voice. "You heard what happened to Dave? Got shot in the groin over at Billy's Bar. But don't worry." Cassandra shrugged. "He's gonna be fine . . . though . . ." She narrowed her eyes and gave Jenny a sly smile. "I might not have to worry about getting pregnant again."

It was high school all over again, snickering at the expense of a boy. Jenny reached out and squeezed Cassandra's arm, a signal they both knew the painful joke beneath the words.

After checking out and promising to stay in touch, Jenny pushed the buggy to her car and stowed her slim bag of groceries in the trunk. She slammed the lid and looked around the full lot. A tall man standing next to a dark-blue pickup was watching her. The man, only a silhouette against the high sun, leaned back on his truck and crossed his arms.

She went to open her driver's side door, put a hand up to her eyes, and looked back at him.

Johnny Arlen waved, then pushed slowly off from the truck as if he intended to walk over.

Jenny didn't return Johnny's wave. She didn't wait. She got in her car, started the motor, and pulled out of the parking lot before her strangling emotions got the best of her.

Chapter 10

A man looked up from the kitchen table when Jenny got back with the groceries. Maybe early forties, stocky, with curly black hair. Jenny guessed he was Mom's new carpenter.

A scar on his left cheek gave him a kind of worn look. The same with the narrow, dark beard outlining his chin and cheeks. Not your ordinary Bear Falls man with the usual open face and friendly eyes. The man stood when she walked in, leaning slightly against the table edge. He held out his rough hand to take hers when Dora introduced them.

"Glad to know you," Tony Ralenti said in a husky voice hovering between a whisper and a growl. A firm shake. A long shake. He gave her a smile that spread into a charming grin.

Jenny, flustered by the man, said she was happy to meet him, too, and turned away to hide her flushed face. She set the grocery bag on the counter.

Mom was at the stove. "I called Mr. Ralenti while you were gone. It's been so hectic. People from everywhere offering help—most with books to donate, a lot wanting to know what was happening over here. I'll be getting more books than I can ever put into one library box—unless we make the box a lot bigger. Some even offered money to get it built again. Of course . . ." Mom smiled at Tony, "I wouldn't take money. My husband would be appalled. I wrote down the names of all the books I could remember on the sign-out sheet. I want to pull everything together fast."

She turned to look over her shoulder at Jenny. "I feel so bad about Adam, then here I am, all excited about a new library. Ordinarily, I'd be too tired to think about starting over, but I'm not. Truly, I think I want to get it going again."

Her face was bright as she chattered too fast for Jenny to keep up.

"I guess she's changed her mind," Jenny said to the man sitting at the edge of his chair, hands between his knees. "When I left, she wasn't so sure about rebuilding."

He looked at her directly, his eyes seeming to know her. She felt the tiniest buzz of electricity run down her back.

"I was sitting on the porch." Dora wiped her hands on a dish-towel. "Feeling sorry for myself, I'll have to say. And sad about poor Adam. Louise Dyer called to say she couldn't live without my library. It's so far to Traverse City." Dora clucked and shook her head. "Minnie Moon called. Poor thing was crying. Everybody's just distraught. No one should be deprived of books. That's what Louise said, and that's what I believe. And my husband, Jim—wished you'd known him, Tony. He would've liked you. I just know he'd be saying, 'Full speed ahead.'"

Tony nodded and looked down at his hands. "I've been by here. Saw the house. Nice job. It's too bad about what happened. Think I've got an idea of how the book box should look."

"Jim wanted it so much for me. I guess I'd feel like a traitor if I just shut up shop without trying."

Mom chuckled to herself and went back to making coffee, measuring grounds and water into her machine, flicking a switch, then standing back to see if she'd got it right. When the machine began to bubble, perk, and drip into the carafe, Dora clapped her hands and turned to the two at the table.

"That's when I called Tony." She smiled at Jenny. "We were just talking about things. I thought maybe we could add a children's wing—or another whole house, as I said before. Tony, here, says that's no problem. He's going to do a drawing for me. I'm happy you're back, Jenny. Maybe the three of us can come up with something splendid."

With the mugs filled, Dora fussed over the sugar bowl, knocked a hunk of dried sugar from the rim, then pushed the milk carton toward Tony.

She busied herself examining the groceries Jenny bought and then put things into the refrigerator and the pantry. "Did you get bread, dear? I don't see it."

Jenny had to shake her head. "Forgot the bread."

"And dish soap?"

Jenny shook her head again and searched for excuses. "So many people there. You know what Draper's is like. Everybody wanted to know what was happening over here. I . . . just . . . wanted to leave."

The last, at least, wasn't a lie.

Dora frowned, looking as if she suspected something could be up. "No bagels?"

"Oh, Mom. I forgot . . ."

"I shouldn't have asked."

"Don't be silly. I'm a dolt." Jenny smiled from Dora to Tony, then pulled her mug to her, making a big deal of blowing at the hot coffee, tasting it, then blowing at it again and again.

Tony Ralenti got busy drawing on a large pad of paper in front of him, then stopped to take a sip of his coffee—which didn't require a lot of embarrassed puffs the way Jenny's had.

When he turned the pad, Dora and Jenny leaned close, squinting. Both of the sketched houses were bigger than the old, single house—or seemed to be. Both looked very close to the house Jim Weston built, but somehow not quite.

"They're not . . ." she started to say.

"Two so close together? Looks crowded," Jenny said.

"How about two posts? Two platforms?" Tony thought fast. He smiled at Jenny. "I could make one post shorter than the other."

She looked away from those dark eyes. The rough hands spread wide on the paper were easier to stare at. Work worn with purple veins—and that scar. She had a crazy urge to run a finger over that scar. She held her breath and turned away. When she got up to get a glass of water, she kept her back to Tony. First handsome man to look at her in months and she was turning to jelly.

Ovaries, she told herself. Womb. Ticking biological clock. Another trick of dumb Mother Nature. She was thirty-six, a lot smarter than she'd been at eighteen. Or even at twenty-eight. *Stay on guard*, she warned herself.

She turned back to him with a calm and disinterested face.

"Yes." Dora thought hard. "One of them has to look exactly like the house Jim built. The other can be fantastical, maybe covered with fairies."

"Your boy readers won't go for the fairies."

"Then fairies and superheroes." Dora clapped her hands.

Tony dipped his dark head. "I'll come up with something. I'm taking a couple of photos of your house before I go. Make sure I've got the one just right."

"Talk to Zoe about the other one," Dora suggested, then looked distressed. "But remember, I don't have a lot of money. I can't . . ."

"The whole thing's not going to cost you much, Mrs. Weston. Maybe materials, that's all. You do plenty for everybody. Zoe's filled me in."

"I'm not a charity case, either." Dora lifted her chin.

"Not charity, ma'am."

"Dora," she corrected, smiling.

He nodded as he closed the sketchpad and tucked it under his arm. "I'm going to give you exactly what you want . . . eh . . . Dora. Not just for you, but for Jim Weston."

Dora teared up, and their agreement was set.

Jenny noticed that he limped as he walked toward the door. It wasn't pity she felt for the man, more interest in the way he wore his past.

With his hand on the door handle, Tony Ralenti turned and caught Jenny watching. "Shot in the knee when I was a cop," he said. "Nothing I can't do, though. Just do it a little slower."

He shrugged, smiled, and was gone.

Dora looked at her daughter. "Well!" was all she said and turned to cover a smile.

* * *

Zoe came in after dinner with a big "Yoo-hoo! It's me!"

She sat down, plunked her elbows up on the table, and set her face into her cupped hands. "Chief Warner thinks I killed Adam Cane."

"Heavens, Zoe. He wouldn't think that. Why, lifting a hoe over a man's head—it would take strength. More a man, I'd say." Dora nodded to prove the rightness of her words.

Zoe pushed up the sleeves of her billowy blouse. She flexed one arm to show a prodigious muscle. "I'm always working in my garden. I've got muscles on top of muscles. I saw the chief's face . . . he thinks I did it, all right. First because I had trouble with Adam over Fida—who still isn't back." There was a catch in her throat. "Then Adam was found dead in my garden. 'It would be so nice if something made sense for a change,' as Alice said."

When she turned to face Jenny, her little face was drawn and sad. There were dark circles under her eyes. "I can't think straight. Not with Fida gone. Where is she? What'd he do to her? You know, with Adam coming over to my house like that, he had to have done something to her."

Zoe shook her head. "But then, who killed Adam? Who set that tripwire? Maybe the killer took her. Maybe he couldn't resist a perfect little dog."

Nobody knew what to say. Jenny got up to fill a bowl with leftover chicken soup and set it in front of Zoe.

She looked down into the bowl, at the couple of pasty noodles floating in it, then picked up her spoon and ate without a single snide remark.

When she'd finished, she set the empty bowl back on the table, nodded to Jenny, and sat back. "I've been thinking one awful thought," she said.

Jenny and Dora waited, expecting a quote straight from Alice's mouth. Jenny swore she would faint—keel over and hit the floor—at even one more.

"Maybe he killed Fida earlier. She was out from about three on. If he did, she's probably buried in his yard. But I don't dare go over there and search. If they caught me . . ."

The straightforward, sensible comment unsettled Jenny.

"Why would he come back later? How would someone know he would be there?" she asked.

"Maybe he forgot something. Maybe he did Fida in with that . . ." Zoe couldn't say the word.

"Hoe?" Jenny filled in.

Zoe nodded. "And came back to get it. I wish I could go over there. Maybe look in his shed or see if anything's disturbed in his yard. You know, like something's been recently buried there."

They sat and thought a while.

"Guess I could go," Jenny finally said. "But not until morning. The police should be gone—they keep going in and out. If somebody catches me, I'll give some wild excuse."

"You could be over there looking for a book we're still missing," Dora offered, followed by a devilish grin and a nod at her most acceptable idea.

"I don't know." Zoe sat up straighter. "They might throw you in prison for trespass. Or," her face wrinkled, "for stepping on weeds that don't belong to you . . ."

"As I was saying," Dora went on, giving her daughter a sly little smile, "we don't know where all the books from the library got to. I mean, there were more books out to readers than I can remember. Books were thrown everywhere. Maybe some were even blown into his backyard. Personally, I think those are fine reasons to search Adam's yard." She thought a moment. "But are those just lies?"

Jenny shook her head vehemently.

Zoe spouted, "'The Dodo says the Hunter tells lies, but who believes a Dodo? Dodos don't exist. So the Hunter says the March Hare tells lies. We know *he's* barking mad. The March Hare says both of them are lying so who can ever figure out the truth?' I wouldn't worry, Jenny. If anyone should ask you what you're doing, just give them a blank look, think of the poor March Hare, and demand your rights."

"What rights?"

"Oh, the right to stick your nose in wherever it can go. The right to look for buried books in anyone's backyard." She thought hard. "The right to be a sleepwalker and go wherever your dream takes you. All of those and so much more."

Jenny laughed. "I plan to do that, Zoe, exercise my rights. And if I find a little bottle, I'll drink it down, and then I'll either hide in the policeman's socks or I will lift one foot and step on him—depending on the direction of the drink."

Zoe beamed, her face settling into a happy moon. "Now you're getting the idea. That's wonderful, Jenny. You're learning how the world really works." Zoe clapped her hands. "Maybe a little bit of magic after all."

Jenny grinned and went off to her room, stepping high as, behind her, Zoe's happy face fell back to sadness.

Chapter 11

She saw the yellow notice on the back door and decided she'd better read it—in case her basket of lies wasn't protection enough from the law.

She climbed the back steps cautiously, hoping a policeman in full uniform—flat hat and all, nightstick at his side, gun drawn—wouldn't open the door and jump out at her.

The yellow paper said no one was to enter the premises without permission of the Bear Falls Police Department. She frowned and wondered what the word "premises" covered. Only the house? The yard and all surrounding territories? She chose to exercise her right to look for buried books in anyone's backyard and hurried to part the weeds at the back of the property, searching the ground, hoping for anything but the body of a little dog.

She moved to the leaning shed at the very back of his overgrown yard. The old building hadn't seen a coat of paint since she was a little girl. She pushed the half-opened door with her shoulder. Inside, the air smelled of musk and raw earth. Packed straw from old birds' nests and leaves blown in a dozen autumns ago littered the shadowed dirt floor. On top of a crooked workbench lay a dusty array of rusted hand tools: a saw, an awl, two trowels, and a set of wrenches—all fated for the place old tools go to die.

Beside the tools stood a crooked oil lamp with a dust-covered glass shade in what looked to be an intricately set mosaic pattern. *Tiffany*, she thought, then got her mind back to what she'd come for.

Everything was beaten down, dead looking, and undisturbed. No new grave in there.

Jenny shut the door the best she could behind her and started a slow walk back and forth, across the center of the yard. She stepped hard as she walked, testing for soft ground underfoot. She made her way over the furrows of an abandoned vegetable garden and then out to what must have once been a well-kept lawn.

"Hey, there!" a voice called from the back porch of the house on the other side of Adam's. "Whatcha doing? You from the newspaper?"

The large man in a T-shirt with a big, red heart on it leaned over the railing of his slightly crooked back porch. Jenny choked her panic back and smiled as he gestured at her with the beer bottle he held. "I can help ya."

"No," she said. "Not from a newspaper. I'm just looking for something."

"Oh." His face fell. "I could have given you a quote or two about my neighbor there, Adam Cane. Knew him. Didn't like him. If you're not a reporter, then whatcha looking for?" The man took a long swig of the beer, set it on the railing, and waited for an answer.

"I'm looking for books."

"Books? You kiddin' me? The old guy who lived there was murdered yesterday. What in hell you doin' looking for books at a time like this? Don't seem right, you ask me. Instead of doing that, we should all be out chasing that little lady over there." He pointed around Adam's house. "There's your killer. I'd say let's get this over with and take that lady off to prison."

She could tell he wasn't a man she'd be able to talk to sensibly but didn't want to say out loud how ignorant he was.

"I'm here because my mother asked me to search. Dora Weston? Your neighbor?"

"You're Jenny, I bet. I remember you. You were a hellion. Warren Schuler—remember me? Heard about what happened to that library of your mother's. Is this about that?"

Relieved he was distracted, Jenny nodded, agreeing that "this" was about "that."

She nodded again, wondering how much time the man had to kill.

"You know who the old guy was?"

"What do you mean?"

"Adam Cane." He sniffed and rolled his eyes as if she was too dense to bother with. "One of the Cane family—that mansion over on Oak Street. Can you imagine him living the way he did? Coulda used help with that yard. Got that old car. What I heard was his sister cheated him outta the family money. You know about that?"

She nodded. "But I don't believe everything I hear."

"You ask me, we should chase all the rich people right outta this country. Get rid of 'em. Nothing but a bunch of bloodsuckers. Along with politicians. Get one big boat—"

"If you chase all the rich away, who would pay your salary?" She couldn't help herself.

"I don't work. Got a disability."

She wished he'd go back inside his house. Maybe if she didn't answer too many of his questions . . .

"Don't you have to look for books on the inside of a house?" The man burped in one hand. He looked embarrassed and grinned, saying he was sorry.

"We thought maybe the people who tore the Little Library apart might have run through here. You know, throwing books away."

The man nodded. "Yeah. I can see that, I guess. Well, I'll let you get back to it. Got to get ready for court. I got jury duty in Traverse City today. Hope you find your books. I'd help your mother out, but I don't think she'd much like the kind of books I read."

The man snickered and went back inside his house.

* * *

Jenny walked faster through the rest of the yard—outer edges to center. One foot after the other. Nowhere was the weedy ground upturned. No mounds of dirt. She got down on her knees to check for soft spots, places where puddles stood, not draining after the rain.

The yard hadn't been touched this spring. Weeds and grasses grew thick, strangling what might once have been flowerbeds. She neared the center of her search grid and found nothing—a relief. She could tell Zoe not to worry. Fida was not buried in Adam's backyard.

As she turned to leave, her toe caught on something beneath a section of bent grass. When she knelt to look, clumps of weeds appeared to have been dug up, then pushed back in place. She ran her fingers along the edges of the clumps—around a line of raised and dying vegetation.

She closed her eyes and dropped her head. This wasn't what she'd hoped to find and not something she wanted to dig up. She didn't want to unearth a mangled white dog with a red collar.

She closed her eyes and thought of leaving it all untouched. It would be easy to say she'd found nothing.

But she couldn't.

It didn't take much to pull at the edges of the separated clumps. Sticking her fingers into the spaces and pulling hard brought up the first one, and then another—two squares with disturbed dirt beneath. The ground was wet and soft. With only her fingers to dig with, she scrabbled at the ground until she felt something and sat back to gulp her breakfast back down her throat.

She couldn't do it. Just couldn't. Another wave of revulsion swept over her. *Not the little, one-eyed, feminist dog.*

She wiped her hands down the sides of her jeans then dug some more until her fingers hit something hard.

She felt along the length of it—not fur—and harder than she imagined a little dog could be—stiff or not.

More like metal.

She pulled the thing from its burial site. A tool. A hatchet, but not rusty. Barely dirty—the soil cleared away easily.

Jenny took the hatchet in both of her hands and stared at it—end to end.

Chapter 12

Jenny set the hatchet on the table. "Didn't smell that coming, I'll bet."

Zoe's eyebrows shot up toward the fuzzy halo that was her hair. "That's all?"

"What's that, dear?" Dora asked, standing to lean forward. "A hatchet? Where on earth did you get that?"

"It was buried in Adam's yard. I'd say it hasn't been there long."

Zoe crawled up on her knees to see better. "Wow! Think he used it on the Little Library?"

Dora looked from one to the other. "I don't think Adam was that evil. We knew him from the moment Jim and I first moved to town. A little odd, you might say. But that was all." She sat down heavily. "I don't understand anything anymore. If Adam did the Little Library in, why did somebody decide to do the same to him?"

Jenny went to call Ed Warner. If he asked how she'd found the hatchet, she decided she would just tell him the truth: hunting for Fida. Maybe Zoe could make fast and loose with reality, but Jenny wasn't that brave.

Before she could make the call, the phone rang.

"Jenny, is that you? For goodness sakes, it's me, Lisa."

Lisa the Good! A voice from a different world, where all the days were sunny and all the citizens tripped merrily about their happy chores.

"I'm so glad you're there with Mom." Lisa's voice went up an octave. "She told me about Dad's library house. And now Adam Cane's been murdered. Awful! Poor Mom. Poor Zoe. Right in her own backyard. I guess you've met her by now. Wonderful person. And so good with Mom."

Jenny pushed her hair back from her face. She looked toward the ceiling.

"You there?" Lisa asked.

"Yeah, I'm here. A lot of things going on."

"I heard. Nothing else, I hope?"

"No. Just that Mom's really upset. I've only been here a couple of days, but it feels like a month."

"Must be awful for you. You sure don't sound good." Lisa's voice slid down the scale.

"I'm okay. It's just . . . well, you know, coming home hasn't been as restful as I expected."

"Is Mom right there? Can you talk in front of her?"

"And Zoe, too."

"Oh. Say hi for me." Lisa seemed to be thinking. "You don't have to say anything but yes or no. Is the divorce final?"

"Yes. But—"

"And you're okay with everything?"

"Happy as a clam."

"Okay, so did they find whoever murdered Adam Cane?"

"Not yet. It's early."

"How about the library mauler? They get him yet?"

"No."

"Terrible."

"Even worse."

"Oh no. Not Johnny?"

"Guessed right."

"Oh dear. How was it?"

"Like you'd imagine."

Lisa's voice flattened. "I'm starting to feel bad I ever suggested you go home. I thought it would do both of you—" She interrupted herself. "Bad timing, I guess."

Lisa the Good sounded repentant. Jenny took pleasure in the rare event.

"Anyway, I called to say I'm coming home. I'm catching a plane on Sunday. I should be at Cherry Capitol about eight. Could you pick me up?"

"Sure. Mom'll be thrilled to hear."

She looked around at the two faces turned her way. She raised her eyebrows.

"I'm giving you to Mom."

"Sure," Lisa said without her usual enthusiasm.

Jenny handed the phone to Dora, who chatted merrily, so happy to soon have both her girls at home with her. "The way it used to be, Lisa. I can't wait."

"I'll call Chief Warner as soon as Mom's through," Jenny whispered to Zoe.

Zoe wrinkled her nose. "Thanks for trying. I still don't know . . . Guess I'll go home and wait for a knock at the door."

"This has nothing to do with you, Zoe."

"You want to bet?" She slid off her chair and left with only the tiniest wave of her hand.

* * *

Ed Warner sent a deputy to the house to pick up the hatchet and take a brief statement. When she told him her story about looking for books—which she decided to use after all, leaving Zoe completely out of it, the deputy raised an eyebrow at her.

"You see the sign on the door over there?" the cop asked. His back stiffened as if every time an infraction of the law was mentioned, he was required to stand at attention.

"I didn't go in the house. I was only in his backyard."

"Looking for books?"

She nodded. Dora rolled her eyes, but he couldn't see her.

"Yes. Adam checked out a few of Mom's books, and we need them back."

"Thought he hated that library."

Jenny, thinking now what a lame excuse she'd used, smiled cheerily.

"So you were digging in Mr. Cane's yard, searching for buried books." He squinted down at her.

"No." Jenny shook her head. "Not exactly. I was just looking around when I tripped and fell. All I did was check the ground to see what tripped me. I found a place where the dirt was disturbed, so I checked it out and found the hatchet." She raised her eyebrows at the young officer.

"You didn't go in the house, did you?"

"No. Of course not. The man next door saw me. You can ask him."

"You mean Warren Schuler?" He nodded a time or two, wrote in his book, and stood to take a large plastic bag from his back pocket. Pulling out a handkerchief, he used it to load the hatchet into the bag.

The deputy gathered his things and left without saying much beyond wishing them a good day.

* * *

Back in her bedroom that night, Jenny slid both back and side windows open and sat in her window seat. The warm night air blew straight across the room, billowing the curtains and ruffling the edges of magazines she'd set on the chest of drawers.

Eventually, she got up and slipped into a pair of pajama bottoms and an old T-shirt. She pulled *Alice in Wonderland* from the bookcase where all her childhood books stood wedged together. She climbed into her bed, hoping to stay there all night, then wishing she could make herself small enough to fit in the room as she read by the dim light how Alice grew very small and then very large and discovered a group of very odd creatures.

The bed was too cramped, the nightlight too yellow—bright circles shining on the ceiling. She snapped off the light, even though she felt better with the light on, and wrapped the sheet completely around her. Finally, she gave up and trailed back to the window seat.

A dark night. She heard pine trees rustling and what she thought was the sound of Lake Michigan waves. A night bird called. Once in a while, a car drove up or down Elderberry Street.

Johnny's face was in her head. His brown, unclipped hair hanging past his shirt collar—so different from the clean-cut guy he'd been when they made plans to marry after college. He was unshaven—all she had really seen of him during his slow move toward her. Different but familiar. There was a time when she would have run to him to feel his arms slide around her body, his chin resting on top of her head. To inhale the smell of him—mostly Dial soap and his mother's laundry detergent.

She hadn't dared acknowledge him there in the parking lot and didn't dare let him get close enough to be able to see him mouth her name. Johnny had made the choice for both of them. He was Angel's—now and forever.

She shut her eyes and let herself remember her and Johnny near the high school gym. The last month of senior year. In the fall, they'd be at Michigan State—even that was planned so they could be together. They were standing the way they often stood—with him leaning over her, hand balanced on the cinderblock wall behind her, close, as if he was going to kiss her right there in the school, three doors down from the principal's office.

They'd made love for the first time the weekend before graduation, on the beach, just at dusk, holding each other and later laughing at the sand in their clothes.

The feeling afterward had puzzled her—not what she expected and not such a big deal after all, though he was pleased. He kept telling her how great she was and touching her and leaning in close as if he somehow owned her now.

She'd believed it. She belonged to him after that, and she had a right to hold his arm tight at her side, touch his hair whenever she wanted to, and look up at him with a smile that went so deep, she could feel it in every part of her body. Then her period had been late, and they were both scared. When it finally came, she called him with the almost disappointing news because, in a fog of romance, she'd partially moved on to the white picket fence.

A week later, her father was killed and the police searched for and failed to find whoever did it—probably a tourist or sales-man passing on the way down to Traverse City, the old police chief told her mother. It was a destructive slash through their lives. Nothing was the same. Not a thought went to Johnny as she moved into a strange world of mourning, where only Lisa, Mom, and she knew how to exist. After a solid month, she'd finally reached out to Johnny—only he didn't return her call. She went to his house, and his sad mother said he wasn't there—that he'd gone away with his brother, Gerry. They were in Chicago. She'd told herself it was understandable; she'd been so distant, and he was getting ready to go away to college. Why not have some fun with his brother?

Weeks passed, and when he came home again, they saw each other in the drugstore on Holly Street.

She'd asked, her hand on his arm, "Are you leaving for Lansing next week?"

"Can't go. Mom needs me at home. Gerry moved out, you hear?"

"But . . ." She didn't believe him. "You've got a scholarship. You can't stay in Bear Falls . . ."

He'd shrugged and looked over her head at a wall of pink hairnets.

"Call me," she whispered when she was too choked to talk anymore.

He'd nodded and walked away.

"Are we . . . ?" She called after him. "Are we still . . . together?"

Johnny, his hair already longer than before, his jeans stained at the knees, looked back, and for a moment they were the way they used to be—the same connection. The look gave her hope. Especially when he walked back and leaned down to whisper in her ear.

He said, "Angel's pregnant."

A piece of gossip? She'd looked up at him, wanting to laugh.

"It's mine," he said. Nothing showed on his face but anger.

He left her standing in the store feeling as if she would fall into one of the glass-fronted counters, feeling as if her legs were melting under her.

She called him from time to time but always hung up before the call went through. He never called her.

She heard about their wedding, and then in the months after she moved to Lansing, she heard they had a baby girl.

She married Ronald much later, after she'd graduated and had a job in Chicago. Years later, she heard Angel had another girl.

After that she stopped listening to news of Johnny Arlen.

Jenny rested her head back against the window casing. How she wished she could be like Zoe and have a fairy story to rewrite everything in life. So much easier to quote a piece of nonsense than explain how someone you thought loved you as much as you loved him could make love to another girl. So much easier to spout a nonsense riddle than to explain how that man could walk away and never explain what happened between them.

"Everything's got a moral, if only you can find it." One of Zoe's Alice quotes.

Jenny laughed and then bit her lip. So a moral for everything. *Hogwash, Mr. Carroll*, she thought.

No moral to being dumped by Johnny Arlen. Unless it could be that the dumpables are always in danger of being dumped.

Maybe it happened so she could meet Ronald Korman, who was surely waiting patiently in line to find her.

Ah, the lesson of the lines. Ronald, waiting his turn to be the second man to dump her. All of it writ large in some book somewhere. And who would be the third? And the fourth to break the heart of the eminently dumpable Miss Jenny Weston?

A dog barked somewhere nearby.

She listened.

Another bark echoed farther down the street. Not the bark of a little dog, but she heard Zoe's back door open.

"Fida? Fida?" Zoe called in a hopeful voice. "Is that you?" Zoe whistled.

A few minutes later, the door closed.

Chapter 13

"Ed Warner wants me down at the station."

Zoe stood in their living room the next morning dressed in a jumbled outfit straight from the children's department of a whimsical boutique: colorful animals on the shirt and trees on the mismatched shorts that fell below her knees. Her wild, uncombed hair was held back by a pink headband.

Zoe's outfit might've been colorful, but her face was dead white.

"I can't go alone." The words were a moan. "And I can't ask you, Dora."

"Calm down, dear," Dora bent to put her arm around the little woman, almost burying Zoe's head against her breast. Dora stepped back. "Why can't you ask me? You haven't done anything. I'd be happy to go with you."

"I wouldn't put you through it."

Dora sputtered, but Zoe looked toward Jenny. "Could you go?" she asked. "I smell the guillotine."

Jenny rolled her eyes. "Michigan doesn't have the death penalty, nor a guillotine."

"You know what I mean. The first thing Ed Warner will say will be, 'Off with her head.' That's what anyone would say."

Jenny lowered her voice to a big-dog growl. "Cut it out, Zoe. You pull that stuff in front of the police chief and you'll end up confined forever."

Zoe had the good grace to blush. "Sorry. A bad habit. I blame Lewis Carroll. I think he gets a hold of a person's mind and . . ."

Jenny gave her an exasperated look. "If you want me to go out in public with you, the quoting and the living a fairy tale stuff will have to stop. Understand?"

Zoe's head drooped. She nodded. "I'll try my best," she promised.

Jenny took a deep breath, certain the victory would be short-lived. "Now, why does he want to see you?"

"He didn't say." Her voice was small.

"Okay. When does he want to see you?"

"Now. As soon as I can make it."

"May I get dressed first?" Jenny motioned to her mismatched pajamas.

Zoe nodded. "Maybe it's about the hatchet. I looked in my shed. Mine is still there. So it can't be that one."

"Let's get to the station and find out."

"Maybe he only needs a gardening tip or two. You have such a lovely garden," Dora said, nodding and smiling now, hoping she'd solved the riddle of a policeman wanting to see Zoe.

Jenny threw on the clothes she'd worn the day before. Her long hair took all of thirty seconds to brush. Lipstick. Sandals from under her bed.

She drove her car because Zoe was too nervous, especially if she had to use the elevated pedals that were on hers. She swore she'd fall right off of them—she was that shaky.

* * *

The station was at the far end of Oak Street, a block beyond the old Cane mansion where Adam and Aaron's sister, Abigail, lived alone in her big house, except for the people who worked there.

The house, the grandest in Bear Falls, sat atop a grassy mound—tall and rigid, built of solid limestone blocks. It stood beneath a canopy of old maples. The manicured yard bloomed with crabapples and mock orange, all surrounded by a black wrought iron fence. An arch of the same wrought iron stood above the front gate. The ornate, entwined leaves of the arch spelled out "Cane."

"I've always detested that house," Jenny said. "Looks like something out of a horror movie."

Zoe shivered. "*Citizen Kane.*"

"Abigail must know Adam's dead by now. I wonder what she'll do about a funeral."

"Humph. Throw him in the lake, I imagine. Might as well do him in all the way. Treated him badly when he was alive, I heard. Her own brother."

"Brothers," Jenny corrected. "She was like that to both of them. Aaron is the younger one. Both somewhere in their late sixties, older than Abigail. Before their father died, they got along okay. That's what my mother said. I never heard much about it. Whole different generation."

"I wonder if Aaron knows about Adam yet. He lives out in the woods somewhere, doesn't he?"

"Abigail must have told him," Jenny said as she pulled into the police station parking lot. "Ed Warner, if nobody else. Maybe Ed should think about that brother first when he looks for a killer. Kind of biblical: Cane and Abel. Or Cane and Cane."

"Yup." Zoe thumped her hands in her lap. "His brother could've done it to him. Or maybe Abigail. She's maybe sixty-six or seven, only a little younger than the boys. But what she would be doing in my backyard at night, I can't imagine. Still, anyone's better than me."

The red brick building bore the discrete sign "Bear Falls Police Department" affixed to one of the heavy oak doors. Jenny let Zoe go in first, waiting for the little woman to straighten her colorful top and set her shoulders straight.

* * *

Ed Warner, head bobbing to one side, said no when Jenny asked if she could come into his office with Zoe.

"You wait out here." He gestured to a row of wooden chairs along one wall. "I'll talk to you when I'm through with her."

"She's very nervous . . . alone," Jenny made the mistake of saying.

Ed narrowed his eyes, first at Jenny and then at Zoe. "What's got you so nervous, Ms. Zola? If you don't have anything to hide, you've got nothing to be afraid of."

Zoe gave Jenny a "they're going to fry me for sure" look over her shoulder and followed the chief back to his office. Jenny sat and crossed her hands in her lap.

And waited.

A very long hour later, during which Jenny got madder and madder, they were back, with Zoe leading the way, face blank. She hurried to Jenny, putting her small hands out.

She whispered, in a stunned voice, "He says he's got evidence. He told me not to leave town. Oh, how I wish I had a place to hide."

The chief bent toward Jenny. "Could you come on back for a minute? Just have a question or two about the hatchet."

Zoe worked her way up into a chair, feet not reaching the ground, and said she'd wait right there. Jenny followed Ed Warner to a large, utilitarian office with file cases lined along two walls. She took the only chair, other than the desk chair, that was in the room.

"Zoe didn't do anything to anybody, you know." She sat forward, signaling she wasn't staying long.

Ed settled slowly in his chair. He sighed and gave her a rueful look.

"Don't know much of anything yet. Got a ways to go, I'd say." He cleared his throat and opened the folder in front of him. "You found the body. What would you say happened?"

She shrugged. "I know Zoe didn't kill him. First of all, can you see her swinging that hoe and striking the back of Adam's head?"

"Remember, he fell over a trip wire first. The man was flat on the ground. Anybody could've gotten him." He leaned back, entwined his hands behind his head, and looked up at the ceiling. "And who else could have put that wire in her garden?"

He leaned forward to hit the floor with the legs of his chair. "But first of all, as I said before, it's good to see you, Jenny. Been a long time. How're you finding things back here?"

"To tell you the truth, Ed, not too good."

He chuckled. "I understand that well enough."

She asked about his wife, Milly Sienkievitz, and how his kids were doing. There was no rushing talk of murder, not when old friends met.

Ed launched into a five-minute monologue on his son, Wally, and his football prowess. Then there was another five minutes on Rebecca, his youngest, who was a math whiz.

Jenny answered questions about living in Chicago and then, after the proper interlude, they got down to business.

"Why did you tell Zoe not to leave town?" Jenny asked. "Sounds to me like you're suspicious of her."

He pulled his smile down slowly and shook his head. "Standard thing to say. I don't want her gone until I find out for sure what happened to Adam Cane."

Ed's voice was slow and deliberate. "Ya know, Adam was threatening that dog of hers. Hated the dog. No reason in particular except Adam hated a lot of things."

"Like what? Maybe that's where you'll find the killer."

"Like his sister and his brother, Abigail and Aaron. Like just about every neighbor he ever had—except maybe your mom. Always said what a fine woman Dora Weston was. Talked a lot about your dad. Blamed us for not catching the guy who left him to die like that. But that's about the only thing Adam ever felt bad about."

"What happened when you told his sister he was dead?"

"You know Abigail. Didn't say much. Shook her head and asked if she could see him."

"See him? Isn't that strange? After all the years they've lived in the same town and never bothered to see each other?"

"I thought it was, but the Canes are like that. Long as I can remember. All over the money. Just teaches you not to go thirsting after gold. Comes back to bite you in the—"

He cleared his throat and sat thinking. "That little friend of yours out there's got quite a mind for investigation. She asked me about fingerprints on the metal stakes that held the trip wire. We had 'em tested in Traverse City. Told her nothing on 'em. Asked about the shoe print on the one book." He shook his head. "Forensics lifted it, but it's a kind of ordinary shoe. Big though. More like a boot than a tennis shoe or anything like that. Guess your friend is cleared on the library thing, what with those little feet of hers. Then she wanted to know if I talked to the other neighbors, see if any of them had a problem with your mom's library. Said there must be some connection—two crimes like that within a day of each other. She talk to you about that?"

Jenny shook her head, then asked, "What about Adam's brother, Aaron? Does he know his older brother is dead?"

"Couldn't find him. Went out to that little house of his. Had a devil of a time finding it, too. He wasn't there. Knocked for five minutes. I'll try again later. Can't quite imagine Aaron killing him though. Aaron was the small one. Kind of timid. Bet if he tried anything, Adam would've knocked him cold."

"Think about the way it was done, Ed. Adam was a target, stretched out on the ground. You told Zoe even she could've killed him that way. Same goes for Aaron."

Jenny got up, but he stopped her.

"About that hatchet you found at Adam's . . . Shouldn't have touched it, you know. Fingerprints. Now the only prints we'll get off of it are yours."

She winced.

"I know you're worried about your friend." He shook his head.

"Not exactly a bosom buddy. I just met her."

"Well, whatever. I know you don't think she had anything to do with Adam's death, but I just don't see anybody else."

She almost laughed at Ed. "Come on now. You take Zoe for a crazed criminal?"

"Seen stranger things."

He reached into the top desk drawer and pulled out a large glassine sheet, laid it on the desk, then pushed it to Jenny. She immediately felt tricked by her laid-back classmate. When she turned the sheet around, she saw it was a letter. Typed.

"We found this in Adam Cane's house," Ed said, watching her closely. "Now you tell me what I should be thinking about your neighbor."

She read,

Mr. Cane,

I found an axe in my shed carved with *WS*, for your neighbor, Warren Schuler, along with pieces of the broken library wedged in the handle. That proves you had nothing to do with destroying Dora Weston's Little Library. You come over tomorrow morning—just about dawn so nobody sees you. Wouldn't want more trouble for you. I left the axe in my shed, on a shelf, because I don't want anything to do with it and I wouldn't want the police chief thinking it was funny I found it. Be happy to have you take it to the police chief yourself and clear your name once and for all. In return, I hope you'll lay off my dog. And I'll do my best to stop her from urinating on your front lawn.

Jenny looked up, in disbelief. "It's typed. Anybody could have done that."

"Who'd want to make a deal for Zoe's dog but Zoe?"

"Come on! This is a setup." Jenny was angry. "Everybody in this town knows the problems Zoe had with Adam Cane. I hope you aren't taking that seriously." She gestured toward the paper. "And Warren Schuler? Sorry, I can't see Mr. Schuler out there in the middle of the night whacking my mother's library with an axe. Lucky if he can find his way up and down his own steps. Did you find that axe? The one that's supposed to belong to Warren Schuler?"

He shook his head. "But Ms. Zola was the first one who thought it was an axe used on the library. How'd she know that?"

"Even you said that's what it was."

He gave a slight shrug.

"This letter's only a ploy to make Zoe look guilty. You talk to Mr. Schuler?"

"Just got back. Said he was down to Traverse City. Spent the night the library was destroyed with his son. I called his son on the way back here. Said his dad was there all right, too drunk to drive. And he never saw an axe with his dad's initials on it."

He reached back and scratched hard at his neck. "So you see, doesn't look too good for your little friend."

Exhausted from trying to follow Ed's logic all over the place, Jenny stood to leave. "Chief, listen, your killer left that note for Adam. I'll agree with you there. But it wasn't Zoe Zola. First of all, it would have been better written. Second, she never would've said 'urinating.' Zoe's a lot more direct than that. Third, none of that's true. She doesn't know who destroyed the library, and you said there was nothing in her shed for Adam to get." She threw up her hands. "You believe anything you want to believe. I know she can be a big pain in the neck, but I won't stand around while you take the easy way out and arrest Zoe for something she didn't do. I'm not crazy about her, I'll admit that, but I'll get her a lawyer if I have to."

He stood slowly, unfolding and stretching. His eyes were hard on her. "Not planning on getting in my way, are you, Jenny? I wouldn't do that if I were you."

Red faced, Jenny looked back from the doorway. "I'm going to do whatever it takes, Ed. Charging Zoe would be crazy."

"Suit yourself. Maybe I should go a little slow. But one thing I'm not going to stand for is interference on this." He raised his eyebrows. "You want to think hard about that before you give me ultimatums."

Jenny's mouth dropped. Had she just been threatened?

In the small lobby of the station, Jenny motioned to Zoe, sitting on the edge of her chair, to follow her out of there. They had things to do, and warning or not, Jenny was going to see that Zoe didn't get railroaded just because somebody was outsmarting the chief.

Chapter 14

The ride home was quiet. Zoe sat slumped in her seat, head barely reaching the window. She didn't look out and comment on gardens the way she usually did, finding fault with people who didn't have a single fairy house.

"It's 'cause I'm a stranger here," she groused after a while. "'Cause I don't belong. He's looking for an easy answer. Wants something that won't disturb the townspeople too much. That's what it is, you know. Throwing a bone to a bunch of dogs, and that bone is me."

There was something in Zoe's voice Jenny hadn't heard before: a flattened spirit. Her usual happy sparring was gone.

The bright June day turned flat and artificial, a tinge of gray behind it, like a faint storm on the horizon. Or something more ominous, Jenny thought as she drove.

She recognized Zoe's depression, the sense of being overwhelmed, the sense of being a target and not knowing why. It was the same thing that hit her after she'd called Ronald repeatedly, certain he was dead on a Chicago street corner, then hysterically telephoning the police and hospitals until he called to say he was in Guatemala with his client—Tootsie or Monique or whatever—and wasn't coming back.

Ever.

In the driveway, Zoe slowly sat up straight, her head popping above the windowsill to look around. She turned to face Jenny. "It's not even what Ed Warner thinks that's bothering me so much. It's Fida." Her lips went white around the edges. "Not in Adam's house. Not in his yard . . ." She struggled to get a breath. "Not buried or anything. At least not where we can find her."

"Maybe she really is lost."

She shook her head. "I've been through this town at least ten times looking. With everything else happening, Fida's disappearance has got to be a part of it somehow. I keep thinking and thinking. Usually I come up with something pretty quick. It's from getting into Lewis Carroll's mind, you know. Figuring out the 'Jabberwocky' made me into a code breaker, and not just because that first stanza is in mirror English." She sighed and shook her head. "It's the words, Jenny. *The words.* Listen: "'Twas brillig, and the slithy toves / Did gyre and gimble in the wabe; / All mimsy were the borogoves, / And the mome raths outgrabe'"

"And that helps?" Jenny was incredulous.

"Of course it does. Once you know that 'brillig' means four o'clock, 'slithy' means 'lithe and slimy,' and 'toves' means badgers or lizards or corkscrews, who live under sundials and eat only cheese."

Jenny shook her head. "And that tells you . . . what? You lost me, Zoe."

"What you're looking at is a suitcase word. Meanings packed in on top of meanings, and all you have to do is dig deeper, down to the bottom, to discover what was meant to begin with. This whole murder thing's like that. Look at what happened to

Adam and then dig deeper and deeper until you get down into the labyrinth and find the criminal brain behind it all."

She sighed. "Ah, 'Jabberwocky.' What a mind Carroll had. Everything tight together in his head, like little pieces of spaghetti—wound round and round. Don't you wonder sometimes where all our thoughts are stored? And why we can find some and have to wait for others to arrive?"

"Nope. Never thought to worry about that, Zoe."

"Humpty Dumpty knew all about words, remember?" She looked out the window as Jenny turned on Elderberry Street.

Jenny shook her head.

"Well, you'll have to read it again. *Through the Looking Glass.* You could use a good dose of magic. So many buried artifacts—like the hatchet. Don't you see? Humpty Dumpty said, 'I can explain all the poems that ever were invented—and a good many that haven't been invented just yet.' That describes genius. If we could get to the interior of words, I'll find Fida there. And I'll find a murderer."

Jenny pulled the car onto their driveway. "How can you be buried in 'Jabberwocky' with so much going on around us?"

"Better there," Zoe said after thinking a good two minutes, "than in a world where they call me a murderer. Or maybe 'murderess.' Or it could be 'Sseredrum?' You see? If only I had a mirror, I could show you how to make words your captives."

Jenny, knowing by now that it was no use to talk to Zoe when she was in an Alice funk, opened her door and got out. Zoe followed, letting her small body slide slowly to the driveway. She stood still, listening.

"I always hope Fida will come running." She shook her head and, shoulders bent, started across the lawn toward the tall pines between their houses.

"Tell your mom I'll be there later," she said over her shoulder. "Tony's coming to your house tonight. He made another drawing. Maybe I'm wrong, but I get the idea Dora wants to cheer me up with happy thoughts about the new library, and Tony's excited about the job." She gave Jenny a wan smile and walked off, soon disappearing under the trees, only a disembodied voice trailing behind her.

"A good man. A really good man, Jenny. Have you ever known a really good man besides your father? You might want to take a look at this one. Wouldn't hurt."

Zoe was gone.

* * *

"What happened?" Mom asked from the porch.

Jenny hurried up the steps to drop into a chair. "Looks like Ed Warner wants to make Zoe into the murderer. Man's crazy. At least, he's in over his head."

"She couldn't hurt anybody, and everybody knows it." Dora rocked and fanned herself with a folded newspaper, then tapped one foot angrily on the porch floor. "Always so much easier to blame the stranger from out of town. As if we don't have enough sinners right here in Bear Falls to choose from."

"Heard anything about Adam's funeral? I don't suppose I'm going." Jenny leaned back and thought about doing nothing.

"Of course you are. Everybody goes to funerals. Have to pay your respects, you know. Funeral is tomorrow. Vera Wattles stopped by while you were gone. Vera said Abigail's secretary and her lawyer took care of everything, and from what she heard from Tom Tannin over at the funeral home, they spent almost nothing on Adam's funeral. Poor man. Probably Abigail's orders."

"Do we have to go?" She was whining and didn't care.

Dora raised her eyebrows. "Of course we do. Adam was our neighbor. Do you remember that line from *Death of a Salesman*? 'Attention must be paid. He's not to be allowed to fall into his grave like an old dog.'"

*　*　*

That settled, they rocked. Dora fanned.

"I hear Tony Ralenti's coming over." Jenny stopped rocking to think about a shower before Tony got there. She felt grimy and hadn't washed her hair in two days. She pulled a fan of her long black hair out so she could see how it shone with too much oil. Yes. A shower was in order. And a change of clothes. She might even go for *pretty*.

"He's got sketches to show us. I'm eager to see what he's come up with. I wish it was rebuilt already and everybody was coming by with the books they promised, and we could throw a party. And I wish everything in Bear Falls was back the way it used to be—without the violence and people getting killed."

Jenny understood "the way it used to be." Back when there weren't dead bodies among the fairies houses. When tiny neighbors weren't accused of murder. When she didn't run into Johnny Arlen—anywhere. When a little dog wasn't missing . . .

"Ed Warner wants me to come up with a list of my patrons. The sign-out sheets are gone, but I know most of them. I told Ed I'd do the best I could for him, but between the two of us, I think he's barking up the wrong tree. Only nice people read books, you know. Bet anything there's not a big call on death row for *Wuthering Heights* or *'Tis*."

"Or *Lord of the Flies* or *As I Lay Dying*," Jenny teased.

Dora got up slowly. "I think you are making fun of me. To think I went to college to be a librarian. Who would have thought Bear Falls was where I'd end up? Still and all, I think a library is a library is a library, don't you? No matter how big or small. Books are important."

Jenny, feeling guilty because she had been making fun of her mother, vehemently agreed.

* * *

After a shower, with her hair brushed until it shone, a good dose of cream all over her body, clean underwear, clean white shorts, and a low-cut cotton shirt with inserts of white lace, Jenny went downstairs, following the smell of pot roast.

Dora had gone to the market herself after Jenny's abortive shopping trip. She was boiling little potatoes to go with the pot roast. And carrots with herbs. And a salad. Strawberry shortcake for dessert, made with fresh Michigan berries. A real meal.

If she was going to stay in Bear Falls and be any kind of help to her mom, Jenny figured she'd better reclaim some of the wifely skills she'd lost when Ronald abandoned her. And maybe find a market in Traverse City.

They ate, relaxed, feeling better than either had felt in the last two days. They talked about the books they were reading: Jenny reading *M Train* and rereading *Alice in Wonderland*. Dora back into Jane Austen. Things felt almost normal in the Weston house. As soon as the table was cleared and the dishes placed in the dishwasher, there was a knock at the screen door. Tony Ralenti walked in, the slight hesitation in his gait hardly noticeable.

Tony carried a scroll of papers under one arm and spread them across the cleared table with a flourish. He bent forward, lowering his dark head and planting his hands directly on the papers. He looked up at Dora. "I think I've solved the problem," he said, smiling broadly.

He turned to Jenny, eyes widening. "Well," he said with clear admiration, "you clean up pretty good, Jenny Weston."

His face wrinkled into fine creases when he smiled, making her blush like a teenager. She wanted to kick herself for making the effort.

"What problem was that?" Dora frowned.

"The two houses." Tony's voice was a deep baritone. One of those male voices Jenny found reverberated in her head. Something of a deep well to it. Almost haunting. Easy to recall.

"Here's the children's house. You were right. It should be separate from the other one. We'll just stand them side by side on separate poles. Room for about twenty books in each one, though I think this one should open from the front so the kids can reach in easy."

"The children's house . . . hmmm," Dora said.

"I've got yours right. You agree?"

"It's perfect, as far as I can see. Jim would love it," she answered.

"So I thought I'd make the other one look like your neighbor's place. That way Zoe can paint fairies on the outside and Superman flying up the pole, or Spider-Man hanging by a thread from the eaves. She can put anything she wants inside: maybe a *Cat in the Hat*. Anything she wants. An extra surprise. Could maybe plant a kind of fairy garden behind the posts."

Jenny leaned in close enough to see these two perfect houses. One was a copy of their house. The other house was Zoe's—white siding, red door, and all.

"They're fine. They're truly fine." Dora smiled happily from Tony to Jenny.

"Thought your neighbor's would work." He looked back at the women. "She writes about fairy tales and little people."

"She'll be pleased," Dora said. "Now there will be two perfect libraries. And to think Lisa's coming home in a few days. She'll be so excited. Lisa met Zoe the last time she was here and just loves her. Things are certainly getting better. I didn't want to change what was, but now we'll have more children stopping by, along with the adults. And I'll get to read books I haven't read in ages." Her mind drifted. "*Mary Poppins* and the Nancy Drews."

"*The Indian in the Cupboard*," Tony joined in.

"*If You Give a Mouse a Cookie*," Jenny said, making them laugh.

Tony rolled up his plans and promised to begin work in two days, after Adam Cane's funeral, because, of course, everyone in town was going to that.

He left as Zoe walked up the steps. They stopped to talk a minute before Tony went on his halting way. Zoe came in, screen door slamming shut behind her.

"Tony said you've got a surprise for me?" She looked from Jenny to Dora.

"We're going to build two Little Libraries," Dora said.

Zoe smiled a tepid smile. "That's good, Dora."

"Tony's building a children's house. Remember? You wanted that."

Zoe lifted one side of her bottom to get on a chair and then slid the rest of herself up to bounce into place.

"That will be a very fine thing." Zoe smiled again.

"Tony's drawn up plans for the children's library to look exactly like your house."

Now her eyes flew open. For a minute, she said nothing, as if picturing such a place in her head. "Would there be room for fairies?"

"Paint some on the pole," Dora said. "And how about a couple of superheroes for the boys?"

"And maybe a fairy on the roof," Jenny said. "And fairy faces looking out the windows."

Zoe's eyes were huge by the time they'd finished. "What a fine thing it will be!"

Dora had more happy news. "Also, Lisa's coming home for the weekend."

Zoe was even happier at that. "Be great to see her. I'd like to hear about that documentary she's doing. We should have a party."

Dora hurried to pour glasses of lemonade all around. "It might not look right, Zoe, with Adam's death and all. I mean the party."

She sighed. "Oh well. It will still be so nice to have Lisa home."

Jenny felt her back get a little stiff. All this celebration over Lisa the Good. A tinge of old sibling jealousy zipped through her head.

Zoe picked up the heavy glass in front of her and took a dainty sip. "Good news is such a magical thing," she said. "It changes you inside and pulls you right out of the doldrums."

Dora clapped her hands. "Then you're happy again. I'm so glad."

Zoe's eyes gleamed with mischief. "'About as happy as King Charles the First when he was imprisoned.'"

Jenny rolled her eyes.

Zoe looked offended. "Lewis Carroll said that himself in a letter. But how happy could the king have been when he ended by being beheaded?"

Dora shook her head. "Zoe, you are incorrigible."

"I know," she said. "And other things too terrible to say out loud for fear of frightening the cat. I think I got that one from Emily Dickinson. I'm reading her again, though the pages of your book are crinkled and feel like old cotton."

She closed her eyes to think. "Or maybe it was a dog," she said. "Maybe Emily said that about Carlo, her dog. I don't remember. I've had it stuck in the back of my head for a long time. I'm glad it's finally out."

They talked about fairies to be painted on the pole and went on to other things before Zoe came to the point she'd originally come over to discuss. "I came about the funeral tomorrow. As Adam's suspected killer, do you think I should go?"

"Of course," Dora said. "You had nothing to do with his death. If you don't go, people will gossip."

"They'll gossip if I do go."

"So it seems you have no choice. Either way, you'll be discussed."

"Like the weather." Zoe sipped her lemonade. "I'll only go if I can be with you two."

It was a sad statement, but it was agreed upon. The three would go to the funeral together.

"One thing more I've been thinking about," Zoe said. "I need to go out to see Aaron, Adam's brother—but maybe tomorrow won't be the best day because of the funeral. There's something in that family . . . I don't know what. Maybe Aaron can tell me more about Adam and who wanted him dead. Maybe even tell me where Fida is. You never know. I've been wondering if Adam didn't take her out to Aaron before he was killed. You know, to hide her for a while. Teach me a lesson." A small ray of hope crossed her face. "I was thinking maybe we should ask Tony to go with us. He was a detective, you know. I'll bet he'd know how to get information out of Aaron."

"Third degree?" Jenny teased. "I'll go if you want."

"Are you kidding?" Zoe made a face. "You coming to help or just interested in Tony?"

"What? I . . . fine. Forget it." Jenny wanted to knock Zoe on her head.

"I was teasing." Zoe frowned. "Of course I need your help. I feel like you're almost my friend."

"Yeah," Jenny muttered. "Well, almost. Think your nose should do a better smelling job around me."

Chapter 15

Brown. Brown. Brown. And then more brown thrown in as an accent color.

Brown carpets in the funeral home. Brown couches lining the long hall of the old house. Brown paneling on the wavy walls. Brown wooden lamps on dark mahogany tables.

The funeral home was a cave, a place so dark and forbidding, it should have been left empty with a few bats hanging from the ceiling. She'd forgotten about Tannin's Funeral Home and about Mr. Tannin, standing at the front door, greeting mourners in his old white shirt with a sweat ring at the collar, his smile frozen permanently somewhere between sadness and melancholy.

"Ah, Mrs. Weston and Jenny Weston," Tom Tannin greeted them, ignoring Zoe. "Adam Cane is in the Serenity Room. So sad . . . poor Adam Cane. And only this one day. I would have thought more time would be needed—friends from distant places, you know. A nice memorial. A cortege of limousines to the cemetery." He rolled his eyes.

His patter would be the same to each person who entered, the flick of his limp wrist, his surreptitious glance at his watch to see if it was dinnertime yet. Her father had been buried from here. Jenny caught the smell of overly sweet flowers masking the stench of death. She felt sick—the same light-headed feeling she had all those years ago.

She remembered flinching from people who came up to hug her, eyeing each of them, thinking that anyone could be the person who killed her father. *That one? That one?* She'd become suspicious of kindness. Wondered what lay behind smiles.

A single awful funeral was enough to write off funeral homes and mourners forever.

Mr. Tannin leaned down to whisper close to Jenny's ear. "I heard you discovered the body of the poor man."

Her stomach did a small leap at his unctuousness and the smell of spearmint on his breath.

He turned to the next arriving group, hands out, sickly smile in place.

The large reception room was packed. People, standing along the hall, nodded to Dora, smiled at Jenny, and ignored Zoe. Others turned their backs.

As Dora said, the citizens of Bear Falls went to funerals no matter if they were friends or relatives of the dead person or they'd seen them once in Baldur's Hardware Store. It was what a decent person did—marked each passing. They were here in force, dressed in their Sunday best. Children—forced to be there—wore their Easter clothes, complete with stiff white hats on the little girls and uncomfortable black shoes on the boys.

Jenny, Zoe, and Dora entered the viewing room.

At the front of the brown room sat a closed brown wooden coffin atop a carved, brown bier. Flowers in baskets stood on the floor around the casket, most seeming to be brown, too, along with planters of dying greenery that looked as if they'd never make it through the day. Dora had sent a plant like so many others. Always practical: "Flowers die. The family can take a plant home with them. You get your money's worth with a plant."

Jenny couldn't help but lean toward Dora and ask, "Which member of Adam's loving family will take home your plant, do you think, Mom?"

Dora shook her head and gave Jenny a shushing look as she joined the line moving up to the casket where the bereaved stood.

Jenny hadn't seen Abigail Cane since before she left Bear Falls. When she worked at Myrtle's Restaurant and Grill, she'd watched Abigail make her regal way down the hill from her house to the drug store or the post office: back erect, head high, a smile to the right and a smile to the left. Abigail was thin then, with light-brown, wispy hair that would stand in the slightest breeze and wave. With her nose in the air and handbag over one stiff arm, she'd stop to grace a passerby with a word or two or lift a hand to hail a honking car. Jenny, never being acknowledged by Abigail, knew little of what she said to the loungers on the benches along Oak Street but imagined it would be a solicitous question about their health, their children, or a comment on the weather. Everybody in Bear Falls talked about the weather as if they had inside information. Especially in the winter, when the waterfall at the far end of Oak Street froze solid before it dropped into Bear Lake. Kids climbed the half-iced cascade.

Abigail, along with a colorless woman who stood at her elbow in front of the wooden casket, received mourners with a gracious dip of her head at each expression of sadness. She, heavier than Jenny remembered, wore a black suit with a white blouse, starched ruffles at the neck. The gold in the frames of her glasses glinted in the low light, making it appear as if she gave off sparks. Jenny found herself a little nervous but then felt silly. Abigail Cane meant nothing to her. The woman's name was usually mentioned only in whispers around Bear Falls, along with a few other rich dowagers living in old, dark houses with antique furniture; doilies on the tables; antimacassars on the backs of plush chairs; and huge, Italian-made soup tureens on their polished dining room tables.

The mayor was speaking to Abigail so others hung back As a kid, she'd learned that there was a pecking order to be followed, beginning with the mayor, though she'd never been told why.

Zoe tugged at her hand. "I can't. I just can't. I can't talk to Abigail Cane. She won't know what to say, and neither will I. And then I'll get preposterous. People are looking at me funny as it is. I feel like an axe murderer. I'll go wait in the car."

Zoe spun around and made her way back through the crowd with her head down. Jenny watched the little figure, in an ankle-length black dress and a black headband to hold the blonde curls back, swish out of the room.

*　*　*

After a few minutes, Tony Ralenti ambled up to Jenny, next in line to speak to Abigail. He whispered, "What I heard, Adam wasn't liked much by anybody, but look at 'em." He indicated the crowd. "Think they're here to make sure he's dead?"

He grinned down at her. She frowned, not wanting to laugh and be stigmatized as an infidel. She was here out of duty—first to Dora, who would have been shocked at not attending, and second because she was the one who found his body, which gave her a terrible distinction. Certainly Abigail would have heard.

"You see Aaron Cane?" Tony asked. "Zoe needs to talk to him."

Jenny shook her head and stepped up, nodding to Abigail Cane. Tony politely waited behind her until he was introduced.

"Ah yes, you're Dora Weston's daughter." The woman, her coarse-skinned face red, leaned forward to take Jenny's hand and shake it. "I heard you were back in town."

She quickly dropped Jenny's hand and turned to Tony. She acknowledged him with a smile and a tip of the head, making the comment that she'd heard he was a fine carpenter.

"Very sad," she answered their condolences.

When her eyes came back to Jenny, the friendliness was more assessing. "I understand you found my brother in your neighbor's garden. Awful for you, I imagine."

Jenny opened her mouth to speak, but Abigail didn't give her a chance.

"It *was* your neighbor's garden, wasn't it?"

Jenny nodded.

"Isn't she that little person who came to town a year or so ago? I thought I just saw her in line."

Again, Jenny nodded. "She felt . . . eh . . . that maybe she didn't belong."

Abigail sniffed. "She was right, I suppose. Hardly the place for her at my brother's funeral when she could very well have murdered him."

Jenny was about to defend Zoe when Abigail cut in: "I wonder why she came to Bear Falls in the first place. Seems very strange to me. Of course, it's nice to have new people in town. Makes things interesting for a while. But with Adam found in her yard, and I'm told there were bad feelings. Well, one has to be at least a little concerned. I . . ."

Jenny interrupted back. "She's really a wonderful woman and neighbor. You'd love her if you got to know her."

"Really?" Abigail's brows shot up.

"She's a writer, you know. Quite well known."

Abigail blinked and then smiled. "I'd heard she was a writer, but so many are these days. But . . . published? No one told me. Well, it's good to have an educated woman living here. I must have been mistaken about her. Ed Warner said something, but I'm sure he's got things all wrong. Well, well, a writer here in town—what a coup for Bear Falls."

She seemed pleased and turned to the woman standing patiently behind her. "This is my secretary, Carmen Volker."

The woman, of the faded sort, bowed slightly first to Jenny and then to Tony. She settled back and clasped her hands in front of her like a good servant. Her dyed-black hair was drawn into a classic chignon that pulled back the skin around her eyes, giving her a pained look. She wore a black dress, buttoned to the throat. The dress had seen better funerals, the white collar not as white as it should be. Her black, sensible pumps tipped oddly backward on worn heels.

"Did you know there was a well-published writer living in town?" Abigail asked Carmen.

Carmen, in her late fifties, Jenny guessed—a hard-used late fifties—shook her head, eyes popping open as if the news was astounding. "No. I suppose you'd like to meet him."

"*Her.* It is a she. And no, I don't think I would like to meet her right now. Adam was found murdered in her garden."

Carmen unfurled her big eyes again. "Ah. Well, then . . . of course not. She'll probably be jailed soon, I would imagine."

"And Jenny Weston, here, was the one who found Adam."

Abigail and Carmen shared a look. Carmen clucked in Jenny's direction, giving her no clue what the clucking was about and whether Jenny, too, should soon be jailed.

The woman's nervous, blue eyes flitted from Jenny to Tony before she stepped back behind Abigail, giving the smallest of nods to both.

"I would love to talk to you sometime soon," Jenny said to Abigail, her throat threatening to close with nerves.

"About what, dear?" Abigail leaned forward, her smile benevolent.

"About . . ."

A slight man in his thirties came up behind Abigail, putting his hand familiarly on her back. The man wore a slick navy-blue suit. A gold tie bar held his black tie in place. He was sallow-skinned and thin-faced, with an austere look to him undermined by brown hair so thick, it resembled a wig or a bouncy toupee.

He leaned in to whisper into Abigail's ear.

She listened then raised her hand to introduce him.

"This is my attorney, Alfred Rudkers."

He gave Jenny and Tony an apologetic look. "I was telling Abigail we have to keep the line moving. Sorry."

He stepped forward and put his hand on Jenny's back, giving her the smallest of pushes. She wiggled her shoulders, stepping away from the hand as she turned and shot an indignant look his way.

Abigail quickly thanked them both for coming and turned to the next person in line.

Jenny leaned close to Tony when they were far enough away not to be overheard. "Obnoxious jerk."

"Got a rich client. Probably rich himself," Tony whispered back. "See that kind everywhere."

They went to a corner to watch the crowd, smiling at one person after the other, exchanging remarks on the weather, the dead man, Abigail, and, more than any other topic, where Aaron was and why he hadn't come to his brother's funeral.

"You'd think old feuds would die at the grave, wouldn't you?" Minnie Moon, Dora's neighbor, stopped to say. Minnie was a big woman in a horizontally striped, black-and-white dress stretched tight over a wide frame. Thick, red hair was bound up in a water spout atop her head. She stepped closer to comment on the lack of flowers and ask Jenny how she was doing, "finding the man dead and all." Minnie didn't wait for answers. She never did, Jenny remembered. She moved on to whisper in another woman's ear.

Tony whispered, "Think we can go now? Have we spent a respectable amount of time here?"

She looked up into dark eyes that wrinkled with his smirk. Smiles seemed called for with this man with the scarred face.

They made their way back through the crowd to the porch where Dora had escaped earlier. She stood now in broken sunlight coming through a honeysuckle vine behind her. She whispered to a severely thin woman in a black pantsuit more appropriate for winter than June.

"You remember Cindy Arlen, don't you?" Dora smiled and took Jenny's hand, pulling her in to say hello to Johnny Arlen's mother.

Jenny nodded. Despite what Johnny had done, she'd always liked his mom, a soft-spoken woman who stood with her head bent forward, looking as if she might break into a run at any moment.

"How are you, Jenny?" the woman asked, her voice low. She smiled a fleeting smile and put out a fragile hand, then drew it quickly back.

"I'm fine, Mrs. Arlen. How are you?"

She shrugged. "Better now. I was just telling your mother how I've often thought—" She stopped herself, obviously knowing whatever it was she wanted to say wouldn't be appropriate in this place, at this time.

Dora took Jenny's arm and steered her away from the awkward situation, even as she told Cindy Arlen she'd have to come by for lunch one day. Cindy answered with a tentative, "Why, yes. I'd love to."

Dora led Jenny down the wide steps to stand on the uneven sidewalk in front of the funeral home. She whispered, "Everybody but Cindy Arlen starts by telling me they suspect Zoe. It makes me so angry." She nodded fast. "By the time I'm finished with them, though, they'll know what a treasure Zoe is, not at all the kind to hurt a flea, let alone Adam Cane. Still, that's the word zipping through town."

Dora's disgust showed. "Hope Zoe hasn't heard." She looked around for Zoe.

"Everybody's in a mood, I'll tell you," Dora said. "I tried to compliment Mr. Tannin on how the home looks, but all he did was go on and on that he never expected a Cane to go out the cheap way Adam's going out."

"You mean being murdered?"

"No, no, no." Dora clucked her tongue at her. "He meant how cheap Abigail's being about the funeral. He said the secretary and that lawyer picked out the least expensive coffin—the model usually used for indigents. No flowers from the family. Not from the sister and not from the brother. Aaron isn't even here, you notice? All those awful flowers Sally's florist got rid of are from people here in town."

"I knew Aaron was a recluse, but still, you'd think, even if they didn't get along, that he'd want to be here," Jenny said.

Dora hitched her shoulders. "That's what everybody's saying. He was always the sweetest of the two boys. Far back as I remember, Adam would insult people, and Aaron would hurry in to smooth things over. Oh, and before I forget, Priscilla Manus is looking for you. She was so excited when I told her you were back in town."

Jenny frowned. "Isn't she the one who wrote the history of Bear Falls? I'm not a historian."

Dora nodded, then looked over Jenny's shoulder to welcome Priscilla, who walked up from behind.

"Why, it's Jenny Weston!" Priscilla chirped. The long, thin woman with frizzy blonde hair, dressed in a chic little black dress with a short-sleeved jacket tipped her head to greet Jenny, avid bird's eyes flashing that she was on a mission. "I just heard you were back in town. You've lived in Chicago for such a long time. Are you here just visiting? Or will you be staying for a while?"

"Oh, for a while, I'd say."

Priscilla clapped her hands together. "My goodness! Can I count on you to help with updating our town history? I've tried to get your neighbor involved, but she's rather coy. All I need is a little of your time. I heard you were in law, so you'd probably be good at this kind of thing."

"Paralegal," Jenny said. "In my husband's firm."

"Well, well, well." Priscilla turned her eyes up a few watts. "I hope we get to meet the man someday soon. I imagine he'll be around. I mean, with you staying."

"He will," Jenny lied happily. "When he gets back from Guatemala. Very busy, you know."

"My goodness! Guatemala, you say. Must be an important man."

Jenny smirked as her mother moved her away, apologizing to Priscilla for being in such a hurry.

"It wouldn't take much of your time," Priscilla called after Jenny. "I'd love to have your name in as one of the contributors. A way to honor your poor father, I would say."

Jenny felt her face tighten and settle into a scowl she hoped would keep others away.

Dora, following through the crowd, said, "That's not a bad idea, Jenny. What Priscilla mentioned. You need something other than murder and a ruined library to keep you busy. And that's all you've had since you got home. 'Busy hands make for busy minds,' you know."

Jenny wanted to snap at her mother; her mind was already busier than it should be. Let Lisa do it. Lisa the Good would know how to handle situations without getting mad at everybody. That was something Jenny had promised herself to mend even before coming home to Bear Falls: her temper. Not that it was a truly bad temper. Not that she was ever the one really at fault . . .

* * *

Zoe sat in the backseat of Jenny's car with the doors and windows open to catch what breeze there was. She stood as soon as the three of them walked up, leaning between the seats.

"First thing we've got to do is talk to Aaron Cane," she said, words tumbling over each other. Jenny noticed tears in her eyes.

"Sure, Zoe. We'll go." She wracked her brain for something to distract Zoe. Thinking "Alice," she said, "But, oh dear, 'Which road do I take?'"

Zoe stopped a minute, then returned, "'Where do you want to go?'"

Jenny frowned. "No idea. I forgot the rest."

Zoe clapped her hands. "You've been hiding your light under a bushel."

"I've been studying. Soon I'll quote you into oblivion."

Zoe frowned. "The battle is on, Jenny Weston."

"Doubt it will be much of a battle. The inside of your head is a muddy swamp of quotes without context. Mine is much more scholarly."

Zoe sniffed. "'The lotus flower grows in a muddy swamp.'"

"Is that from *Alice in Wonderland*?"

"Not at all. Not at all. But I'll leave you to find where it came from, since you think yourself so scholarly."

Jenny thought hard for another quip to squash her, but Tony interrupted their fun.

"You sure you want to go see Aaron Cane?" He bent toward Zoe.

Down came Zoe with a silent thud. "I can't come up with anything else."

"You think there's something in it for him? I mean, out of his brother's death? Like maybe inheriting Adam's house or money Adam wrangled out of his sister? I never met the man, but I've seen him around town. Not as much a hermit as people say."

"You'll come, won't you?" Zoe screwed her head around to give Tony a one-eyed stare. "We need your help. You've got experience in—"

"Help as much as I can."

"Does anyone know where he lives?"

"I have the address." Dora, standing quietly behind the others, dug into her pocketbook. "I wanted to send him a sympathy card, you know. They were brothers, after all."

"Then we can go." Zoe took the paper with Aaron's name and address on it.

Dora left to go home and make a casserole to take to Abigail.

Jenny, Tony, and Zoe were on their way, following the sweet voice of Jenny's GPS as they drove south along the Lake Michigan shore.

Chapter 16

After all the brown of the funeral home, Jenny welcomed the green hills along the lake.

"Don't worry what Ed Warren said about not leaving town, Zoe," Tony said from the backseat. "That's standard procedure. It's early days in the investigation, and Ed doesn't want people disappearing as facts unfold."

Zoe smiled, peeking back between the seats. "Think he'd tell you what he's found so far? I mean, detective to detective? He sure won't tell me anything. He had a shoe print on one of the books and checked out my shoes. Mine were much too small. You'd think that would clear me."

He shook his head. "Maybe of the Little Library business, but not Adam's murder."

He looked over at Jenny. "Got any thoughts?"

"There'll be other shoes to look at."

"Don't you think the same person committed both crimes?" Zoe asked. "What about the note they found in Adam's house? Supposed to be from me, asking him to come over to my yard right around dawn." She made a disgusted sound. "I never wrote him such a note. I never would and never did."

"What about that hatchet you found?" he asked Jenny.

"Buried in his yard. Not long ago," Jenny said as she checked her speed. She was going too fast—maybe from the joy of being free of the town. "The grass over it wasn't even wilted, though the roots were all cut."

"Think it was used on the library?"

"Who knows? Nothing made it seem that way," she said.

"Could Abigail have anything to do with this?" Zoe asked.

Jenny shook her head. "Doesn't seem her style, breaking up a library with an axe in the middle of the night. Then killing her brother the next night? I don't think Abigail's a Carrie Nation, fighting against books. And certainly not a Lizzie Borden."

Tony gave a low chuckle. "I've worked stranger cases. You'd be surprised what people do to each other and who those people are. One case in Detroit, a lawyer set up a hit on another lawyer. The other lawyer hired the same hit man, at the same time, to kill the first one. The hit man was so confused, he came into the precinct and ratted them both out." He shook his head. "Another time, a grandmother didn't like the way her grandchildren were being raised, went over to their house, and poisoned the children's mother and father so she could raise the kids herself." He shook his head. "People can be beyond strange. All the way to evil. I quit being surprised by anybody a long time ago."

The three stopped talking and watched as they drove by the quiet lake. Summer people's mansions stuck out like sore thumbs here and there, built along the sandy shore: grassy lawns and gates and architecture so wrong for a Midwest coastline. Once beyond the houses, the lake opened wider, a few fishing boats bobbed on sudden swells, and sails dotted the horizon as small white caps fell over each other, hitting the now-rocky shoreline. A beautiful day. *Not a day for sadness and murder,* Jenny thought, then wondered where all of this fit into her life.

She'd come home to be healed.

Behind her, Tony stared out the window and intoned with exaggerated depth: "By the shores of Gitche Gumee, / By the shining Big-Sea-Water, / At the doorway of his wigwam, / In the pleasant Summer morning, / Hiawatha stood and waited."

He leaned back, arms behind his head. "I love that poem."

"That's Lake Superior," Zoe corrected. "Up by the Pictured Rocks. Not around here."

"So what? Water's water. Still a great poem."

"You think Longfellow was ever in Michigan?" Zoe went on, but the other two ignored her as the GPS warned that their turn was just ahead on the left.

The cottages along here were hidden back among the trees. Most were shacks at the end of overgrown two-tracks. At the head of one of the driveways stood a crooked sign with "Cane" painted in red on a weathered board.

Jenny turned up the weedy road.

She navigated through the scrub and potholes. In places, deep sand threatened to swallow her wheels. Eventually, she pulled into an open clearing, where a small, wooden house stood, all doors and windows closed.

They got out. Nothing moved but tall daisies and grasses bowing in the syrupy breeze. To one side of the house, an ancient truck with broken windows leaned; on the other sat a dusty car about as old.

"Certainly is quiet," Zoe said looking around. She shivered despite the thick sun.

A robin called from the safety of a tall maple at the edge of the woods, bees and wasps hummed among the weeds—all contented summer sounds. But nothing from the house. The unpainted front door stayed closed, curtains pulled over the glass.

If anyone was inside, he or she hadn't heard the car or weren't interested in company.

"What's your nose say?" Jenny leaned down close to tease.

Zoe stared at her with narrowed eyes. "It says you need a shower."

"Fraud. You—"

"Did you hear that?" Zoe interrupted, eyes wide, a finger next to her nose.

Jenny shook her head, nervous at the dilapidated state of the house and how much she felt like a trespasser.

Tony stopped to listen. "You mean that barking?"

"It's a dog," Zoe said, her mouth hanging open. "A lot of yipping . . ."

Her head tipped to one side. She scanned the woods in one direction, then another, a hand up to her ear.

Jenny held still to listen.

"A neighbor's dog," Jenny said. "Everybody keeps a dog this far out."

Zoe sighed. "You're right. How could it be Fida?"

Jenny knocked at the front door: once, twice, then harder. Nothing.

And then a dog barked again. And something thumped against the door on the inside, as if being thrown.

Zoe stepped up and tried the doorknob. It didn't turn. "Fida!" She pressed her nose to the door glass, covered by a faded curtain.

"He's probably got a dog." Jenny read Zoe's face. "Living out here, all alone. I imagine a dog would be the first thing you'd get. It's inside. A watchdog."

Tony reached around Jenny and knocked harder. There was frantic barking now, and not the deep woof-woofing of a large animal.

"We know Aaron didn't go into town for the funeral. But you'd think he would have stayed home. At least that much to mark his brother's passing." He looked around the clearing. "But neither of those vehicles have been anywhere in a while."

Tony walked over to a window on the side of the house. He cupped his hands around his eyes and looked in. When he turned back to the women, he seemed confused.

"Somebody's in there. He's sitting in a chair. Far as I can see, he's ignoring us."

He knocked at the glass, then hollered, "Hey, Mr. Cane. We'd like to talk to you a minute about your brother."

More barking.

Tony shook his head. "Not moving."

"Let me see," Zoe said, elbowing Tony from the window and then standing on tiptoe to see in. "Something's moving in there, all right. And it's not the man in the chair. Too dark to make out, but I saw movement across the floor."

"His dog." Jenny's reminder was met with a flurry of barks.

Zoe stared at the ground, listening. "I'm going in."

"You can't just break in."

"Who says?" Tony stood behind Zoe.

Without another word, he and Zoe got their fingers under the sash and pushed until the window went up—one drawn-out squeal at a time.

"Grab my butt and legs," Zoe ordered, hiking her black dress up over her knees. Tony and Jenny did as they were told.

"Come on, guys. Lift together. I'm not a sack of beans, you know." She grunted and then was over the sill, hanging half in the house, dirty curtains around her.

"Hey," she screamed, "Fida! Fida! Oh my God!"

"Is it really her?" Jenny hung in the window to see.

Zoe was through, landing on the other side with a thud that shook the house. Jenny called after her, then stood listening to happy yips and small barks and then cooing from Zoe.

In a few minutes, the door opened, and Zoe stood there with two fingers pinching her nose and a wiggling Fida nipping at her arms and chin.

"Look who I found." Zoe avoided more licks and held Fida out for the others to see. "Aaron Cane had her. I can't imagine why."

"Is that him in the chair?" Tony, confused, tried to see around Zoe and Fida.

"Yes. Something's wrong. He didn't say 'Boo' when I dropped in. All I could do was pick Fida up or she would've had a heart attack." She stepped back. Making a face, she said, "You won't believe the smell in here!"

When Jenny stepped into the house, it was first thing to hit her. Thick and awful. Earthy and chemical. The stink of heated iron mixed with the fetid odor of a kennel.

"Whew!" Jenny pulled back, letting Tony be the first to approach the man. She pinched her nose shut as best she could.

"Is he asleep?" Jenny didn't bother to whisper.

The elderly man was slumped in the worn, red plush chair. His chin rested on his chest. His arms were draped out to either side of him, hands turned up.

Tony felt for a pulse at the man's neck and then at his wrist. He shook his head, then pointed to a small round hole in the middle of the man's faded red shirt and to the dark stain along the buttons.

"Aaron Cane's dead," Tony said. "Just like Adam, only he's been shot."

Chapter 17

"I'd say small caliber. Pretty close range." Tony straightened and stepped back from the dead man.

Jenny drew in a breath. "Not Aaron, too."

"We're in the ninth circle of hell," Zoe whispered. "Cain and Abel."

She stepped as far away as she could, avoiding the piles of dog poop littering the floor. Something crushed under her foot. She reached down, pulled duct tape from her heel, and threw it on the floor.

"Ask me, he's been like this a couple of days. Maybe since Adam died. Blood's hard. Rigor's gone." Tony turned to point at the floor behind them, instinctively lowering his voice. "Your dog's been in here a while, Zoe."

She nodded and moaned as she gripped Fida harder. "No water pan. Poor Fida. No food." She set Fida down and hurried to a sink on the back wall, found a pot, and filled it as Fida leaped around her and then noisily lapped the water.

"Who left her here?" Zoe asked, hovering over her dog, keeping her eyes away from the dead man in the chair. "Think it could've been Adam? Maybe he brought her out before sneaking into my garden."

"Could've been his insurance that you weren't trying to fool him with that note," Tony said.

"Then somebody killed him," Jenny said. "And it wasn't Aaron. He had to have been dead already. Fida disappeared the same night Aaron was killed."

"Poor Fida. She must have been here when Aaron was killed. Oh, poor baby," Zoe half-moaned and bent to pick up the little dog who sat at her feet.

"Look at the man." She made a gesture toward the dead man almost lost in the big chair. "He was killed right there. I mean, no blood anywhere else. I don't see any smears on the floor, as if he'd been dragged. He mustn't have been alarmed when the killer arrived with my dog. That means he let the man in. Maybe he was even waiting for him."

"You think Aaron was in on the murder? That he'd arranged to have Adam killed?" Jenny asked.

"Could be." Tony gagged when he took too deep a breath. "But whoever that was, the man turned on him. Means he was shot that same morning. After Adam was killed."

Zoe moaned. "Follow my dog. Follow my dog. The killer grabbed her before she could bark. Probably stuck her in his car and then killed Adam. Brought her back here with him to kill Aaron. Maybe he even knew about my problems with Adam. Figured bringing Fida here would make me more of a suspect.

"Oh, Lord!" she moaned again. "I'm trapped in the middle of another murder. And a small-caliber gun! As if the murder was tailored perfectly for me."

Tony leaned down and put an arm around her back. "Let's get out of here. I'm about to heave. And I've got to call Ed Warner."

He pushed both women toward the door.

Outside they took deep breaths.

"This is way over my head." Zoe was in tears.

"Mine, too." Tony pulled his cell from his pocket. "Hope I get a signal this far out."

His phone showed zero bars. He shook his head at Jenny. "Let's go. No signal."

Zoe shook her head at him. "We should stay here. Somebody could come. Nobody knows the body's been found yet. I don't feel right, leaving the poor man alone."

"I'll be fast. Back at that last hill, I'll bet. Just stay out of the house. You don't want your fingerprints all over any more than they are already."

They promised and watched Jenny's car disappear back up the narrow road.

The clearing around them was emptier and more forsaken than it had been before. There was no wind, so nothing moved, and there was no sign of other humans. Insects buzzed and hissed from tall weed to tall weed. A few birds sang dispiritedly. The sun, moving behind high clouds, grew mottled and then weak, as if the sky was wrapped in gauze.

Jenny felt a shiver move along her arms. Zoe held her forlorn dog close to her chest.

"What the heck's going on?" Jenny finally asked.

Zoe wrinkled her nose. "Let's go back in. Maybe there's something we missed. Something the killer left."

"You heard Tony. He's a cop—or was a cop. Last thing we need is more trouble."

"But somebody's doing this, and it looks like they're aiming straight at me." Zoe shook her head and took a step toward the house. "Think about it. Somebody wanted both brothers dead."

"Who else is left but Abigail?"

Zoe nodded. She walked faster toward the house. "Money, money, money. That's the word to follow here."

"But Abigail's got it all."

Zoe stopped at the door to steel herself before stepping inside. "Maybe the boys found a way to get it away from her." Her voice was a whisper.

"So maybe they had something they could hold over her head," Jenny whispered back.

"Maybe a later will she'd hidden?" Zoe wondered. She walked slowly around the room. "Maybe Aaron had something Abigail wanted. That's why she came out here, to find it. She'd been to Adam's house already. Left that note, then killed him when she found nothing there."

Jenny was behind Zoe, pushing a little. "If we're going to look around, let's do it. Tony'll be right back."

The heat inside the little house was even more intense and the stink was worse. Fida scrambled at Zoe's chest, wanting no part of her recent prison. Jenny covered her mouth and nose to shield herself from the smell.

They kept their eyes away from the silent man sitting in his chair and said little to each other. The house was so small, so plain, there were few places to look for anything important— nothing but bare walls, right down to wall studs. An old wood-stove in one corner stood on a pedestal of reclaimed bricks. The black pipe behind the stove snaked up the wall and then through a hole to the outside.

There was a sink filled with dirty dishes, a crusty range for cooking, and an ancient refrigerator standing on three legs against the back wall.

Jenny motioned that she would search the kitchen. Zoe went into the tiny bedroom off the kitchen, first pulling her shirt down over her hands so none of her fingerprints would be found.

Cupboards above the sink held a couple of plates, one cup, and a few cans of stew. Nothing else, Jenny found, but a lot of dust and scattered debris that looked suspiciously like an old mouse nest.

"How did he live like this?" Jenny called out as she opened a drawer filled with a jumble of silverware, cooking utensils, a box of long matches, and a stack of papers that appeared to be paid bills. When she opened another cupboard, she found blackened pots and pans stuck inside. The refrigerator was beyond examining—the few dishes of food were covered with layers of mold. A drawer, built into the handmade kitchen table, held nothing but four dollar bills, a calendar from 1999, a small ball of rubber bands, and a couple of keys.

Zoe came from the bedroom with papers in her bare hands. "Nothing in any of the drawers or in the bathroom, but I found these stuck under his mattress." She waved the papers at Jenny.

"What are they?"

"Don't know."

"We can't just take them."

Zoe nodded. "I'll read them fast." She glanced down at one just as they heard a car pull into the clearing.

"Put 'em back where you got 'em," Jenny hissed.

"Will not," Zoe hissed back.

"Zoe, Tony told us not to come back in here! You can go to jail for tampering with evidence."

Tony called their names a couple of times as he headed toward the house.

"Put 'em back under the mattress," Jenny ordered.

"I'm already in the soup. My fingerprints are all over them." Zoe shook her head and searched for a place to stick the papers. No pockets. With only a few seconds before Tony got to the house, she lifted her dress and stuck the papers down into her pants. She dropped the dress and patted it flat.

Jenny winced. Too late.

"Hey, I told you guys to stay out of here." Tony glared when he came through the door. "Didn't touch anything, I hope."

Zoe shook her head, blue, innocent eyes open wide. Jenny bit at her bottom lip but shook her head, too. They were in this mess together, she figured, and smiled sweetly at Tony.

* * *

Chief Warner pulled into the clearing, his siren smashing birdsong to bits. Two deputies drove in behind the chief. The deputies said nothing to the waiting group, walking straight to the house and disappearing inside.

Chief Warner, hatless, sunglasses pushed up onto his closely cropped head, sauntered over to where the trio stood.

He nodded at Zoe and Jenny, barely acknowledging Tony. "Hear you found another dead man," he said to Jenny.

She said nothing.

He looked hard at Zoe for a while.

"See you found your dog, Ms. Zola." The chief looked at Zoe's feet, where Fida leaned against her. His eyes narrowed to nothing. "You find her here? That what brought you out?"

"No. I had no idea Fida was here. It was just that Aaron Cane wasn't at his brother's funeral—"

"What business did you have with him?"

Zoe shook her head. "None. I thought I should talk to him. You've been coming after me pretty hard."

"You and that dog of yours sure get into a lot of mischief, far as I can tell. Gives me reason to take a long look at you, don't you think? There's nothing personal here, you understand."

"I was with her, Chief," Tony said, stepping forward. "Coming out here was my idea."

The chief frowned at all of them.

"Hope we're not going to find your fingerprints all over the place," the chief said to Zoe.

She looked sick. "On the window. That's how we got in. Maybe around inside. I had to get water for Fida."

He sniffed and looked away. "Wait here," he finally said. "I'll be back out to talk to both of you."

He indicated that Tony should come with him and walked back toward the house.

Zoe frowned. "'Curiouser and curiouser,'" she mumbled.

"'Worser and worser,'" Jenny mumbled behind her. "You're in deep crap, Zoe. Now you've got those papers in your drawers."

Zoe closed one eye and squinted up at Jenny. She sighed. "Probably all true about the deep crap."

"Honestly!" Jenny, exasperated, turned away to wait for the police chief to come out and maybe arrest both of them for trespassing, or worse.

An hour later, a forensics van drove into the clearing. White-suited technicians hurried into the house. An ambulance sailed into the clearing followed by a private car with a pudgy man, a small black case in his hands. The dead man was now in the arms of police procedure.

Once Adam's body was brought out to the ambulance, Ed Warner strolled back to the women.

"As I said, funny about your dog." Ed looked off toward where the trees were thickest, then kicked at the ground with one heavy shoe. Sweat stood out on his forehead. It was the hottest part of the day, when the air was still and the sun flat. The chief heaved a large sigh. "Ralenti swears it was a big surprise to all of you, finding the dog here. You ask me, whoever left your dog had a lot to do with the deaths of both men."

He turned to stare directly at Zoe, whose face burned.

"Got any ideas?"

Zoe shook her head.

He nodded and cleared his throat. "Said, too, he told you not to touch anything in there while he was gone. You listen?"

She nodded, a little too fast.

"So you didn't take anything?"

She stood still, busily looking innocent.

"Won't find your fingerprints all over everything, will I?"

"Told you I was in that house soon as I heard Fida barking. Tony and Jenny helped me get through a window."

Ed shook his head, as if in deep sorrow. "Sure is odd. You and your dog involved in all of this. Right from the beginning when Mrs. Weston's library was broken up—you and your dog, there first thing."

Zoe widened her eyes in Jenny's direction.

The chief went on. "Now, one way to look at it, you been out here, to this place, before."

Both Zoe and Jenny protested, but Ed continued.

"Brought the dog with you. Killed Aaron Cane and left. Maybe you made a mistake and the dog got locked inside. Couldn't get her out. Brought this one—" He indicated Jenny. "—out to help you."

Ed put up a hand when Jenny sputtered. "Not that I'm sayin' you're in it with her, Jenny. Just that she could've tricked you."

"And Tony, too?" Jenny showed her disgust.

"Well . . ." Ed thought a while. "I guess you're right there. Unlikely. But what's going on with the brothers, then? Both dead. Both murdered." He nodded over his shoulder toward the house. "Aaron sure wasn't a suicide. No gun anywhere. I might've said Adam did it. He would have been my first suspect, but Adam was killed first. Aaron second, far as I can tell. The medical examiner thinks the same thing."

"Ever wonder if Abigail Cane was involved somehow?" Tony came up behind them. "She controls the money in that family. What if the boys were coming after her? You know, getting a lawyer or something like that? I don't know why they didn't do it before. I'll bet anything they could've got something from the estate."

Zoe cocked her head to one side, folding both hands across her stomach as if keeping fear locked in there. She took a step closer to the chief and said, in a low voice, "Abigail's sure a better suspect than I am. First of all, I had no reason to want Aaron dead. Saw him a couple of times in town when Dora pointed him out—that's it. Second of all, I don't, nor ever did, own a gun. No cannons. No mortars. No machine guns. And come to think of it, no dead flamingos."

All Jenny could do was grit her teeth and hope Zoe would stop.

Ed's face tightened, but he went on. "Don't forget the note," he warned.

"Ah, the note—inside Adam's house, even though I've never been in there. But I got in somehow and left him a note telling him to come over to my shed at dawn because I had an axe that would clear him of destroying Dora's library. Fida was gone by the time he came to the shed, so I made him tell me where she was, hit him in the head, and waited two days to get over here to get her. Seem logical to you?" Zoe puffed up, spoiling for a fight.

"Well, I guess you wouldn't want your dog left alone like that. No food. A corpse the only thing with her."

"Or maybe I'd do just that kind of thing." Zoe's eyes were slits. "Maybe I'm just that kind of person."

"Don't be crazy, Zoe." Jenny decided it was time to quiet her. Zoe was digging herself a hole so deep, she would soon hit magma and they'd all go up in flames.

"I'm going to remind you to not leave town, Ms. Zola." Ed pulled himself as tall as he could get.

"I'm meeting my editor in New York next week."

He shook his head. "No. You're not doing that. Better have 'im come to Bear Falls. You leave and you'll be sitting in our jail—you and your little dog, too."

Zoe pulled in a shocked breath. For once she was speechless.

Chapter 18

A plane roared over the Traverse City airport. Not Lisa's plane. Not yet.

Jenny had come to the airport early. She needed a few hours away from everyone. Away from the insanity that had struck her hometown.

Alone for the first time in almost a week, she was relieved to sit and relax in the small refreshment room at the Cherry Capital Airport.

The big gate closed off the runway, so no planes were coming or going at the moment. All there was to do was wait.

She stretched her legs and closed her eyes, feeling as if a big gate had closed around her life, too. No place to go. No choice but to stay at home with her mom. No way she would leave her in the middle of the awful stuff going on: murder, the library destroyed, Zoe—her almost friend—under suspicion, and people talking all over the north country.

For just this minute, until Lisa arrived, she wanted no problems. She wanted to be nothing but a stranger sitting alone in an empty terminal, a woman in a wild T-shirt with a pouncing leopard on it and khaki shorts, waiting for her older sister to arrive and straighten out everybody's life. She wanted to be an ordinary woman with long, black hair hanging around her kind of pretty, oblong face. Maybe a woman going to California to meet her husband, the big business tycoon. A woman—so neat and nice—with places to go and people to see.

After a while, an airport agent appeared and rolled back the gate. There was still time before the plane landed, but not thinking wasn't getting Jenny anywhere, so she stood, feeling the excitement of seeing her sister. Let the rest of it wait—all the trouble. They'd go someplace and talk before returning to Bear Falls. First, she wanted to see her sister's face, hug her, and then feel the way a kid sister feels: happy, dependent, eager to get back to sharing their lives.

She walked over to the arrival gate where others were waiting. Travelers came out one by one: tired mothers with tired children, businessmen, tourists. Greeters queued up behind her, hurrying forward, one after the other, to meet their friends or family. Lisa wasn't in any of those groups.

Jenny was getting impatient. Lisa would have called if she missed the plane. She wouldn't leave her standing there.

And then a lone woman, wheeling a red carry-on behind her, made her way slowly up the carpet. She was a woman swathed in blue scarves and a long, off-white dress. A large, puffy bag was slung over her left shoulder; her blonde streaked hair was swept up into a pile on top of her head. Large sunglasses were pushed up into her hair. At first Jenny wasn't sure—too tanned, too thin, too . . . otherworldly.

Lisa waved and hurried forward, big smile on her face, carry-on forgotten as she rushed to Jenny with her arms out.

Lisa was home.

They hugged hard and stood back to look deeply into each other's eyes. Lisa, shorter than Jenny, hugged again and said, "Missed you, kid."

"Me too." Tears sprang into Jenny's eyes.

"Think we can go someplace and catch up?" Lisa asked, her arm around Jenny, who'd taken over the suitcase.

"Absolutely. How about Junior's? I haven't been there since I came home. Nobody to go with. How I've missed you."

"What the heck have you been doing? You come home and the place goes to hell."

It wasn't a real jab, just a sister's way of showing sympathy.

They kept their arms around each other as they made their way out of the terminal and into the dark lot where Jenny's car was parked.

* * *

Junior's Bar, on Cass, was an old place with a lot of history and thousands of glasses of Irish beer behind it. It was both a family restaurant and a place for the good ol' boys to shoot pool and drink beer. And it had real good food. Not a place for tourists, exactly, although they found their way to Junior's, too, eventually. Both women had childhood memories of the place: with their mom and dad on a Sunday afternoon, eating hamburgers and drinking sodas, their parents talking about a vacation they were planning with friends who were visiting.

Neither found a familiar face along the bar when they walked in. Too many years since they'd been there.

They took a booth near the pool table in the second room. With cold Irish beers in front of them and warm smiles and a little shyness, they talked. First Lisa told Jenny how filming was going, about the people she was meeting, about a distributor who'd already contacted her. It didn't take long, though, before Lisa was asking, "Really, Jen. What the heck's going on in Bear Falls?"

Lisa shook her head while Jenny laid out all that had happened since she got home, beginning with the Little Library and moving to two dead men and Zoe Zola. "You know her, don't you? Mom's fairy-tale neighbor?"

"Met her last time I was home. I love her. A little odd, but I figured hanging out in fairy-tale land can do that to a person. Actually, we've kept in touch. I call her from time to time. She calls me. She's friendly with Mom. Kind of keeps an eye on her."

Jenny shook her head, conveying her feelings about Zoe Zola.

Lisa leaned back, rubbing her neck. "Mom loves her, too, Jenny. They share gardening and the Little Library . . . she is building it up again, isn't she?"

They talked on, into a second beer. A group of men entered the room talking and laughing, maybe a little drunk. One racked up the balls on the pool table. Another shoved coins into the jukebox, and a country singer whined through the speakers about his dog loving him more than his girl did.

Jenny looked around for a table they could move to, but the place had filled while they talked. The laughter was loud. The crack from a break shot on the pool table was enough to spawn a headache.

"We should've remembered not to sit here," Lisa said. "You want to move to the bar?" She laughed, but when she looked over the back of the booth, her smile fell away.

Jenny leaned forward. "What's wrong? Somebody you know?"

Lisa screwed her pretty face into one of those warning looks. "Sure is," she said and started to get up.

"Who?"

"Nobody you want to see. Let's get out of here."

Jenny finished off her beer and got up, trusting Lisa to know what she was doing.

"Then why the hell don't you go on home?" a man's voice snarled from someplace behind them.

The voice came from an alcove next to the jukebox. Noise in the room died down. Even most of the half-drunk men at the pool table stopped, looking past Jenny at the commotion.

Jenny froze. "Is that Johnny?"

Lisa nodded slowly. "He's with Angel. And drunk. You are *so* lucky you didn't marry him."

"Get the hell outta here. Go on home," Johnny barked. A mumbling followed, and then Angel stepped from the alcove where they'd been hidden. Her large belly preceded her. Her face was a deep, mottled red. Angel paused and stared straight at Jenny.

Johnny muttered something at her that made Angel scurry for the door, working her way through a gauntlet of staring faces—every patron watching as she stumbled out the door.

"We better go before he sees you." Lisa rose and reached across the table for Jenny's arm.

"Too late. I'll bet I'm what Angel's mad about."

Lisa made a face. "Oh, oh," she said.

Jenny turned to see Johnny walk slowly toward her.

She couldn't catch her breath as he approached—there was no getting away this time. The young face Jenny remembered had been carved by the last eighteen years into an older, unhappy man's face. But it was still Johnny: black, straight hair hanging over his forehead; hooded, hurt eyes fixed on her; a thin, angular body—that of a man wracked by alcohol, cigarettes, and other things.

Her breath caught in her throat. This was her first lover: gentle, sweet, and brimming with plans for their future back then. She almost fooled herself into smiling until his lips curled into a cruel, drunken smile.

"Let's go," Lisa said and pulled her arm.

Jenny couldn't move.

Johnny maneuvered around Lisa and then half-fell into the vacant side of the booth. He leaned back, closed his eyes, and shook his head ever so slowly. When he opened his bloodshot eyes, he smiled a slipping smile at Jenny.

"Saw you the other day at the market. Guess you didn't see me. I was gonna come over and say hi." He put a hand on the table, fingers inching toward hers.

Jenny pulled her hand down to her lap.

"Aw, come on." He leaned closer. He smelled of beer and smoke. "Don't be like that. We used to be . . ." He stopped to smile a bleary smile. "Well, you know what we used to be."

Lisa, looking mighty, grabbed Jenny's arm. "We're getting out of here, Jenny. This guy's got nothing to do with you."

Jenny's mouth opened. Whatever the words were supposed to be, they didn't come out.

Johnny grabbed for her arm, too, ignoring Lisa. His voice was low and lush. "Let's go someplace where we can talk. We've got a lot to make up for."

"*Now*, Jenny." Lisa puffed with anger. Blue scarves wafted around her as her chin dropped into her neck and her body got tight. Sweet Lisa was spoiling for a fight.

"You always were a pain in the ass." Johnny blinked up at Lisa then back to Jenny.

Jenny found the strength to pull away from his hand and stand. There were things she wanted to say, things bottled inside her for years. But now was not the time. She took the hand Lisa held out and followed her through the poolroom, past the row of staring bar patrons, and out the back door to her car.

Chapter 19

How many times can you be a fool?

Jenny sat alone in the dark yard, wishing she could be like this for at least a month or two: unseen and unjudged.

Mom had been so happy to have both her girls at home with her. She hadn't noticed Jenny's pasty complexion, her distress. She made them all sit down at the table for ham and cheese sandwiches and a pitcher of iced tea. There were *ooh*s and *aah*s over the orange chiffon cake she brought out.

After eating and talking, Mom and Lisa went to sit on the porch while Jenny escaped to the backyard. She needed to be alone. Seeing Johnny was an assault, a dark hole she'd fallen into without warning.

She sat on the damp ground under the black walnut tree, arms around her knees. Overhead, the sky was a vision you'd never see in Chicago: billions of stars—dead light from thousands of years ago. She imagined universes, planets, moons, novas, and swirling gases. It was always the sky that reminded her how small and unimportant she really was.

She felt ashamed—nothing nice or kind or any of the good things she used to feel after seeing Johnny. She brushed her hand over the soft grass and felt as if she ought to cry. If she was the kinder, happier self she used to be, she would at least take what happened as only a blip, a misstep. Johnny could change back to who he used to be—of course he could. Despite all the proof to the contrary, she believed in happy endings.

Or used to.

Not anymore. Johnny wasn't what he was supposed to be. Something had derailed him. Maybe alcohol was a big enough demon. Maybe it was something else.

Jenny leaned her head against the tree, brushed an ant from her thigh, and closed her eyes. There were better things to think about. Good things around her: happy Fida barking in the house next door, the library houses they were going to build . . .

But her thoughts strayed to bad things: Zoe practically being accused of murder, the anonymous destruction of the Little Library, a man dead in his own house, his dead body guarded only by a little dog . . .

Lisa called from the back porch. "Jenny?"

She didn't answer.

She slumped down into herself, knowing the dark wasn't deep enough to hide her.

When Lisa found her and dropped beside her on the ground, they said nothing for a few minutes.

"How sorry are you feeling for yourself?" Lisa finally asked.

"Very," Jenny muttered and snuffled to show she'd been crying.

"How long will it take you to get over it?"

"Forever."

"That long?"

"Think so."

"Then I'll give you the wisdom I came out here to impart and go back in, since I don't have forever to waste in the dark."

"Bitch." Jenny felt the word.

"No, I'm not. I just don't buy into self-pity. Don't have the patience for it. I've seen too much of real misery while making this film. A lot of poverty. A lot of alcoholism. A lot of sadness." She took a breath. "And, by the way, I don't call other women bitches."

"Good for you. But none of that makes me hurt any less."

"Right. So dumb of me."

"Sure is. Just because there's worse in the world, you think I'm not supposed to feel what I feel?"

Lisa was quiet, letting Jenny spout off.

"What Johnny did before was about me—something about me. I somehow chased him away. And Ronald . . ."

"Sorry," Lisa said and seemed to mean it. "I don't think you could have changed a thing."

"Then why can't I get over it? Or grow up?"

"Okay. So give me a date. When's it going to end?"

"I may never get over it."

"I'll give you a week."

"A week?" Jenny went from shocked, to hurt, and soon to laughter.

"No good? A year? A decade? Poor you. We'll all play little pity violins. All the while, the years will pass you by—only you'll be alone because we won't be able to stand your moping. Then one day, when you're old and decrepit, you'll wake up and say, 'Why the hell did I waste all that time?'"

Lisa got up, a small figure against the night sky. She swept her hands across the back of her jeans. "Anyway, I was sent out with messages."

"Messages?" Jenny asked.

"Zoe's here. She said to tell you her pants are empty. Whatever that means. I didn't dare ask for fear of getting a long passage on pants that rhyme with ants but really mean aunts, and therefore we will move on to relatives—meaning you, to whom the message was sent."

Jenny laughed, breaking up a tight place in her chest. "What else?"

"Tony's here, too. I thought everybody went to bed at nine o'clock in Bear Falls. Guess things have changed. So he's the carpenter Mom hired to rebuild Dad's Little Library. Seems like a nice enough guy."

"What's *he* doing here?"

"He's got final plans for the twin houses—or something like that. He said he won't show anybody until you come back in."

Jenny made a noise and struggled to get up. "Glad somebody needs me."

They headed up the dark lawn to the house.

"A week, huh?" Jenny mumbled.

Lisa reached over and put an arm around her sister's slumping shoulders. "I take that back. A couple of hours. That's about all the self-pity I can take."

* * *

Iced tea was poured. More cake was sliced and passed around. The group settled into conversation—mostly welcoming Lisa home and, on Tony's part, asking about her documentary. That led to a lengthy conversation about small-town kids in peril.

"Why Montana?" Tony asked. "There's plenty of 'em here in Michigan."

"Plenty of 'em everywhere. I'm setting the template for local filmmakers to follow—I hope."

Zoe—tired, she said, of coming only armpit high at the table—sat on two phone books. She sipped a glass of tea with her pinky in the air, eyeing people as they talked but keeping mostly to herself.

Tony took center stage, rolling out his blueprints for the two library houses and smiling ear to ear when he heard the *ooh*s and *aah*s and Dora's satisfaction.

"They're perfect. Jim would be so happy."

He pointed out how the front of the children's house would open to allow access to the books and the roof of the other would seal when it's closed to keep the rain out. He showed them a pocket for a notebook and a pen. "Sign-out sheets," he said.

"Oh, yes." Dora put down her fork and sighed. "About those. Ed Warner stopped by earlier and asked for any I'd remembered. I wrote down what I could."

Dora turned to Zoe. "Ed felt bad about warning you not to leave town. Said he didn't want to do it but didn't know what else to do until he finds the real murderer. I think he's sorry, Zoe."

"Humph. He keeps looking in the wrong direction," Zoe said. "The man's got to dig into that family—the Canes. That's where the skeletons are buried."

"Just picture that house all painted with fairies and super-heroes," Dora interrupted, pointing to the blueprints in front of her.

"Oh, the fairies." Zoe was easily distracted. "Of course, I'll get a few to pose for me and, as to the adult post, how about an escaping Madame Bovary? Don't you wonder where she went?"

"An Atticus Finch, too," Lisa hurried to put in. "I'll always believe he was the hero Harper Lee made him out to be in the first book."

"What would an Atticus Finch look like?" Zoe frowned, thinking.

"Like Gregory Peck, of course," Dora said, then began to laugh. "Oh my. Then how about Hercules Poirot? He's easily recognizable with his fine mustaches."

"Or Vito Corleone. You know, from *The Godfather*," Tony joined in. "Paint him in his garden, Zoe. Dead or alive."

"How about you, Jenny?" Tony asked. "Any character you especially like?"

Jenny wasn't in the mood to be funny. "How about the girl in *The Girl with the Dragon Tattoo*? Lisbeth Salander."

Lisa made a face. "She's your favorite character?"

Tony winced.

Zoe shrugged.

"She will do," Jenny said, reminding herself she had only an hour left to be nasty.

Zoe slid off her chair. "But before all of that, my editor is coming in from New York tomorrow, about noon. I'll be busy most of the day. Why don't we all meet at Myrtle's for dinner at six? I want you to meet him. He's a very nice man." She started for the door. "Oh, and I'm buying. It's nice to have something to celebrate."

Jenny stopped her. "Zoe, what about . . . your pants?"

"Oh, yes." Zoe turned back from the open door. "If you've got a half an hour in the morning, could you come over? I've got some . . . er . . . things I need to show you. It would be good if we got a chance to talk."

"Ants in your pants, Zoe?" Lisa laughed.

Zoe, straight-faced, threw both hands in the air. "Ants in my pants, a bee in my bonnet, butterflies in my stomach. All little things. Little things. No importance, really. Except little things can be powerful things, and that makes them big things when they become words. Line the words up and you have so many answers. Do you see?"

"Of course not," Lisa said. "But I'll take your word for whatever the heck you're talking about."

Zoe grinned and nodded.

Tony rolled up his drawings and exited behind Zoe.

* * *

Lisa, Dora, and Jenny sat rocking on the porch and talking about things having nothing to do with killers. They made plans for Lisa's short visit, beginning with a trip to one of the lonely beaches on Lake Michigan the next afternoon.

"Only if it doesn't rain," Dora cautioned to groans from her daughters.

"Mom! My cell phone says seventy-five and sunny."

"Cells!" Dora dismissed the idea. "What do they know? Joe, my Traverse City weatherman, will tell me in the morning. Joe's got maps and weather quizzes and fronts and things. No cells. We'll go if Joe says so."

Dora went inside when she got a chill from the damp in the night air. Lisa and Jenny sat quietly rocking. Every once in a while, they shared a funny memory of their father.

Unable to contain herself, Lisa finally asked, "So, okay, what's with Zoe and her pants?"

Jenny weighed whether to rat Zoe out or not. She decided she needed a completely sane person on her side. "She stole papers from Aaron's house after we found him dead. She stuck them in her pants when Ed Warner arrived."

Lisa made a painful noise. "Should she have done that?"

"No. But I'm having trouble blaming her. Ed keeps talking as if he thinks she's a killer."

"Yuck! Couldn't he find somebody his own size?"

"Size doesn't matter with him. It sure doesn't matter to Zoe, but she's new to town. Well, 'new' in Bear Falls years. I guess that makes her a suspect."

"She's so alone."

"She's got Mom on her side."

"And me. And you," Lisa said.

"I suppose so," Jenny grudgingly agreed.

"Why'd she take the papers? Do you know what they are? Is there some way to sneak them back where they came from?"

"I don't have answers to any of those questions. I only know she's getting desperate. I'll talk to her in the morning. Maybe there's something there that will help her."

The phone rang inside the house. Lisa clamped her feet to the porch floor and got up. Jenny did the same and then led the way back in, hoping the phone would stop. Nothing good ever came of a phone ringing after eleven o'clock.

She answered on the sixth ring.

"Is this Jenny Weston?" a harsh woman's voice demanded.

Jenny racked her brain—who was calling?

"This is Angel. Angel Arlen."

She froze. "Angel. Hi. Was that you I saw at Junior's earlier?"

"You know that was me. You were practically begging for Johnny's attention. I'm just calling to warn you to stop playing games. In case you don't remember, he married *me*. He's *mine*." Her voice broke. "He's got responsibilities here."

"I . . ." Jenny couldn't think of a comeback.

"Just a friendly warning. Don't take it personally."

Angel hung up.

Jenny didn't know whether to laugh or cry.

Chapter 20

"Christopher's coming at noon." Zoe flew from room to room, waving a feather duster over the surfaces of tables and lamps. A dust mop leaned against the wall in the kitchen hallway. Zoe—despite her nerves and flitting—was resplendent in a red flowered dress that ended just above her ankles, white-flowered earrings. She had a red headband around her hair, so curly today that tendrils waved like tiny snakes.

She stopped dusting to scan the room.

"Does it look okay?"

"Fine," Jenny said. "Looked fine when I got here. What are you worried about?"

"Nothing. Nothing." Zoe waved a nervous hand. "Christopher wants to see what I've gotten done so far with this new book on Alice. I'm a little behind, what with—" She gestured around her. "—everything. I think it will be okay because he wants to talk about the illustrations, too. We're using the same woman we used on the last book. And he wants to talk about the next book. Can you imagine? It seems the Oz book is still selling well—at least I'm getting very nice checks. I want to be the most cooperative writer he's ever worked with. Mainly,

I would say, because Christopher is one of the finest men I've ever met."

"Did he ask why you couldn't come to New York?"

She nodded. "I said I haven't been feeling well, which is, of course, a lie." She sighed. "A mark on my immortal soul—but there are so many. I hope it's a small mark."

Jenny pitied her. Word was spreading fast through town, the townspeople only too happy to put the blame for murder on a stranger: *She's lived here only a year, after all. An interloper. What do we know about her?*

She'd only known Zoe for a few days, and though she wasn't completely crazy about her, she couldn't see her as a murderer. It wasn't her size that made her an impossible suspect; it was who she seemed to be and how her mind worked—catching things other people didn't know existed. If not "catching," then "smelling" out odd possibilities.

Jenny got up to look out Zoe's front window. A sunny morning. Mom was wrong—no rain. It was a beautiful day for the beach and maybe a picnic up at Norwood where they'd spent hours as children hunting for Petoskey stones along the beach.

"Do you have time to show me those papers you took from Aaron's house?" she turned to ask.

"Of course. I want you to take a look at them."

She hurried away, calling over her shoulder as she ran, "Bank statement. Nothing much. But there are two letters . . ."

Her voice faded away.

"This." She was back and handed a single sheet of paper to Jenny, then warned her to hold it by the edges. "Fingerprints," she warned. "It's odd. I mean, at first I took it for a blackmail letter, but how can that be? You've seen Aaron's house. Your mom said the two of them, both the brothers, built it years ago, back when they were still friends. Barely more than a shack. Do you think he was someone you'd try to get money from? And if you did, what would you get?"

Jenny shrugged and looked at the letter she held. A plain sheet of computer paper, smudged at the fold across the middle. A short message was set precisely at the center of the page. There was no salutation or date on it. The letter was typed but unsigned. It began,

> You boys can't cheat us anymore. I hear you've got what I'm after but you're hiding it. All three of you are cheating us, just like him. A pack of cheaters. Time's up on that. You cheated her way too long, and now you're cheating me. I'll get it, you know. One way or the other. Adam ignored me. Hope you aren't that stupid. I'm not finished. Do what you want to do, but I'll get what's mine.
>
> Put an ad in the *Record-Eagle* saying, "WE ARE READY," and we can make arrangements to deliver what you've been hiding.

She looked up from the paper. "'*Three* of you'? Who are the three? And what does 'it' mean? *Or* 'him'?"

"And who is that 'her' in the letter?"

"How was it delivered, I wonder?" Jenny shook the page, thinking about the hands that might have touched it.

"No envelope. Not folded the way a letter would be. Had to have left it in the mailbox, I suppose," Zoe said.

Jenny read the letter again then handed it, by its corners, back to Zoe. "What's it all about?"

Zoe shrugged. "Where does the family money come from?"

"I think it was shipping." Jenny went back to conversations she'd overheard as a child. "Freighters. Ore carriers on the Great Lakes. Then lumber, maybe."

Zoe was quiet for a tick. "There's probably only one person who knows the truth about any of this."

"Abigail." Jenny nodded. "But I don't see her sitting down with you, or me, for a heart-to-heart about the family business any time soon."

They sat in silence, both thinking hard.

"Why didn't this person call them instead of putting it in writing? Seems dumb," Jenny said.

"You see a phone in either house?"

"Okay. So what's this 'thing' he's talking about?"

"Who knows? But it's sure about money. What I don't get is, the only one in that family with money is Abigail. Why didn't the man—or woman, I suppose—go after *her*?" Zoe paused, clearly working through these riddles. "Maybe he did and she ignored him, too. So Abigail's the only one left on this man's list."

"That lets Abigail out as the murderer. She must have been threatened just the way her brothers were."

"Look at that other letter." Zoe motioned toward a paper laying in Jenny's lap. "It's a letter from an attorney. Justin Princely. He's in Traverse City."

"Who's it to?" Jenny took the letter and read it for herself. "Aaron Cane?" She looked up at Zoe, confused.

"Aaron must have written him asking for an appointment. That's what the letter says. Says he had an appointment on June ninth at four o'clock." Jenny screwed up her face. "Doesn't sound like this Justin Princely was Aaron's regular attorney. They don't seem to know each other."

She read the letter over again. "Nothing here to say what Aaron wanted to see him about. You've got to get all of these to Ed Warner as fast as you can."

"Not possible." She shook her head as she slipped the papers into a cabinet drawer. She turned back to Jenny. "I was starting to think maybe Abigail was giving Aaron money but none to Adam. Or the other way around. That could've caused the trouble between them. But neither way fits. If it hadn't been for Fida being stolen, I'd have thought maybe Adam killed Aaron. But that can't be. If Fida was in that house with him, Aaron had to have died after Adam. Or . . ." She clapped her hands to her cheeks. "Maybe Aaron killed his brother and took Fida because she's so cute."

"Come on, Zoe. You're driving yourself crazy."

"I am. I am. I truly am." She twirled her finger in one of her curls. "Seems to me we have to find out what the letter writer was after. That's at the heart of everything. Oh my! If this keeps on, the next thing you know, it will be Fida charged with murder because she was the only one out there."

Zoe sighed, dropping deeper into confusion. "I'm sinking into a murky mind. You know what happens in a murky mind? You can't see anything clearly. Flotsam and jetsam. It all floats by, but there's no use putting your hand out because it will just fade away."

"I'm calling Tony." Jenny eyed Zoe as she pulled out her cell. "We're getting in way over our heads. Maybe you can't see beyond the shipwreck, but I'm not going down with you."

Chapter 21

When they heard footsteps on the porch, they thought it must be Christopher Morley. Zoe hurried to the door with Jenny close behind. Chief Warner stood there, nervous head tipped forward, stiff hat in his hands, his long face more ashamed then official.

"'Day." He looked around Zoe to where Jenny stood. "Jenny." He nodded. Back to Zoe. "I've come to take you into the station with me, Ms. Zola. We've got more questions."

"I don't have any more answers." Zoe stood flat on the ground, her fisted hands at her hips. She leaned way back to look up into the man's eyes.

Ed cleared his throat. "What I've got here—" He pulled a paper from a folder and waved it at her. "—is a search warrant for your house and property. Judge in Traverse City signed it last night. Gives me the right to have a crew search your house, Ms. Zola. Same time, I'd like you to come into the station with me. We'll just be talking. Unless there's something in there—" He nodded to the interior of her house. "—that'll incriminate you and you want to tell me now."

Zoe's face froze in horror.

"Ed!" Jenny couldn't believe what she was hearing. "You've got to be joking."

"Wish I were. I'd like to get going, Ms. Zola."

"I'm busy right—"

He lifted his hand to stop her. "Not my problem."

"My editor will be here . . . soon. He's from New York. Remember, you told me not to leave town? *He's coming.*" Her voice took on a waiflike plaint.

Again Ed shook his head. "Just get whatever you're going to need or we'll provide it for you."

"Need for what? I don't understand."

"You might be lodged in our jail a day or so. I can hold you for forty-eight hours. After that, we'll see." He turned and looked far off.

"This is crazy," Jenny said. "You must be kidding, right?"

"Not kidding about anything. Ms. Zola could very well have somebody working with her. In Adam's case, there was a trip-wire. Perfect thing to bring him down and then hit him in the head with that hoe. Don't have to be tall for that. And as for Aaron—anybody can hold a gun and shoot a man in the chest. Maybe took the dog out there to ask him to watch her a while. Any excuse to get inside his house. When she left in a hurry, the dog got trapped. These are serious charges. She could be with us a while."

"What's 'a while'?" Jenny demanded.

He shrugged. "Not my place to give out information. What I'd say is, get her an attorney."

"You're damned right she'll have an attorney." Jenny looked down at Zoe's stricken face. "Don't worry. I'll call somebody right away. We'll get you out . . ."

"Go get Lisa. She always knows what to do," Zoe begged, giving Jenny the slightest of jealous twinges.

"And Fida!" The little dog ran from behind a chair at the sound of her name. "Oh no. Can you watch Fida?"

"Course. I'll keep her until . . ."

"Her food's under the sink. Oh, and don't forget her pills." She pointed to the drawer of a nearby cabinet, smiling at Jenny. "They're in that drawer. Remember?" She lifted her eyebrows.

"Can Jenny take those things?" She turned to the chief.

He frowned but nodded. Zoe handed the dog over and gave Jenny a hard, telling look she didn't understand at first. "And be on the lookout for my editor. He should be here around noon. Explain . . ." She checked herself. "Tell him whatever you want to."

Zoe turned to look up at Ed Warner. "You didn't read me my rights," she warned him.

"Don't need to, Ms. Zola." He put his head down, as if this was a thing he was far from proud for doing. "I'm not arresting you."

Zoe waved a hand at him. "Fine," she said. "Have it your way. Still, no matter what, I'm choosing silence."

Chapter 22

Jenny stood in the tall grass between the pines, quietly holding the shivering Fida in her arms. An outsized bag of dog food sat at her feet. Aaron's papers, from the table drawer, were shoved up under her T-shirt. She'd accomplished everything Zoe had expected of her and now waited to see what would happen next.

Poor Fida shook in spasms. She needed Zoe. She needed a bath. When Jenny set her down, she whimpered and turned that sad, one-eyed face up to her. All Jenny could do right then was put a finger to her lips to shush her.

When a police patrol car and a white van drove slowly down Elderberry and parked in front of Zoe's house, Jenny pulled back among the trees. One of the deputies she'd seen at Aaron's house got out of the car; took a swipe at his pants, straightening the crease; and then leaned back into his patrol car to retrieve a folder. He strode up to Zoe's front door, where he opened the folder, pulled out a key, stuck it in the lock, and turned to wait for the three officers in the van to join him.

Tony's pickup came around the corner a few minutes later. He was parking behind the deputy's patrol car when Jenny hurried out of the trees—dog in her arms and bag of dog food pulled along behind her—to stop him. She waved him to back up and park in front of her mother's house instead.

Tony parked and got out. He eyed the police car and van and then went to the back of the truck to unload the cedar posts and a bag of cement. He pulled a post-hole digger out and laid it in the grass.

She watched him work. His dark hair was wind-blown, the limp no more than an interesting quirk that made him braver, more worldly—at least more worldly than most men in the tiny world of Bear Falls. And just the kind of friend a woman needed at times like these, she decided. A man dressed for hard work in ripped jeans and a paint-stained T-shirt.

He walked over to her. "What's going on?" He nodded toward the police cars.

"Ed took Zoe down to the police station. Those men are searching her house."

Tony made a face and scratched behind one ear. "What a mess."

"What can we do?" she said, feeling the tears in her voice. "Her publisher's arriving from New York today. I've got to watch for him. And there's Fida to take care of." She patted the quivering dog she held.

"They going to find anything?"

She shook her head. "There were papers, but I got those before the police came."

"What kind of papers?"

"Papers Zoe found the other day in Aaron's house."

"When I told you two to stay out of there?" His face bloomed red.

She shrugged. "We didn't know what the papers were until this morning. At least, I didn't."

"So? What are they?" He laid his hand on Jenny's back and directed her toward her mother's porch, out of earshot and eyeshot of the searching officers next door. He lowered his head close to hers to catch what she was telling him. She'd forgotten how good it felt to have a man's concern centered on her.

"There was a letter. It looks as if the writer wanted something Aaron and Adam had. And then there's a letter from an attorney addressed to Aaron setting up an appointment for June ninth. Oh, and there was a bank statement with what looks like a very small savings account."

"Who are the letters from?"

"No signature, except for the attorney's letter."

"What'd they say?"

"I've got them." She gestured to her University of Michigan T-shirt under Fida. "I took them just now before the police got here."

Tony rubbed his forehead hard. "And got yourself in this up to your ears."

Jenny didn't feel a bit sorry for what she'd done. She felt resolute, certain that she was on the side of justice.

"Let's go inside," he nodded toward Dora's house. "I'll take a look at what you've got, then we can decide what to do next. You can't be hiding evidence, Jenny."

"I'm not hiding anything. I want them to go to Ed— eventually. I see this as proof that Zoe's not the killer."

"Unless she's the one who sent the letter." He took the steps two at a time. "First thing, you've got to find her an attorney. Lisa seems like a detail person. Let's get her moving on that."

For a swift second, Jenny let herself feel put out at the faith everybody had in Lisa the Good while all she seemed to do was screw up.

* * *

Inside, Dora waited for them. "I saw men go into Zoe's. Is every-thing okay over there? And why do you have the dog? What have they done to Zoe?"

"Ed took her to the station," Jenny said and handed the quivering lump of fur to Dora. "This one needs a bath."

Dora patted the little dog's back. "My poor friend." She nuzzled Fida.

* * *

With everyone sitting around the table, filled coffee mugs in front of each, Jenny laid out what happened.

Lisa slowly shredded a napkin as she listened. Tony studied the blueprints of the dual libraries but listened closely.

"We've got to get her an attorney," Jenny said to Lisa.

"I'll take care of it. Anybody know of one here in Bear Falls?" Lisa asked, looking at Tony and Dora. "Or how about Traverse City?"

Dora, Fida in her arms, licking her face, thought awhile. "What about that Alfred Rudkers? Abigail's lawyer? Met him at the funeral home. He seems nice enough to me."

"Mom!" Jenny couldn't hide her exasperation. "He's an awful man. There's got to be more than one lawyer around."

"But if he works for Abigail, I'm sure he's perfectly fine."

Jenny rolled her eyes.

"I'll find somebody." Lisa squinted down at her cell phone and started a search.

"Remember Penelope Farnum? From high school? She was in my grade," Jenny said. "Penny?"

Lisa shook her head.

"You'd remember if you saw her. We went through elementary school together and right on through high school. Really smart, ready to take on anybody—even back then. But also a real pain in the ass. Straight as a stick, with that much personality. What I do remember, in high school, was how she fought for one girl who wanted to try out for the football team. Didn't make it onto the team, but Penelope said it was still the morality of the law she was upholding."

"Okay. So what about her?"

"I heard she's an attorney. Think she's practicing here in Michigan. Look her up."

Lisa went into the dining room to make phone calls. Dora took Fida to the porch to rock her. Tony went out to dig holes, which was actually the reason he'd showed up.

Jenny made a peanut butter sandwich for herself and sat down to eat and think.

When Tony came clumping back into the kitchen, he went directly to the sink to wash up, then turned to Jenny as he methodically dried his hands on paper towels. She noticed his limp was worse today.

"Weather?" she asked, nodding to his leg.

He looked down as if he didn't know what she meant. "Oh, that. Yeah. Weather can get me. There's still part of the bullet in there. Couldn't get it all out without more damage."

"Sorry," she said.

"About what?" Tony finished drying his hands. "If you're sorry I was shot, so am I. If you're sorry you asked—don't be."

She didn't know why she wanted to keep him talking, maybe just not to be alone.

"Are you in pain?"

He shrugged. "Once in a while. If I work too hard. Or if the weather changes. That bullet turned me into a barometer."

He grinned, walked to where she sat, and leaned down in front of her.

"Don't be afraid to ask me anything, Jenny. Nothing you can ask will hurt me more than that bullet did. Or my ex-wife."

"I didn't know you had one."

"You don't belong to an exclusive club, you know."

His dark eyes were so deep. It was like looking straight into the man's head. She had an overwhelming urge to reach out and softly touch his cheek, to run a finger delicately over the faded scar and then over his narrow beard. She wondered if she had a sappy look on her face.

"Got to talk about those letters," He put a firm hand on her back. The surprise of those warm fingers left her briefly breathless.

Avoiding her eyes, Tony looked down at her peanut butter sandwich. "Glad I ate already," he said and laughed.

Jenny got up. She knew the way her body worked, how it could betray her. She wasn't going to be tricked into emotions she didn't trust. Not again.

She went to the dishtowel drawer where she'd hidden Zoe's papers.

When he took them from her, he shook his head and warned again, "You're in this now. Right along with Zoe. Don't know what in hell the two of you were thinking."

He read the letters carefully, then went over them once more.

"I'll give them to Ed, tell him I found them," she said.

"Where? In the bulrushes?" Tony wasn't happy. "Typed and unsigned. Ed'll be sure you and Zoe trumped this up between you. Maybe I should—"

Tony was interrupted by a knock and a deep "Hello there" through the back screen door.

* * *

Fida came running through the house, woofing and growling. Jenny went to the door to greet a tall and impossibly thin man in a rumpled light-blue summer suit. Middle-aged and slightly stooped, his thinning brown hair stood up at the back of his head as if he'd been blown to the door by a very high wind.

The man pushed wire-rimmed glasses up his nose, stared myopically at Jenny, and set his briefcase down beside him on the porch.

"Christopher Morley." He stuck out his hand and bowed slightly. "I'm Zoe Zola's editor."

Jenny groaned inside as she shook the man's limp hand. She'd completely forgotten to watch for him.

"I was next door," he hurried to say, blinking at her. "A man there said Ms. Zola . . . er . . . Zoe is at the police station. Do you people know her? Can you tell me what's going on?"

Jenny drew the fidgeting man into the house, apologizing as she offered him a chair at the table. She asked what she could get him to drink.

"Water. Just a tall glass of water, thank you," he answered, bowing his head formally. "Flying makes me thirsty. And driving here from the airport, well, I made a turn in Elk Rapids, which was obviously wrong. A few more wrong turns after that and I ended up in a corn field." He looked worriedly at the watch on his wrist. "Oh my. I'm an hour late getting here."

"And I forgot to keep an eye out for you. Zoe told me you were coming. I'm so sorry." She introduced Christopher to Tony, who nodded to the man.

"Whatever has happened?" He glanced around the kitchen as if taking in foreign territory. "I don't have a lot of time. I have to be back in New York tonight. Is everything okay with Zoe? I'd like to help her. I can make a few phone calls, if needed."

"It's all a mistake, Mr. Morley," Jenny assured him. "Truly a mistake. I don't imagine she'll be there long."

"I'll wait, of course." His long face was a moving mass of worry. He pushed gold-framed glasses up his nose, then glanced at his watch again. "For a while. Unless I can't wait and have to leave. But I hope not. Oh dear, I hope not. I do care about Zoe. She's a wonderful writer and a wonderful woman. I only hope . . . oh, how I hope. I mean, I can't stay forever, but—at the police station! What on earth is she doing there? Could it be research? She's a meticulous researcher, you know."

His twice-magnified eyes looked from Jenny to Tony. "Do either of you know what's happened? If I can help . . . of course I want to wait, but I'm not certain. You see, I have my return flight." He swallowed hard, glanced at his watch again, then back at them. "I do hope it's research."

"It shouldn't be too long," Tony reassured him. "I think the police chief only wanted to ask her some questions."

"About what? What could Zoe be involved in that would interest the police? She's such a dear person. If she needs me to vouch for her character, I'll be happy to go right over there and . . ."

Dora and Lisa walked through the back door and stopped midconversation when they noticed the stranger. Jenny introduced Christopher, who began quickly with his disbelief that anything could really be wrong with Zoe and his worry about catching his plane on time and his offer to vouch for Zoe's character. Dora looked over his head to Tony.

Lisa filled his water glass, as Lisa would, then sat beside him, calming him, one hand on his arm.

"I can see you care about Zoe, Mr. Morley," she said in a quiet voice. "I'm really happy she has someone like you in her corner."

"What corner is that?" he asked, startled.

"I meant on her side," Lisa tried again.

"Which side would that be? I don't like the sound of this at all."

Lisa smiled and gave up.

Dora brought a plate of cookies to the table.

In a very short time, it seemed too maddeningly cordial and ordinary to Jenny. Talk of Zoe was suspended. Dora wanted to know about the writers he published and his life in New York. Through all of it, Christopher glanced again and again at his watch, then leaned back to roll his eyes up to the ceiling.

When conversation waned, Christopher sat straight up in his seat. "Could we call that police station? Find out if she's on her way home?" He turned to Tony. "They aren't actually holding her in a cell or anything, are they?" Christopher frightened himself. "I certainly hope not. I certainly do."

"Why don't we go down there?" Dora was delighted with her idea. "She will be so happy to see you. It's too bad all of this nasty stuff had to happen."

"Just what is this 'nasty stuff' you all talk about without actually saying? Did she jaywalk? We get a lot of that in New York, but of course no one pays any attention. I can see how a small-town sheriff might take umbrage at jaywalking, though. Crime seems to be relative. Don't you agree?"

"Well, no, it isn't jaywalking." Dora smiled to calm him. "There have been a couple of murders here in town."

"Surely they don't think my good friend had anything to do with murder!"

Jenny slid down in her chair. With her hands covering her face, all she thought was, *We're all mad. Barking mad, the whole lot of us.*

Chapter 23

They weren't allowed to see Zoe. It seemed, the stout woman behind the front desk said, that Zoe was being interrogated at that moment. "If you want to, you can wait," she said to Jenny, who'd done the asking.

"It's part of the processing," the brassy blonde went on. "Could be out soon." She hesitated. "Or not."

Tony began to argue with her, but Jenny pulled him off to one side.

"Please take Christopher to Zoe's house. He's driving us crazy," she begged. "One minute he's worried sick about her and the next minute he's worried sick about catching his plane."

"Take it easy, Jen. I imagine you'd be nervous, too, if you had to explain to the board of your publishing house why one of your best-selling authors is in jail."

"He's a wreck and making me into the same thing. Take him to Zoe's. The police will be gone by now. Let him look at her work. That's what he came for. Maybe later . . ."

Christopher, pacing the floor, walked over, his face one long scowl. "Just where is this attorney you spoke of? They can't do this to our Zoe." He'd skewed himself into a high-pitched snit.

"An attorney's on her way," Jenny assured him, fingers crossed behind her back. "But Tony can show you what's she's working on. It's magnificent, from what I've heard. You'll be amazed."

"Really?" At first he was pleased, then muddled. "Have those men left her house? But I shouldn't care about that now, should I? The poor dear . . ." He looked at his watch again. "Maybe if we go for a little while."

Tony put his hand on the thin man's bent back, directing him toward the door. Tony talked as fast as he could about Zoe's house and how he'd worked on it and knew it well enough to show him into her office. His voice faded as the door closed behind them, leaving Jenny with a last impatient sigh from Christopher and the nervous words, "Poor Zoe. Oh dear, poor, poor Zoe. I hope this doesn't take too long."

Chapter 24

Heads turned when Jenny and Lisa walked into Myrtle's Restaurant that afternoon. Delaware Hopkins, daughter to Demeter, the head waitress, wore a short, brown uniform covered with a somewhat white, frilly apron. She was excited to see the Weston sisters again.

"Thought that was you two." Delaware hurried toward them, soles of her thick shoes sucking at the linoleum floor. "Heard you was both back. Things sure getting wild around here."

"Don't blame me." Lisa made a face at her. "I just got here."

"Wasn't me." Jenny shook her head at the woman.

"Well, Myrtle was just saying how she'd never seen the town so worked up."

"Say hi for me," Lisa said.

Jenny leaned close to her sister. "You know Myrtle? I've never seen her. She doesn't come out of her kitchen."

Lisa scoffed. "Of course she does, silly. She wears a green hat. That's how you know her."

"That lady waiting for you?" Delaware pointed to a booth where a thin woman sat. "Guess what she ordered? Hot water and lemon. Can you beat that? Neither one cost a penny. Some people!"

"Is that Penny?" Lisa asked.

Jenny took a hard look and nodded.

Penelope Farnum looked exactly as she had eighteen years before, when they graduated from Bear Falls High together: same hairdo—straight brown hair lopped off around her ears and straight bangs over her eyes—same blue-framed glasses, and the same wrinkling nose and pursed mouth instead of a smile. *Amazing*, Jenny thought when she slid into the booth across from her. *Like time stopping—but only for Penelope.*

Lisa started to apologize for being a couple of minutes late. Penelope waved the excuse away.

"Who do I bill?" She cut right to the chase, skipping over routine small talk.

There was no "What have you been doing these last eighteen years?" The kind of thing most people said to fill awkward spaces.

"Me." Jenny raised her hand. "Or Zoe. She's a pretty well-known writer. She's good for it."

Penelope nodded. "I checked her out."

She gave them both a stern look. "I want you to know, when I'm in, I'm all in. I'll stay with this to the bitter end, no matter which end is bitterest: I get her off or she swings."

"You'll do fine with Zoe." Jenny had to laugh at what a great pair the two would make.

Penelope finally smiled, though it wasn't an improvement on the severe face. "I haven't seen you since high school. You're not still living here, are you? I thought you'd turn out to do something big. Especially after what that awful Arlen boy did to you."

Smack! Right in the face. Jenny swallowed words she felt like spewing.

"I did." Jenny smiled a smile so tight, her cheeks might've cracked. "I'm just visiting from Chicago."

"What are you in?"

"In?"

"What do you do? What profession?" Penelope was impatient.

"Legal aid." Jenny said, which was a bit of a stretch, since she'd been a paralegal in her husband's office and never worked with the poor. Charity wasn't Ronald's idea of the way to run his office.

"Married?" Penelope demanded.

"Divorced. You?"

"Never married."

"Didn't think so," Jenny said and smiled sweetly.

"So . . ." Penelope smacked both hands on the table, making waves in her lemon water. ". . . I'll get her out of there as soon as possible. I have to tell you, it won't be until tomorrow. Your police chief said he's holding her, at least for twenty-four hours. What a one-track man! Where's she going to run, after all? Does he think no one could identify her? She owns a house and has a job. She's pretty well known, from what I see." She squeezed her last tiny lemon slice into the cooling water.

"Is she okay?" Lisa asked.

"She's complaining about the food. She said they must have a large mustard mine nearby. Then she said, 'And the moral to that is the more there is of mine, the less there is of yours.'"

"Welcome to Zoe's world," Jenny said.

Penelope shook her head and made a face. "I don't like playing games with clients." She pushed her glasses back up her nose. "Still, I thought it was funny."

"She's a writer. Working on a book about the two 'Alices.'"

Penelope nodded. "The mustard mine was from *Alice in Wonderland*, if I remember right. Still one of my favorite books. In law it's good to know a little nonsense language."

"I get about half of what she says," Jenny admitted. "But I'm working on it."

Penelope shrugged. "That's to be expected, I suppose."

Jenny wondered if she'd just been insulted and then got madder because the insult flew over her head.

"She doesn't like her cut-off, striped outfit. Doesn't like the cell they put her in. Doesn't like her cot. She said it will be like sleeping in the middle of a doughnut. I guess the edges folded up around her when she took a nap."

She gave a sharp laugh without smiling, then went dead-pan again.

"What am I looking at? Any way to clear her if this goes any further? And will there be a point where you toss her to the wolves?"

Jenny bristled. Penelope was the same nasty girl she remembered from high school. She wished she'd remembered this person better than she had. "We're not tossing her anywhere. Me, Lisa, and Tony Ralenti, an ex-cop—we're working hard to get to the bottom of all this."

Penelope screwed up her face. "Keystone Kops?"

"We know what we're doing." Lisa took over because Jenny was speechless.

"I hope so. You want to let me in on just what that is? What you're doing? Or am I supposed to be kept in the dark?"

"All we're asking is that you get Zoe out of jail. You don't have to worry about anything else," Jenny said.

"I will worry. I'll get her out, but then I'm not throwing her to the lions."

"I thought it was wolves. Got any more clichés?" Jenny puffed up like a setting hen.

"I was always better than you were in English." Penelope almost smiled. "So here's what I'm saying. I met Zoe. This is a ridiculous charge. That little woman didn't murder anyone. I want to help however I can. It's too easy to go for that 'stranger from out of town' stuff. I just want you to know that I'll be here from now on."

Jenny and Lisa looked at each other in wonder.

"Well, sure," Lisa said, drawing out the words. "As long as you mean it."

Penelope frowned. "I don't bother saying things I don't mean. Okay, what's he got against her?"

Delaware was back beside them with her pad in her hands. Jenny and Lisa, knowing the menu well, ordered Reubens and Diet Cokes. Delaware pranced away with her head high, ignoring Penelope.

"The chief has got a letter they found in Adam Cane's house. Supposed to be from Zoe, asking Adam to meet her out by her shed early that next morning."

Penelope frowned. "Signed?"

Jenny shook her head. "The thing's all typed. No signature."

"Why early the next morning? Why would he go? It's not like they were friends, right?"

"The note said Zoe had proof he wasn't the one who destroyed my mom's Little Library. Supposed to be a hidden axe with a neighbor's initials carved into it and bits of the library caught in the handle."

"I don't get it."

Lisa explained the rest of what had been going on in town. "Anything else?"

Jenny looked at Lisa before answering. "Adam died in Zoe's backyard. I found the body."

"I've got all of that. What else?"

"Zoe was the one who found his brother's body."

"She told me. You were there, too. Maybe you're the killer. It makes as much sense as Zoe. What else?"

Lisa, frustrated, said, "Adam threatened to kill Zoe's dog."

She nodded. "I got that. What else?"

Lisa shrugged. Jennie shook her head.

"Who do you think did all of this?" Penelope asked as Delaware delivered their drinks. Penelope asked for more hot water. Delaware turned away as if she hadn't heard.

"Who do you think did all of this?" she repeated.

"I found a hatchet buried in Adam's backyard."

"What's that got to do with anything? Neither man was killed with a hatchet." She consulted papers she'd set on the table. "And anyway, what were you doing in Adam's backyard?"

"Looking for something, anything I could find."

"That would be what?" She leaned forward.

"You really want to know?"

"You think I'm sitting here, on the clock, for nothing?"

"I was looking for Fida, Zoe's dog. Zoe got the idea that Adam killed Fida and buried her in his yard."

"And that's how you found a buried hatchet." Penelope thought a while. "Native Americans buried hatchets. Two hatchets, if I remember correctly from my early American culture class in college. It was to unite the Indians and their enemies: 'Hurling the hatchet so far into the depths of the earth that it shall never again be seen in the future.' I liked that idea. If only we could bury nuclear bombs . . ." She sighed, closed her eyes, then opened them and zeroed in on Jenny.

"I understand the brothers weren't speaking. They had been mad at each other for years. What if, say, Aaron—because he's the younger man and the nicer one, from what Zoe said—what if he chopped up your mother's library with a hatchet to get in good with his brother? Then he buried the hatchet?"

"Farfetched," Jenny said. "So then Adam went out and killed his brother as a thank-you? Pretty tough, especially as Adam was killed first."

"I don't need sarcasm," Penelope said as Delaware went by their booth. Penelope reached out to grab Delaware's apron, stopping her. "I said I need more hot water, miss. And lemon."

Delaware smiled a mechanical smile, stood still beside them for a minute, then looked over at Jenny and Lisa. "Your orders will be right out," she said.

Delaware looked at Penelope from the sides of her eyes and walked off, only to come back immediately with the sandwiches, a pot of hot water, and a whole lemon, which she set in front of Penelope, asking if she needed a knife.

Penelope absent-mindedly shook her head, then turned her focus back to what they'd been talking about.

"Of course Adam didn't kill his brother. And it's unlikely Aaron killed Adam. Nothing I've heard points to that. So? Do I have anything else to work with?"

Jenny hesitated only a minute, imagining how she was going to trust Penelope.

"Okay." Jenny leaned in close so people in the booths around them couldn't hear. "We found some papers that Aaron had hidden in his house."

"What kind of papers?"

"Two letters. One looks as if it's from a blackmailer or somebody with something against the brothers or who wanted something from the brothers. And then there's a letter from an attorney confirming an appointment with Aaron. That was a week before he died."

"You've got these letters?" Penelope's voice wasn't quiet. She narrowed her eyes. "Are you hiding evidence?"

"No!" Jenny's shock sounded almost real. "Zoe found them. We gave them to Tony, and he took them to Ed Warner."

Penelope put a hand up to stop her. "I don't know if I believe you, so I'll just warn you to be careful, okay?" She rolled the lemon back and forth on the table. "Tell me what's in the letters and who took the letters from Aaron's house."

"As I said, Zoe did. That was the day we found Aaron dead."

"So? How'd *you* get them?"

"I took them out of Zoe's house before the police came to search. The ex-cop we're working with took them to the chief of police."

"She stole them. Just what I thought," Penelope said. When she spoke again, her voice was very low. "What's done is done. So here's what you're going to do now. Are you listening?"

Jenny and Lisa nodded.

"Did you make copies of the letters?"

Jenny nodded again. Penelope smiled. "I want a set of the copies. Get it to me as soon as you can, okay?"

Penelope reached out and put a surprisingly soft hand on Jenny's. "Be careful, Jen. I know you want to help your friend. And I know you were always a tough kid. Almost as tough as I was. And I know what you've been through—with Johnny and with your dad. Just don't screw this up. I don't want you to be the next one I'm getting out of jail."

Her smile was genuine as she slid over, got up, and stood beside the table.

Despite having no bill to pay, Penelope laid a twenty-dollar bill down as a tip as Delaware approached.

"I'm full of surprises," she said to an astounded Delaware. "Remember me next time."

She headed out the door, leaving Jenny and Lisa scrambling to pay and follow her.

In front of the restaurant, Jenny reached out to hug her old schoolmate but was halted by Penelope.

"I don't hug." She tightened her shoulders. She informed them that she was staying at the Woods Motel, out on the highway, for the duration. "It's cheap," she added with what passed for a smile. "You're paying."

* * *

In Jenny's car, Lisa leaned over to laugh. "What a horrible human being. 'I don't hug. I don't smile. I don't like people. And I'm a terrible witch.'" Lisa sat back. "You know what, Jen? She may be all of that, but she's just what Zoe needs, And I'm happy to have a witch of her caliber on our side."

"Lisa! Where did my sweet big sister go? You have now officially shocked me. A real swearword! And said as if you meant it. My, my, what has Montana done to you?"

Chapter 25

There was no time for a beach trip, although it was one of those soft Michigan summer days when the sun was circled with haze, eagles and turkey buzzards flew in lazy circles, sprinklers dashed and dotted front lawns, and the voices of playing children were absorbed by the leaves on all the trees and bushes along the streets.

Jenny thought how she and Lisa could have been lying in the sand by now, the way they used to, and burning because they didn't pay attention to how long they'd been in the sun. They could have been talking about nothing all day followed by some swimming—challenging each other to races.

Instead, it was another brown funeral.

Jenny pulled into the parking lot of Tannin's. People standing on the front porch turned to stare as she drove in. She ignored the stares, too occupied with thinking of a way to talk to Abigail Cane without Carmen Volker, the hovering secretary, or Alfred Rudkers, the rude attorney, on guard beside her.

She needed time alone with the woman. She had copies of the letters to show her.

She'd been to the jail to sit with an unhappy Zoe, all the life sucked out of her. Strained, dumb back-and-forth followed: "How's the food?" "Lousy." "How's your cell?" "Perfect, glad you asked."

The only thing to hold on to was Penelope's promise to have her out sometime that morning.

Zoe had echoed Jenny's need to talk to Abigail. "Show her those letters," she'd begged. "See what she thinks. Something is wrong in that family, I'm telling you. The answer's there. Words! Words! Words! You've got to listen for them. 'Cheat.' 'Cheating.' 'Cheaters.' 'Cheated.' Now what could all of that mean? At cards? At what? They have no money—except for Abigail, and she's not dead. But then there's that 'what you've been hiding.' What could that be? Hiding something lets out cheating at cards. Something else. All of them in it together? 'All three of you.' You three: Adam, Aaron, and Abigail. My head hurts from thinking so hard."

Zoe'd looked around at the bare, gray walls, gathered her strength, and turned her attention to how Fida was doing.

"Mom's giving her a bath this morning. I'm going over to the funeral home a little early, see who's there. Maybe I can get Abigail alone for a few minutes. Mom and Lisa are coming later. Lisa's leaving soon. Got to get back to Montana. They're shooting some finishing shots."

And then there had been nothing left to say, so Jenny hugged Zoe, told her not to worry, and left for the funeral home, hoping there'd be time later that afternoon for her and Lisa, maybe even with Zoe, to head over to the Lake Michigan shore and have a couple of real "sister" moments before Lisa had to go.

Jenny's cell phone rang as she pulled into the parking lot.

It was Penelope.

"I'm bringing her to the funeral home."

"That's crazy, Penny. People will treat her like dirt. They've already made up their minds that she's the one who did this. Please don't put Zoe, or the rest of us, through that."

Jenny had a couple of reasons for disagreeing, one of them having to do with wet sand in the late afternoon, which in no way was going to include Penelope Farnum.

There was a long, cool pause on the other end of the line. "My name is Penelope, Jenny. Not 'Penny.'"

"Okay, Penelope. My name is Jennifer, not 'Jenny.'"

"Don't be an ass," Penelope said.

"You either. Remember, I knew you when you wet your pants in third grade."

There was a pause. "And I knew you when you tried to kiss Bobby Solomon in the coatroom."

Laughter broke out on both ends of the phone.

"Okay. 'Penny,' if that's what you want," Penelope said. "Just write the correct name on my checks."

"Deal." Jenny laughed. "Penny and Jenny. Sounds like a comedy team."

"So what about Christopher Morley?" she asked. "He still in town?"

"He had to get back to New York, but he told Tony the work looked good and he was in the process of drawing up a contract for two more books on magic people or fairy tales. Whatever she wants to do. He said he hoped she'd approve."

"Great!" She actually sounded happy. "I like to be the bearer of good news. Lord knows, she can use it. So we'll see you at the funeral home," Penny said. "This woman is innocent and doesn't have anything to hide. You'll be there?"

"I'm just parking. I hope to set up a meeting with Abigail Cane. Hope you don't make a mess of things."

"I know what's best for my client. And I want to see first-hand how people react to her."

Jenny hung up, thinking how she was stuck in a world full of lunatics. Nothing was the way it should be. Jenny knew enough about law to realize that none of this was the right thing to do: not Zoe getting detained in the first place, not having her still under suspicion, and not bringing her to the wake of a man many in town think she'd killed.

"Curiouser and Curiouser"—watchwords to live by. Jenny wished Zoe was there to be proud of how she was progressing with her "Alice" studies. She was in a place much like the inside of Zoe Zola's head. It wasn't a mind she welcomed breaking into, but at the moment, it felt like the sanest place to be.

* * *

Jenny stepped onto Tannin's porch and greeted old neighbors: Millie Sheraton and Louise Dyer, fanning themselves with their handkerchiefs and smiling wide at Jenny. Vera Wattles, another neighbor, was looking aggrieved at Sarah Plenty, who always said the dullest things—and in a monotone.

Jenny ran into Minnie Moon, who lowered her voice, then raised her thick eyebrows as she asked something Jenny didn't catch.

A few of the men had already pulled off their ties because of the heat. Sullen children whined that they were hot.

Once inside and past Tom Tannin, she pushed through the very warm and crowded vestibule into the viewing room. She got in the mourners line to talk to Abigail, happy to see her secretary and attorney were nowhere in sight.

She watched the people around her, so many drawn into little cliques, their heads together. Jenny could easily imagine what they were gossiping about and dreaded again the moment when Zoe walked into the room.

Dora arrived and stood in the doorway, looking for Jenny. When she saw her in line, she put up her hand and hurried forward, her face frazzled, her body stiffly awkward as she made her way through the crowd.

"I want to show you something," she whispered loud enough for people to turn, then jerked her head toward the back of the room.

Once alone, Dora put a fist out to Jenny and dropped a small key into her hand, an old key—tarnished brass.

"What's this?"

"I don't know."

"Where'd you get it?"

"I gave Fida a bath. She was filthy. I thought it would be a nice surprise for Zoe."

"Yes?" Jenny knew enough to wait until her mother was ready to get to the meat of the message.

"That red collar of hers was hidden under a lot of dirty hair, so it wasn't until I soaped her up and took the collar off that I found the key. Duct-taped to the inside." Dora leaned in close. "Duct tape. Can you imagine? Wrapped around and around."

"Maybe an extra house key?"

Dora shook her head. "That's no house key. You take a look at it?"

"Okay. Any idea what it opens?"

"Some kind of box, I'd say. Bigger than a diary key. Smaller than a safe deposit box key." Dora couldn't come up with a better answer.

"Let's ask Zoe when she gets here. Should be any—"

There was a cessation of sound around them, a dropping of voices, a kind of holding of breath throughout the viewing room.

Penelope and Zoe stood in the doorway. Zoe was out of prison orange and back into a long flowered top and white cuffed pants that brushed the tops of her white sandals. No black this time. When the pair spotted Dora and Jenny, they made directly for them.

Zoe hugged them. She didn't say anything, just smiled a wan smile, ignoring the shocked faces around her. Her eyes were fixed only on her friends, and then on Penelope, who icily stared down the looks coming their way.

Dora opened her hand and showed Zoe the key she'd found taped to Fida's collar.

"Where?" Zoe was incredulous, taking the key and turning it over and over in her hands. "Taped to her collar? I didn't put it there. The only time she was out of my sight was when Aaron had her—other than now. And she's been with you. I don't understand."

Jenny looked up to see Tony edging his way through the crowd. *Here comes the cavalry.* Jenny wanted to laugh. His rugged face lit up when he saw her. He straightened his shoulders and ran a quick hand over his unruly hair. He was dressed in dark-blue summer pants, white shirt, and black tie. Jenny smiled. Clothes sure could change a man.

Dora saw him, too, and would have *yoo-hoo*ed, but instead settled for a wave.

After the greetings—a big hug for Zoe, smiles for Jenny and Lisa, and an introduction to Penny—Dora put her closed hand out to him.

"I found this taped to Fida's collar," she whispered.

He took the key.

"I didn't put it there," Zoe said.

"You know who did?"

She shook her head.

Tony turned the key over. He fumbled in a pocket, pulled out his cell phone, and took three photos of the key.

"Anybody know what it belongs to?"

Penny threw up her hands. "Nothing to do with me." She hesitated, looking straight at Tony. "I understand you were a detective in Detroit."

He nodded.

"Think you can find a way to identify what kind of key that is?" Penny asked. "Maybe what kind of box it fits?"

"I know a man in Detroit. Helped me more than once. A locksmith. A real expert on keys. I'll text him these pictures, see if he knows what it belongs to."

"Will you tell the police chief about it?" Penny slowly asked.

He shrugged. "I've agreed to work with him—when I can. Let me take a shot at identifying this first. See what I come up with."

"Jenny Weston," a woman's deep voice behind them said.

Jenny and the others turned to Abigail Cane.

The stately woman's eyes were pained behind her gold-embellished glasses. She looked from one face to the other, finally stopping at Zoe. "I'm so sorry you've been drawn into this," she said, then stopped, overcome with something that wouldn't let her finish.

It took a minute for her to turn to Jenny. "May I speak to you?" she asked, then turned and walked off with a privileged woman's certainty, knowing Jenny would be right behind her.

Chapter 26

Abigail, up close, looked tired. What she'd been through had aged her. There were dark circles under her eyes and her face was pale. She was no longer as beautifully dressed as she'd been at the last funeral. This dress was black but without style. More like something her secretary, Carmen Volker, would have chosen for her.

"So much . . ." Abigail started to say as they moved to a quiet corner of the room. "I can't imagine what's happened to my family."

She closed her eyes and tilted her head. When she could speak again, Jenny saw tears.

"I think I might need your help. I know you are working with Ms. Zola."

Jenny had no idea what to admit and so said nothing.

"You mentioned that she's a writer. I would have loved to talk to her . . . before . . . all of this." She motioned around the room. "My entire life . . . I've gotten along best with creative people."

"We'll set up a time and . . ."

Jenny was waved to silence.

"Please listen," Abigail said, her voice very low. "I need to talk to someone. I will call you."

Behind them, Carmen Volker wove her way through the gathered people. She touched Abigail's arm to let her know she was there, then whispered something in her ear. Abigail's face cleared of emotion as she listened.

To Jenny, she finally said, graciously, in her normal voice, "It's been lovely talking to you, Jenny. Thank you so much for coming."

Carmen took Abigail's arm and pulled slightly. "Alfred is trying to get your attention."

"Abigail," Alfred called from where he stood with a group of people. "Times up on that, dear. We have *important* people waiting."

Jenny went back to where her group stood watching, away from the others.

"What did she want?" Zoe asked.

"I told you we should call her. Too bad she was dragged away by that . . . that 'frumious Bandersnatch,'" Zoe hissed though gritted teeth.

"Or 'a Borogrove who lives under sundials and eats only veal.'" Jenny came up with a line she'd read the night before.

"Stop studying, please. You'll never know as much as I, and really, is this the time for a competition?" She narrowed her eyes, then clucked at Jenny.

"You'd better get to her without those two around," Tony leaned in to say.

"I'll call her tonight if I don't hear from her first," Jenny said.

"Give the poor soul at least until tomorrow," Dora said. "Let's not forget, she's burying another of her brothers today."

They were shushed when a minister stood and raised his hands for quiet.

* * *

Tony went home. The others sat in rockers in the twilight of the Weston's porch. Zoe held a happy Fida on her lap and the brass key in her open hand. The tarnished key glinted strangely when the light of the moon caught it just right.

"What could this fit?" Zoe asked again and again.

"No idea. But even knowing what kind of thing it fits, how will you ever find the exact box or locker or whatever it goes to?" Lisa asked.

"I'm afraid the box was put somewhere in my house to make me look even more guilty. I'll bet the police found it today." She looked glum. "I can see the Perry Mason moment at my trial when Ed walks in with some funky box and holds it up for everyone to see the body parts I keep there."

"Zoe, we have no idea what that key is to." Lisa plumped a pillow behind her head.

"Look at what's happened so far. I feel like a—" Zoe stopped to think of an appropriate image.

Jenny groaned. "I don't want to hear any more of this tonight, okay?"

"You be quiet, Jenny Weston. I'll say exactly what I need to say. Nothing more and nothing less." Zoe spat the words at Jenny.

"And just what were you saying, dear?" Dora asked.

"I was going to say . . ." Fida leaned up to lick Zoe's chin. "I feel exactly like Alice trapped in Wonderland. It's as if someone is trying to snare me in my own book. Now here I am, arrested by the Queen of Hearts . . ."

"Is that Ed Warner?" Jenny asked, a gleam in her eye. "I never pictured him as—"

"Quiet, please," Zoe ordered. "Let's be serious. I have a brass key someone left for me—attached to my darling dog. The key might as well be sitting on a table way above my head for all the use I have of it. So the first question is, what or who does this key belong to?"

"And don't forget the two men dead in close proximity to you." Jenny joined the game. "One by a bullet. One by a hoe."

Zoe ignored her. "A letter," she went on, her pretty face balled up in worry. "A letter that came from me but didn't come from me, since I didn't send it, was found in Adam's house. If I did send the letter, how did I get it in there? There was no envelope with a stamp. I'm not in the habit of breaking and entering. Still, someone had to write it since it wasn't me who invited Adam to visit at dawn. That someone, as I've said before, has to be the killer. He or she would be the only one expecting to run into Adam in my yard at that time of night. He or she was the one who laid the trap. Now, the next question is, who is he or she?"

Jenny thought her head was going to explode. "Does all of this have a point we haven't looked at already?"

"My point is, I didn't do any of the things I'm being accused of, so it must be someone else. Somebody alive—since the Cane boys are dead. Somebody with a grudge against both of them, even though they had a grudge against each other. Someone who has chosen me as dispensable since I'm rather odd all the way around."

"Not all the way around," Jenny said.

Dora hushed her. "There is nothing odd about you, dear," she said to Zoe, and Lisa the Good agreed. "Okay, maybe not odd but . . ." She thought a while. "Unique. Will that do?"

"So," she went on, "It could be Abigail who is doing all of this, or someone she's directing. She's the only family member left. Still and all, I don't think the woman has the meanness for it, even though everybody says she stole the family fortune from her brothers. Which brings me to—"

"This is Lisa's last night home," Jenny interrupted. "Could we talk about something other than cruelty and death?"

"No," Lisa demanded. "I want to hear what Zoe's come up with. I'm just so sorry I have to leave and can't help anymore."

"That's all right, Lisa," Zoe nodded to her friend. "I'll call you as soon as the story's worked itself out and we know for sure I wasn't the one who did the killing."

"I know that already," Lisa scoffed. "What I want to hear is who is doing this to you. And why."

"Can we talk about the key again?" Dora said from a chair closest to the outside door.

Jenny rolled her eyes.

"Taped to Fida's collar. What we have to look at is where Fida has been." Dora said as Zoe lifted the fluffy dog to look deeply into her one bright eye.

"She won't say." Zoe set Fida back in her lap with a tremendous sigh.

"We could beat it out of her," Jenny suggested.

"She was missing those two days," Dora said, ignoring Jenny. "I wonder who took her."

"Probably the person who killed Adam," Lisa said.

"But why? And why take her out to Aaron's house?" Dora was into the puzzle with all her might.

"And why tape a key to her collar?" Zoe put in. "Maybe it was Aaron?"

"Or Adam," Lisa offered.

Zoe stuck a finger into the air. "As I remember, I stepped on a roll of duct tape on Aaron's floor when we found his body. You remember, don't you, Jenny?"

Jenny shook her head. "With a body and all that dog crap on the floor, I wasn't watching out for duct tape."

Dora rocked back and forth, ignoring all of them. "As I see it, somebody knew you'd find Fida at Aaron's house and wanted you to have the key. Everybody knows you'd keep searching for Fida until you found her. Whoever murdered the men knew Aaron couldn't show up for his brother's funeral because he was dead, which would, of course, send people looking for him. You'd get Fida back. And with her, you'd find the key."

Zoe sat up. "Who else could it have been? Maybe there was time between when Fida was dropped off and when the murderer came back to kill Aaron. He must've sensed something. Had to find a place for this." She held up the key in a Sherlockian moment.

"All we need to do is discover what this key opens," Dora said as if she'd solved the crime.

"I vote we concentrate and figure out who committed these terrible murders," Zoe went on.

"Why are we voting?" Dora asked, distress in her voice.

"Who called a vote?" Jenny demanded.

"I'm going to bed," Lisa said and got up, leaving the last three gathered to think deeply until nothing came to anyone and they followed Lisa's example, all going off to bed.

Chapter 27

It was the time of day on a June afternoon when Bear Falls went quiet. The faux Swiss chalet stores and old-fashioned plain shops along Oak Street were empty. There were few cars parked along Oak Street. Sprinklers in front yards turned lazily or flipped themselves over and dug deep water holes in the grass. Children's voices were subdued, the games quieter. Cane Park, curving around the waterfall, was empty.

Jenny and Lisa decided to come to the waterfall because there'd been so little time to be alone.

They leaned against the railing, watching and listening as the towering water cascaded over bare rocks—loud when it fell, then loud again when it hit the river, spewing upward in clouds of vapor, and louder still when it thundered on into Bear Falls lake.

Lisa turned her head and smiled. "I wanted this so bad," she said, her hands gripping the wooden railing. "I needed to come home." She leaned back to take in the very top of the falls. "Wish I didn't have to go back, but I'm getting distress calls from the crew."

"I'll miss you," Jenny said. "I don't know how we're going to handle all of this without you."

Lisa shrugged and gave Jenny a smile. "I'm nothing but moral support."

"Where will I get *that* from?" Jenny sounded like a miserable kid, even to her own ears.

"That Tony's a pretty good guy. Got broad shoulders. Worth a second look."

"Thanks." Jenny made a sour face. "Maybe I should get over the last one first."

Lisa turned back to the falls. "Isn't it something?" She stared at the water.

Jenny knew with certainty, and for almost the first time, what was in her sister's head. She was talking about them: how they were friends again. Jenny laid her hand on top of Lisa's and watched the water falling, barreling over itself to hit the bottom and splash up high, again and again.

They didn't say much, just stood together.

"Is that your phone ringing?" Lisa tipped her head at the noise.

It was. Jenny fumbled in her shoulder bag.

"Mom?"

"Is Lisa with you? Where are you?"

"At the waterfall."

"Well, that's nice." She hesitated. "But could I ask you to come back to the house?"

"We've got an hour before we have to leave for the airport."

"I called Tony. He'll take Lisa. I really need you here, at home. Minnie Moon was here. She needs to talk to you."

"Who?"

"Minnie. She'll be back in an hour. Please? This all seems so very . . . strange."

She couldn't refuse her mother. She sounded nervous and not able to handle a *no* right then.

When Jenny told Lisa, she agreed to leave, but not happily.

A few minutes after getting home, Lisa was hugging everyone, then she and Tony were off to the airport.

The sadness hit Dora and Jenny immediately. And the bottomless quiet that comes when someone you love has gone.

They finished a supper of scrambled eggs and toast before Jenny asked unhappily, "Where's Minnie, Mom?"

Dora shrugged. "She'll be here. Said she would be."

"That was hours ago."

Dora shook her head quickly but didn't say any more.

Dora rolled piecrust for a rhubarb pie and Jenny read *Alice in Wonderland,* memorizing new quotes, though the old quotes ran out of her head even as she read. Dora talked on and on about all the books being donated and how a party was in order when the libraries were up and running.

"We'll have an amazing cake," Dora said happily. "And refreshments." Dora turned her piecrust into the waiting tin.

"How about a raffle? Give away some of the books?" Jenny suggested.

"Oh, I don't think so. I might need them all."

Jenny was about to say that with the dozens of books they were getting, she wouldn't need new books for years, but she didn't.

As Dora set her filled pie in the oven, Zoe and Fida came through the door, Minnie Moon behind them.

"Glad you came back, Minnie!" Dora waved her to a seat at the table. "Come on in. Come on in. Jenny and our neighbor are here now. You know Zoe, don't you?"

Minnie Moon fell into a chair, trying to catch her breath. It was a long walk from her house. She nodded to Dora and Jenny, then colored up and bit at her bottom lip.

"Don't think we've been introduced, Ms. Zola. Seen you around, mostly at funerals. Nice to know you."

Minnie Moon, in red slacks, a red T-shirt, and all that messy red hair, looked somewhat like a pregnant volcano. She huffed, then puffed, then pounded at her chest as if to dislodge a plug.

"I remember you especially." She grinned at Jenny when she could talk. "Used to get in trouble, is what I recall. Wasn't it you and that Arlen boy threw a park bench down over the waterfall that one time?"

Jenny gave the woman a weak grin and started to shake her head but gave it up.

"And your Halloween trick? That dog stuff you kids put in a bag and lit on fire, left it on my porch so I'd get it all over my foot when I went to step on it? Bare foot, too, I remember."

Jenny smiled again, though she thought she smelled retribution, not nostalgia here.

Dora brought Minnie a glass of iced tea, which she took with gratitude.

With the tall glass in her hand and her breath coming back to her, Minnie said, "Anyway, heard you talking about a party, Dora. That's what brought me here to see you. Well, not the party. Though that sounds like a nice thing to do. I'm talking about what happened to the library in the first place."

"What's on your mind, Minnie?" Dora asked.

"I would've gone to Ed Warner, but people are starting to say he's trying to push everything that's happened off on to you, Ms. Zola. People starting to think he's being lazy. Not really looking into things." She gave Zoe a slightly pained smile. "Maybe I should have come right out with it when I came before. I guess it mostly has to do with you, Dora." She smiled almost sweetly. "What I didn't want to do was get in the middle of anything and make it worse. So I've been thinking. Sometimes I tell myself to stay out of stuff. None of my business. Then I tell myself it's my civil duty to let you know what went on the night the Little Library was busted up."

"You saw something?" *At last*, Jenny thought. *Something beyond a list of my sins was coming out.*

Minnie nodded.

"What'd you see?"

"I'll tell you exactly as it happened."

They waited.

Minnie gave a weak cough and settled slowly into being the center of attention. "Would you have another glass of tea, Dora? Little more sugar this time, if you don't mind."

Minnie gave Jenny a long look. "You really were an awful little girl, Jenny. So much trouble. But look how you turned out." She shook her head. "Gives me hope for my Deanna. She's into everything. Can't keep her hands off anything. Especially not off a man."

"How old is Deanna, Minnie?" Zoe asked after catching a look at Jenny's reddening face.

"Oh, she's nineteen now. But she's one of those girls who just don't want to go to college or anything. You know, not too quick to get a job, either. And going with boys I don't much like."

"What's the point here, Mrs. Moon?" Jenny leaned back, feeling tired and too stressed to sit there listening to Minnie's list of grievances with her daughter.

A massive tear rolled down Minnie's wide cheek. "I've got to say something I don't want to say."

"You're not going to hurt my feelings," Jenny said. "I mean, no more than you have already."

"Don't be hurt by anything I say, Jenny." She moved uncomfortably around in her chair. "The reason I mentioned Deanna . . . well . . . much as I hate to say it, Deanna's been seeing Johnny Arlen."

"Seeing him?" This wasn't at all what Jenny expected. "Johnny's married. With a couple of kids. One more about to be here any day."

Minnie nodded. "I told her what's going to happen to her. And that poor Angel pregnant and probably fretting because of my daughter. Can't tell you how bad I feel."

"Pretty lousy, I imagine. Have you talked to Deanna?"

"A hundred times." Lines of tears ran down her face. "Oh, if you only knew. I mean, what happens if Deanna gets pregnant? What will any of us do?"

"Is that what you came to tell me?" Jenny asked while the others stayed silent.

She shook her head fast. "No, there's more. Maybe you'll see why I wasn't in any rush to tell somebody what I saw. The night the Little Library got all busted up, my Deanna was out with Johnny. Night after night, I'd be out looking for her and chasing him away, then taking her back home."

"What are you saying?" Dora asked.

"I was coming down Elderberry. It was about five in the morning, I'd say. I was damned and determined I'd find them and put an end to her seeing him once and for all. That's when I saw Johnny's blue pickup parked across the street from your house, Dora. That's when I saw these two people just whaling away at the library. I couldn't believe it. Johnny Arlen and my daughter. Both of them. You couldn't really hear anything. I mean, because of the hard rain and the trees shaking and the wind. It was like one of those pantomime things. I stopped my car and crossed the street, and they didn't even see me. Laughing and whispering and chopping up that dear little house and throwing the books around. Can you imagine the two of them doing such a thing? It looked like something straight outta hell."

She settled her shoulders back.

"They were drunk," she went on. "I told them I was going to call the police on 'em, and that kind of woke them up. I got Deanna into my car, though she was crying and reaching out to Johnny—a big drama queen, you could say."

She heaved a lung-emptying sigh. "So there, now I've told you. Guess you could sue us. Can't blame you. Or maybe you can talk to Johnny Arlen. Tell him to leave Deanna alone from now on. Maybe get him to go talk to Ed Warner, confess it was his idea. My daughter would never have come up with such a thing by herself. I know that for certain."

Jenny shook her head. Her voice was firm. "I won't be talking to Johnny."

"You got any other idea? I didn't come here to throw my daughter to the dogs, you know." Minnie straightened her back and looked down her nose at Jenny.

"My mom's having it rebuilt. Paying for it herself. I think somebody owes her that money."

"As I said, better talk to Johnny. Deanna was only there because of him."

"Did Deanna tell you why he wanted to do it?" Zoe asked.

"Only thing she will say is Johnny was just mad. Somebody was coming back to Bear Falls. Probably you, don't you think, Jenny?"

"Are you sure it was Johnny?" Dora asked.

Minnie nodded.

"I'll bet that's not exactly how the story went," Zoe said.

Minnie rubbed hard at the red polyester stretched tight over her legs and shook her head. "That's what Deanna said. She's the one heard you were coming home, Jenny. So I thought back to the time you and Johnny were supposed to get married and figured there was still bad blood between you. That's all I know. If it's money for the library you want, you go see Johnny. The only reason I told you in the first place was to get the truth out and let the chips fall wherever they're going to fall. I've got my hands full with Deanna as it is. Girl's going to get in a lot of trouble."

She turned to Jenny. "I was even thinking maybe you could talk to her about Johnny. I mean, if it's all true, what he did to you, you could lay it out for her and open her eyes."

Minnie got up slowly from the chair, looked at nobody, then walked straight out of the room.

Dora and Zoe were dead quiet. Jenny couldn't feel herself breathe. She didn't know if she could move.

Johnny, that bastard. All over again.

"We should call Ed Warner," Dora finally said.

Jenny nodded.

"Bet that shoe print on *Tom Sawyer* will match Johnny's shoes," Zoe said.

Jenny shook her head. Her stomach hurt—a sucker punch to the gut. She couldn't stand the sound of even one more voice, not in the place she was now, somewhere between throwing up and screaming. She had to get out of there. Nobody spoke, but even silence felt crushing and expectant. Any minute, someone could say another word and the room would explode.

She stood.

"Don't go, Jenny," Zoe called softly.

"It'll be all right, dear." Dora put her hand out.

She went back to her room and fell into her small bed, praying for sleep.

That day had been a hard one.

Chapter 28

Jenny wished it was darker. She wished she was in a place so dark she couldn't find herself. So completely invisible she'd never be found again by anyone.

She lay in her undersized bed and tried to sleep, tried to hide from thoughts that might dissolve her right back into her old, unlovable self.

When she was engaged to Johnny, she'd been a much better human being, a nicer, kinder human being. She'd been a girl who trusted everyone to be true to their word and the world to be more like an ideal Hollywood movie, where the happy story ended with a kiss, a white wedding, children, good careers, a house in the suburbs, and anniversaries celebrated. There would always be an enduring love and a long, happy life. That wasn't who she was after Johnny. Scarred now, as if he'd taken a knife to her instead of words.

Feeling sorry for herself didn't seem warm and fuzzy all of a sudden. She should call Ed Warner—immediately. But if she was the one to call, there would be whispers again among Bear Falls people: "Poor Jenny Weston. She's getting even, you know."

What was wrong with Johnny? He got exactly what he wanted. He had Angel and a few kids, another on the way . . .

so what was he doing with Deanna Moon? And why had he destroyed the library?

She lay still listening to the soft wash of wind in the pines. Again and again, she flipped from one side of the bed to the other and then finally got up to sit at the window and look at the stars and that sliver of moon. She thought about the two men she'd let into her life. Neither of them wanted her.

Johnny didn't. He'd heard she was coming home and was determined to make her miserable.

The pines waved in eerie shadows, geometric triangles, ragged squares.

She hugged herself though the breeze coming through the window was warm.

Before she knew what she was doing, Jenny snapped on the light and got back into the clothes she'd shed and laid over a chair earlier—clothes she'd been wearing all day. It didn't matter. Who cared what she wore? Not to the place where she was going.

She brushed her hair then stuck it back into a ponytail, wrapping a red rubber band around it.

She bent to look in the dresser mirror and thought she needed at least a little makeup, then asked herself if it was for her or someone else.

When she decided it was for her, she patted on blush and a good, hard swipe of lipstick.

When she looked as good as she wanted to look, she grabbed her shoulder bag and left the room, closing the door behind her, making her way down the hall and out the back door on tiptoe.

* * *

It was dead dark and scary. Deer moved in the darkness—or were they raccoons? Could be a bobcat—no, a bear. She drove only as fast as she felt was safe, never overdriving her headlights. There was no plan, only driving up and down the main streets of town, beginning with Johnny Arlen's house. The lights were on in almost every room, but only one car was parked in the driveway. That car wasn't Johnny's blue pickup.

She drove past Bear Falls' two saloons, then went back down Elderberry to where Deanna Moon lived. No blue pickup.

No Johnny anywhere in town. Useless quest, but she couldn't leave it alone now that she'd set her mind on talking to him. She drove out of town toward the turn on to US 31, the place where her dad had been killed. But she couldn't think about that right then. No thinking about loss.

She drove the twenty-five miles to Traverse City, and then over to Cass Street, to Junior's Bar. She turned into the parking lot behind the bar and checked the cars parked there. No blue pickup—not one among the many in the lot.

She sat a while, wondering what she'd missed, where she hadn't checked. A car honked behind her, forcing her to move. No sense going home. She parked, got out, and went into Junior's, being stopped on the way in by a drunk who wanted to buy her a beer, which she politely declined.

A few couples sat along the bar, heads together. A trip to the ladies room told her Johnny wasn't in the poolroom.

It was after midnight. The place was emptying out. A workday for most.

She had a beer at the bar and nursed it so she wouldn't have to order another. The bartender, maybe feeling sorry for her—a lone woman—tried to strike up a conversation, but she only stared and didn't answer.

Twelve thirty. People were no longer coming in. She told herself to give it up, that she hadn't thought anything out well enough, that she didn't know what she'd say to him if he did show up, that she was beginning to be embarrassed sitting on a barstool and giving her phony expectant look every time the door opened, glancing at her watch as if waiting for someone. All of it was wearing thin.

She paid and left the bar, walking out to the dark parking lot and looking for her car, since she hadn't been thinking straight when she'd walked in.

A man stepped out of the dark, from beside a dumpster near the alley.

"That you, Jenny?" The voice was familiar.

Johnny stepped in front of her, putting his hands up to stop her.

All she wanted, now that he stood in front of her, was to get away. Why did she feel she had to talk to him about any of what happened? He was drunk when he destroyed the Little Library. It had nothing to do with her.

"I'm glad to see you." Johnny's voice was soft. He swayed slightly, a shadowy smile on his face. His hands reached out to take her by the shoulders. "I hope you're looking for me."

She felt his hands on her and remembered how strong Johnny was. She tried to pull away. He wouldn't let her. She gave in, stood still, looking up at him—small knives of moonlight in his eyes, shadows over his face. She felt sadder than she'd ever imagined she could feel in Johnny's hands.

His dirty brown hair hung to his shoulders. She wanted to reach up and push it back, away from his face. Crazy thoughts and feelings ran through her head. She ached to lean in and hold him gently. She'd loved him. He'd loved her. There were remnants there—of wanting to take care of him, of thinking she could save him. He was still the man she'd loved completely.

"You were lookin' for me, weren't you?" he asked, trying hard to stand straight and smile at her directly with both eyes open.

Jenny said nothing. She couldn't have spoken if she tried.

He pulled her closer. She put her hands against his chest.

"I knew you would come around," he said.

Love didn't come with a conscience. Parts of her body responded in ways she didn't know she could feel again.

It took her a few minutes to get enough breath to speak.

With her hands against his chest, she said, "I'm here about what you did."

He stumbled back. "What did I do now? All of you blame me for everything anyway. Could stop all this and we could still be—"

"You destroyed Mom's library. To get even with me for . . . what?"

He fell back another step, righted himself, and peered hard at her. "Who told you I did that? Liars. People make trouble for me, ya know. Ever since we had our, you know, with Angel and all. Just make trouble for . . ."

"Deanna's mother stopped you."

He looked at the ground and finally shrugged.

"What gives you the right to hurt my mother the way you did?" she demanded.

Johnny blinked a few times. "You don't know anything, do you? You don't know what I've been livin' through."

"You're the cause. Always were. You wanted Angel."

"No, no, no, no . . ." He shook his head. "Before that. When . . . you know . . . when your father got killed."

His face was wet. He reached toward her with a pathetic hand.

"Jenny . . ." He moaned her name.

Jenny took one last look and ran toward her car. She got in, locked the doors, started the engine, and backed out, moving around Johnny, who stood under a streetlight with his head down. A sad and ridiculous, staggering figure.

Poor Angel, Jenny thought. *She thought she'd won the prize.*

Chapter 29

When the sun came up, Jenny stood beside the place where Lake Huron and Lake Michigan met. She stood on the shore in Mackinaw City, small waves covering her bare feet. Overhead, the span of the Mackinaw Bridge stretched north into a thick morning haze. She could breathe here, as if she'd found the one spot on earth where nothing could touch her.

For hours—straight through the night—she'd driven, trying to keep her thoughts from falling into piles of squirming worms. There should be a neat stack of thoughts about Johnny in her head. Another stack about Ronald. A neat stack about her future. A neat stack about the murders of the Cane men. One stack for Zoe Zola. Maybe a small stack for Mom's Little Library. Oh, then "poor" Deanna. And a stack for "poor" Angel. A stack for "poor" Jenny Weston. All of it orderly, delivered on demand or wiped away.

The sun burned through the mist and lit the eastern side of the impressive bridge, turning the towers a deep gold, the cables between towers a sharp green, and the Straits of Mackinac a metallic gray. So much power—natural and man-made. So much beauty and majesty.

She always ran to water when the world was too much with her, always to a place where she could stare out and see nothing but the curve of the earth or the passing away of a spring torrent. She had been near the water when she'd arranged her teenage thoughts into a hierarchy of importance: White dress for marrying Johnny or off-white, now that she was an off-virgin? Major in education? It had to be more practical, since she and Johnny would be married right after they got their degrees. They'd probably settle in Bear Falls, though Johnny was taking business and they might end up living anywhere. She'd dreamed then that their future was limitless.

She dragged her toe through the water, down into the sand. What a waste of her life. From here on, she was going to think about crucial things, not dreams or old hurts. Not the people who hurt her but the people who loved her. She looked over the water and thought about Tony Ralenti. Another daydream. He wasn't exactly chasing her.

The light on the bridge changed. The magic was gone. She walked across the park, her mind already turning to practical things.

First she had to go see Chief Warner. She would turn Johnny in.

But then Deanna would be in deep trouble, too.

Served her right. She was old enough to know better than to run around with a married man.

There was also Angel, about to go into labor, and Johnny's two other girls to consider.

And how was all this going to help Zoe? There had to be a clear thread that led straight to a killer. There had to be a clear reason he or she was killing. The only person connected to Adam and Aaron was Abigail, and she couldn't see Abigail—the dowager queen of Bear Falls—murdering anyone.

"Off with their heads" jumped into Jenny's mind as she started her car. *"Off with their heads!"*

Chapter 30

Zoe, sitting on the lawn with a paintbrush in her hand, waved when Jenny turned up the drive and pulled to a stop next to her.

Tony, attaching a platform to one of the support posts, looked up and smiled.

On the shorter post, Zoe was painting figures with wings in wild, bright colors. Fairies. Jenny had to smile, then thought, *What kind of world am I caught up in? Fairies and little people and one-eyed dogs with secret keys . . .*

"How do you like these?" Zoe motioned, paintbrush in hand.

"It's all coming together." Tony walked over to stand near her car, stretching his back muscles hard. His hair was mussed. His work clothes were covered with sawdust. His smile was as it always was—reassuring. Maybe she had a new "idea stack" to consider. A stack labeled "Tony Ralenti." She smiled at him. Just an idea. After all, she told herself, all she had left was possibility.

"I see you two are hard at work."

Tony nodded. "Be ready in a couple of days. I've got finishing touches yet: shingles and the screened porch. Last thing will be a coat of paint. If you've got something special in mind—"

Before she could reply, Zoe spoke up. "You stop to see Ed Warner?"

Tony raised his head fast.

Zoe's mouth fell open and stayed there. "Oh . . . did I put my foot in it?"

"Something happen I don't know about?" Tony narrowed his eyes and looked from one to the other.

"Nothing . . . I was just . . ."

Jenny wouldn't let Zoe flounder. It shouldn't be a secret anyway, not from Tony.

"Minnie Moon, our neighbor, came by yesterday," she said. "She told us she saw her own daughter, Deanna, and Johnny Arlen destroying the library. Minnie didn't want her daughter brought into it, so I'm not sure what . . ." She hesitated.

Tony gave her an odd look. He shook his head. "Of course you'll tell Ed. I'd say let your mom and Johnny settle it between them, except we've got a couple of murders worked in here. Not saying Johnny had anything to do with them, but . . ." He frowned. "What was he doing out with Ms. Moon's daughter anyway? Isn't Angel about to have a baby?"

Jenny nodded. "If it weren't for the two deaths, this would just be a cheap, sleazy thing."

"Yeah. Grown man. Responsible for his actions. But is he a murderer?"

She shook her head.

"Guess you better go see the chief as soon as you can. If he hears you know about this . . ." He looked over at Zoe. "Time we worked up a couple suspects besides you, right?"

He was teasing, but Zoe didn't laugh the way she usually did.

"Want me to go with you?" he asked Jenny.

She nodded. She'd had enough of being alone.

* * *

"I hope this doesn't turn into a huge event," Jenny said to Ed Warner, who sat behind his desk with one hand on a stack of papers. Since Jenny didn't much trust Ed, her voice took on a tone she didn't use with ordinary people.

"Angel Arlen's about to have a baby," she said. "Maybe you should keep that in mind when you spread the word about Johnny."

"Have to do my job, Jenny. I understand you think I'm wrong about everything, but I can't worry about that. I've got two murders in a town where we've never had a murder. I've got your mother's property being destroyed. I've got people coming in every day like they're sneaking into the White House—a rumor here, a suspicion there."

Tony, beside her in the chief's office, cleared his throat. She put up a hand. There were things she still had to say.

"Maybe you'll leave Zoe Zola alone now. Crazy idea anyway. She barely knew Adam and didn't know Aaron at all. Just from the size of her—who would believe?"

"I said it before. You don't have to be tall or a man to kill somebody." His face wrinkled as he spoke. "She's only been here a year or so. Who knows what the real reason was she moved to Bear Falls? You see many new people moving in?"

"She writes books. What better place for quiet than Bear Falls?"

"Writers use computer paper. What we found in Ms. Zola's house looked just like the paper that note to Adam was written on."

"Computer paper's almost all alike," Jenny said.

"Cane family could be the reason she moved here to begin with. We don't know her people nor her background. Could be she smelled money. Heard her brag she's got quite a sense of smell on her. Maybe she's writing a book about the Cane family. Who's to say?" Ed shrugged. "I know you don't think much of me, Jenny. Living in Chicago so long, you're probably used to squads of police and forensics and a lot of things we don't have here. But I've still got a brain. I've still got eyes and ears and can figure out most things, given enough time."

His craggy face softened as he went on. "So you're handing me Johnny Arlen."

"I'm not handing you anybody. I'm just telling you what Minnie Moon said."

"Then I want to go talk to Ms. Moon and her daughter." He shuffled his feet and leaned back in his chair. "Have to tell you, though, the *Record-Eagle* in Traverse City has been sniffing around. They ran a week of stories on the murders and are hot to do follow-ups. Can't control the press, you know. If they get ahold of this, Johnny's name will be all over the front page. Nothing I can do about it."

"This isn't about the murders," she said. "It's about a man with a huge problem who needs help. And it's about his kids and wife and not destroying their lives. There's nothing in this for the newspaper."

She looked to Tony for help. He stared at the floor.

"You think maybe Johnny was over there again the next night when that dog went missing? And over there, too, about the time Adam Cane was being hit in the head with a hoe in Zoe's backyard? Or out at Aaron's when somebody put a bullet in him?"

"That's not Johnny—"

"Was breaking up the library the man you knew?"

She had nothing more to say.

"I'll tell you this, Jenny. I'm going out to talk to Ms. Moon, and I'm having Johnny brought in for questioning. I'll call your mother and see what she wants to do about him. Press charges, I hope. Or make him pay to replace the library. I think I'll kind of follow her lead on that, but on everything else—questions about the murders—well, that's got to be up to me. I won't spare anybody. Not your friend and not Johnny Arlen. That's the best I can do for you."

"Johnny would never kill anybody."

She looked around at Tony, who only shook his head.

"Call Mom," she said finally. "She's got better sense than I have."

Jenny got up and left with Tony right behind her.

There was no avoiding the heavy silence on the way home. It wasn't until he parked in front of her house that Tony opened up.

"That's how I knew about you and Johnny Arlen." He turned in his seat, putting a hand on her arm to stop her from getting out. "Town like this, everybody knows everything about everybody. But it looks like you've got to get your priorities straight, Jenny. Either you're fighting to clear Zoe—who we both know didn't do any of this—or you're willing to throw her overboard to protect an old boyfriend who jilted you. I think you'd better decide who it's going to be. Or drive yourself crazy."

"Neither one of them. There's no side to choose. I do have my priorities straight, Tony. And by the way, they are *my* priorities and *my* life."

She shook his hand off her arm. She jumped out of the truck.

Chapter 31

Dora's first words were a pained cry. "Where have you been? Minnie was here this morning begging me not to go to the police. She doesn't want Deanna to get a bad reputation. I had no idea where you'd gotten to and couldn't promise her anything." She stopped. "You've been out all night! You worried me to death."

She moved on without waiting for Jenny to answer. "Now Minnie's mad at me and says she will never take one single book out of my library ever again in her whole life if we ruin her daughter."

Jenny put her arms around her quaking mother. "Mom, I talked to Ed. He says what's done to Johnny and Deanna will be up to you. You don't have to press charges if you don't want to. Maybe just get Johnny or Deanna to repay what it's costing you."

"Johnny Arlen doesn't have a pot to . . . well, you know he's got nothing. Barely works. Drinks. I can't tell you, Jenny, how happy I am you never married that boy." She sighed, looking hard into her daughter's face. "I'm not pressing charges and I won't make them pay. The books cost me nothing. People have been dropping off more than I can use in a month of Sundays.

Anyway, Tony gave me a very fair deal on the new houses. Neighbors are already offering to man the libraries on given days to take the pressure off me—though I don't mind it at all. Still, it will be nice to see my neighbors more often and share the books with them. Especially with children. A few little ones have come to the door asking if their library's open yet."

"So you won't press charges?"

Dora shook her head. "There's just one thing I'd like. I'd like to talk to them. I want them to know what your dad's library means to me and to the town. I'd like them to know about books—for real. That they're not just paper and cardboard. It's about learning what people think and do outside of Bear Falls. It's like . . ." Dora spread her arms wide. "Your father offered me a whole new world with his gift. And a whole new—bigger—world to the town. I'd like to say that to them."

"Oh. Something else. What was it now?" She shook her head. "Anyway, Lisa called. She's so nervous. Can't stop thinking about us. She says I could be in danger, living here where two people got killed. I tried to tell her I'm just fine, and I've got you. Maybe you should call her."

"Was that what you forgot?"

She shook her head and put her hands to her cheeks. "No. It was Abigail Cane. She called, wanted to talk to you. I told her you were out and I didn't know when you were getting home. I asked if she wanted you to call back but she said no. She'll get ahold of you as soon as she can."

"What's that supposed to mean? 'As soon as she can'?"

Dora shrugged. "You know Abigail. Everything in her life's always been the most important thing that ever happened to anybody. Personally, I think money does that to people, makes them important in their own head."

"I'll call Lisa." She headed to the kitchen to get hot tea and lemon slices to go with it. She felt in need of a little pampering. "You see that house Zoe's painting?"

"Darling. Just darling. And she just got a new house for her garden. Funniest fairy you ever saw is going to live there. Little being's got a wig on her head, with a tiny daisy sticking straight up."

Jenny, halfway to the kitchen, turned to say, "Think I should get into fairy houses?"

"That would be nice, dear," Dora called after her.

"Kidding, Mom. Just kidding."

* * *

By late afternoon, Abigail Cane still hadn't called. Jenny phoned Lisa to tell her everything that had been going on and was given a stern warning to call every day.

"If you don't, I'm going to go crazy worrying. I can't tell you how many times I've wanted to drop everything and get on a plane."

The conversation ended with Jenny promising a phone call every day.

"Love you, Jenny." There was a break in Lisa's voice. "Don't want to lose you."

"Me, either. I don't want to lose me."

"Brat," Lisa said and hung up.

Jenny heard nothing from Abigail in the next hour. She gave up waiting and went next door to see Zoe, missing her daily dose of mayhem and madness.

A voice yelled, "Come on in!" after after Jenny toured the fairy gardens to visit the new fairy with a daisy growing out of her head and then said hi to each of the other peeking faces, all having moved since her last trip around. An unsettling idea—that the fairies watched her from different houses and different windows. Even worse, that they'd seen a man murdered. But even worse than all of it, Jenny told herself, was the fact that Zoe'd gotten her to believe in fairies.

Zoe was on the phone when Jenny walked in. She was giving all short answers. Nods and smiles and big, wide-opened eyes. "Of course I want to go. Oh, that. Don't worry. I'm certain I'll have no trouble. Why, after all, what human being would want to stand in my way. You'll come here? Why, Christopher, you don't need to . . . of course, I understand. Yes, I'll be on time. Waiting. Time is of the essence. You'll have it planned to the minute, I'm sure."

She hung up and turned to Jenny. "Three weeks!" she crowed. "Three weeks! The White Rabbit's coming for me. Heavens to teacups! What a surprise! An award!" Zoe clapped her little hands. "A big, New York award. That was Christopher Morley. He said he's very proud of me and my work."

"An award? For what?" Jenny asked before thinking.

Zoe put her hands at her waist and an exasperated look on her face. "For my book, of course. What did you think it was— best fairy garden in the world?"

"Could be," Jenny said.

"Well, it isn't. It's the National Award for Literary Research. Me! Can you imagine? Me and my Oz book, *The Wizard of Oz as Dream*. Christopher said this will make the book a classic." Her face slowly darkened. "Oh goodness, what does one wear to such an affair? I won't know a soul."

"You'll know Mr. Morley."

"But will I enjoy myself?" Her happiness slipped down a long slope. "You met Christopher. No frivolity. Time. Time. Time. A very busy man. No, no, no. I'll go with him and act happy."

"But you can't leave town!" Jenny felt like Mary Poppins at the up-in-the-air tea party, all brought down by a sad thought. "Ed Warner warned you."

"Three weeks, Jenny! We have three weeks to put all of this to rest. I think I'm onto something new right now. Something I've been trying to figure out about those letters."

"Ah, Sherlock. I should never have doubted."

"Don't make fun. If I'm not out of trouble by three weeks from now, I'll be hanging in the town square. A warning to future writers."

"Zoe," Jenny chided, "I've had enough drama for one day. I think I've got Tony mad at me." She told Zoe about her reluctance to believe Johnny murdered anybody and how Tony took it.

"He should be angry," Zoe said. "He's a good man, Jenny. You don't seem able to pick a good one from a bad one."

"Pick! Pick!" Jenny mimicked her. "Is that like picking apples? So far two have had worms."

"Silly analogy."

"You said to look behind words. Pick. Pick. Pick. Pick my nose. Pick my seat. Pick!" She stuck her tongue out at Zoe, which made both of them laugh.

Chapter 32

Abigail called at eight thirty that evening.

"Jenny Weston?" The voice was cool. She didn't give her name, as if expecting Jenny would, of course, know who was calling.

"I don't mean to be cryptic, Jenny," she went on. "I told your mother I would call you back when I could. What I meant by that was, when I was alone. I do seem to have people around me at all times. They mean well. Alfred and Carmen take such good care of me, but there are moments . . . well . . . when I do have private business to attend to. Not that I'm complaining. Please don't think I don't value the friendships that I have. Especially after, well, my brothers let me down so badly, turning on the family the way they did."

"Did you want to come here and talk?" Jenny finally broke in, afraid the woman would wander forever and never get to the point. There was something almost charming about Abigail's meanderings—an open, talking-to-remind-herself feeling to it.

"Yes. That's why I called. I'm very sorry your little friend's been dragged into all of this. I truly doubt she has anything to do with my brothers' deaths. The story goes back such a long way. But I'm puzzled, truly puzzled, how it came to this. I've been racking my brains. Over and over again I've been asking myself, is there something different I could have done? They were always such independent thinkers, you know. I've done my best, but that's neither here nor there. What I was contemplating was, my dear girl . . . I hope you appreciate how difficult this is for me . . ."

"What's difficult, Ms. Cane?"

"Why, everything I've been telling you. Haven't you been listening?"

"Yes, but . . ."

"Then you should understand why I'm being so cloak-and-dagger. I must protect my family's reputation. Murder's never been a part of our lineage. I hope you understand and respect that fact, even as we speak of murder."

"I'm sorry, Ms. Cane. I—"

"I will be over to see you tomorrow evening. Precisely eight o'clock. That is unless my companions have other plans for me. They do carry on about my health and welfare—especially at times like this, when I'm under such stress. But then, I can come up with reasons to go off on my own for an hour or two. I'm not a prisoner, you understand. Nothing of the sort. Just . . . when people care for you as deeply as my secretary and attorney care for me, well, you understand. I don't like to disappoint them. But this is different. So much history. And you do understand, I hope, not a word of anything I divulge to you can be passed to another living soul. I've chosen you because you've somehow insinuated yourself into the middle of Cane business."

"I did nothing of the sort," Jenny protested.

"No blame on your side. How could I blame you for having this whole ugly business thrust on you? Why—"

Enough was enough. "I'll see you at eight o'clock tomorrow evening. You know where we—?"

"Don't be silly. I know everyone in town. Eight o'clock." Abigail hung up.

When Jenny told Dora that Abigail was coming the following evening, Dora was thrust into a frenzy of vacuuming, baking, and dusting.

"What time did you say she was coming? Eight o'clock? That doesn't give me near enough time. I should make new cushions for the rockers. What kind of tea does she drink, do you think?"

"Mom, enough. She'll never notice."

"But this is the first time she's come here." Dora wrung her hands. "Abigail Cane! Why, that's like the Queen of England visiting. Everything must be right."

She headed toward the kitchen. "Queen Abigail of Bear Falls—for heaven's sake. Imagine that. Coming here. How Jim would laugh at me."

She muttered all the way out to scour her teapot.

Chapter 33

When she awoke to screaming, Jenny thought it was a part of her dream: she'd been swimming beside a boat headed for Guatemala. The water was so cold it could have been the Arctic Ocean. Her legs hurt from kicking. Her arms were about to give up and let her sink. She thought the screams were her own.

"Help!" The word came again in a high, squeaky voice. Then unintelligible words. Then barking.

Zoe!

She hopped out of bed and, in only her very short pajamas, ran out into the hall and into Dora, fumbling an arm into a proper housecoat.

"It's Zoe," Jenny yelled at her. "Call the police. I'm going over there."

"Oh, don't, Jenny. Wait . . ."

She was outside and through the trees. She ran into Zoe, whose arms were waving wildly.

Fida leaped and barked around her.

Jenny grabbed an arm. "What happened? What's going on? Zoe? Zoe! Mom's calling the police."

"Someone's in my house. I heard him. I got up and saw him in my living room. He was tearing things apart. You should just see. I yelled, and he ran out the back door. I thought he came this way . . . did you see anybody?"

Jenny shook her head. "No one," she said. "There's no one. Let's go to my house until the police get here."

Zoe didn't like the idea at all, trying to pull away to go chasing nothing in the dark, but she gave in and went back to Jenny's.

* * *

Ed Warner stood in the archway of Zoe's living room surveying the damage. Pillows and books were thrown everywhere. Drawers were pulled from tables and dumped on the floor.

In the kitchen, every cupboard had been ransacked. Even the refrigerator door stood open, with dishes moved aside, packages of meat from the freezer taken out and left on the counter. A deputy took photographs. Another deputy dusted for fingerprints, sneezing with every sweep of his brush.

"So you didn't see who did this, even though you were in the house with your dog—which barks at everything, far as I've heard—sleeping beside you in the bed?" Ed made notes. "Can't find any forced entry. Nobody saw who did it."

The chief shook his head.

"I told you, I didn't hear anything. When I did, I yelled, and he scrambled across my living room and out the kitchen door. I didn't really see him. But at least I heard him."

"What was the guy after, you think?" Ed was skeptical.

Zoe shrugged. "I know Tony and Jenny brought you those letters we found at Aaron's. I can't imagine what else someone would be hunting for. I just don't know what it means."

Ed shook his head. "Doesn't mean anything, far as I can tell. And those letters—looks like they were threatening both men over something. Can't tell what. And a letter from Aaron Cane's attorney. Your fingerprints all over them. And Tony Ralenti's and Jenny's. Sure wish you hadn't messed 'em up like that. Another strike against you, Ms. Zola, if you ask me."

He eyed her closely. "You take a copy or something—I mean of those letters? You've got no business interfering the way you have been."

Zoe looked from Ed to Jenny and back.

"I copied them, Chief," Jenny spoke up.

"Sticking your nose in everywhere—both of you." Ed showed as much emotion as Jenny'd ever seen him show. If what she'd done was a criminal offense, she wasn't sorry. Helping Zoe was more important than any slight miscalculation—or deliberate act—on her part.

"Anything else you keeping from me?" Ed looked from Zoe to Jenny.

Zoe was slow to shake her head. Jenny said nothing.

"If there is, you'd better hand it over pretty quick. Don't like to say this, but with your prints all over Aaron's house, the fights with Adam Cane, the letter we found in his house . . . things aren't exactly looking up for you, Ms. Zola." He shook his head. "And I'm not convinced anybody was in here tonight. Could've done all this yourself to throw me off."

Ed looked closely at Zoe's indignant face.

"Could've been your dog, nosing around while you were sleeping."

"Have to be a lot bigger than she is," Zoe muttered.

He leaned in closer. "Could have been nothing at all."

Zoe's eyes, when she looked up at Ed Warner, gleamed with tears. "Wish you didn't hate me like this, Chief." Her voice was tiny.

Ed stood back, blinking hard and shaking his head as if trying to get things inside to fall back into place. "Sorry, Ms. Zola. I didn't mean all that. Don't usually go around hollering at people. Just, well, I'm starting to feel like I'm chasing my own tail."

He left soon afterward, leaving a trio of depressed women behind.

At first, the three stood staring at the mess around them.

"I'll help you clean," Dora offered and began picking up jars of spices from the floor where they'd been dropped.

Zoe didn't answer. When she looked around at Jenny, her face was pale. She bit at her lip harder and harder.

Jenny put out a hand. "What is it, Zoe? Something else you remembered? What's wrong?"

"The key," Zoe whispered. "I didn't tell him."

Jenny held her breath. Last she knew, Zoe had it in her hand, wondering what it belonged to and why someone had taped it to Fida's collar.

Dora stopped arranging silverware in the drawer. "I forgot about that key. I'm forgetting everything—so much going on." Her eyes were wide. "Maybe we should turn it over to Ed. It's just—well—Fida. The way things were, I wasn't thinking murder. I was just thinking somebody doing something to the poor dog."

"Don't worry, Dora," Zoe said as she pulled up to her full height, arms crossed in front of her. "I still have it . . . or I had it."

"Where?" Jenny asked.

Zoe walked across the kitchen, shuffling through the mess on the floor. She left the room and was gone for only a minute.

When she came back, she held a book in her hands. A gray book. Very old and ornately decorated.

Zoe ran her fingers on a cover with gold-embossed diamond shapes in the form of two columns and what looked like a fat rabbit between the columns. She held the book up carefully to show Dora and Jenny, her face radiant, almost beatific.

"*Alice in Wonderland*. A very special, very old copy."

"Lovely, dear," Dora smiled sweetly at her. "But—"

"The key's in here." She set the book on the table and opened it carefully, one finger turning page after page until she came to a drawing of a small glass table with a key on top.

Stuck in the gutter, between the two pages, lay a glassine envelope.

Dora and Jenny hovered over Zoe as she pulled the envelope carefully from the book and opened it. The key fell into her hand.

There was a sigh of relief from each of them.

"That's what he was after." Zoe looked at the key with a kind of wonder.

Zoe slipped the key back into its envelope, then set it in the gutter of the book. "Alice will guard it for us."

"Call Tony," Jenny said. "He e-mailed a photo of it to a friend. A locksmith. Maybe he's heard something."

"I hope so. It seems to be important, doesn't it? Most especially to me." Zoe turned in the doorway, her round face deadly serious. "And I didn't make up somebody in the house. He was here. Or she was here. Somebody was definitely in here. I'll bet anything they're coming back for this."

She held up the gray book, gold embossing sparkling for just a moment in the artificial light of the kitchen fixture.

Chapter 34

"Penelope called." Zoe was at the breakfast table in Dora's house, where she'd spent the night. "She heard about the break-in. Want to meet her at Myrtle's for dinner?" Zoe looked to both of them, her bright face hopeful.

Jenny asked, "What time? Remember, Abigail's coming at eight." Dora broke in to say good-bye. She was off to find very special teas.

Tony, invited to breakfast to talk about the break-in, glanced up from the iPad he was using as though his mind was elsewhere.

"She said six thirty. Maybe she's got something new." Zoe, book in her hands, sat back on her stack of phonebooks, legs straight out in front of her. She leafed through the book of fairy tale characters she wanted to trace and paint on the pole of the children's house.

"Fine with me," Tony said.

"Me too," Jenny, going over the copies of Aaron's letters, answered absentmindedly.

"Want to hear what the locksmith has to say about Fida's key?" Tony looked up from his screen, stopping as if to tease.

He turned the iPad to the others and pointed to an antique humpback chest on the screen.

"That's it? The key fits that chest?" Zoe asked.

Tony shrugged. "Or one like it. My friend says this particular key is from the late nineteenth or early twentieth century."

Tony used the eraser of a pencil to point out places on the image of the key.

"See the shaft? Three decorative circlets on a bow end. No collar. My friend says it's a simple key. From the size, probably opens a wooden box or small chest—like the one pictured."

"Great," Zoe groused. "How many of those you see around these days?"

"This could be what the killer's after. First thing to look for," Tony said. "Or he could have the chest and needs the key to open it. Nah—in that case, he'd just smash it open. So maybe he doesn't have the chest." He snapped the iPad case closed. "Finding this box is crucial. And finding it quick, before the killer does."

"So," Zoe thought out loud. "It's definitely got something to do with the Canes. It's the Cane men who are dead, after all."

Tony nodded at her. "And it's the Cane men who each got a letter."

"And look what they say . . ." Jenny pointed to the letter she was holding, then read aloud. "'You boys can't cheat us anymore. I hear you've got what I'm after but you're hiding it. All three of you in on cheating us, just like him. A pack of cheaters. Time's up on that. You cheated her way too long and now you're cheating me.'" Zoe was lost in her head for a while.

"Were the boys in on something with their sister?" Zoe asked but didn't appear to be listening to herself. "Abigail got all the money. I don't get it."

Jenny was thinking hard. "It sounds as if whoever wrote the letters knows the Canes pretty well. Calls Adam and Aaron 'the boys.'"

"Everybody in town calls them that," Tony said.

"Not really. Only people who have lived here a long time." Zoe frowned.

"Or who know the family pretty well," Jenny added. "A family friend. An old teacher."

"A butcher, a baker, a candlestick maker," Zoe said.

"So," Jenny put in, "somebody who's been around a while. Other than Abigail, I can't think of anybody in that circle, except for some very elderly folks. How about Carmen Volker, her secretary?"

"She's not that old. And she's not from here."

"Anyway, you think she'd want to jeopardize her job?" Tony asked. "Doesn't look like the type to give up her little bit of safety."

"I wonder why Adam or Aaron didn't go to the police when they got their letter," Zoe said.

"Maybe they did," Jenny said, feeling as if they were all trapped in a circle, running hard to stay in place. "Maybe Ed couldn't find anything wrong. Or he didn't trust them. He said Adam was always coming in to make a complaint about a neighbor."

"Where are we then?" Zoe, shoulders sagging, looked over at Tony and Jenny. "Anywhere?"

"Here's where I think we are," Tony said. "Aaron and Adam must have known who wrote these letters. Maybe there were other, earlier letters. The writer wants something. It doesn't seem to be money, though." Tony hesitated, then looked hard at Jenny. "No dollar figures in here. Was there ever a question about their father's death?"

Jenny shrugged. "I remember a big funeral. Two statues of him going up: one in Cane Park and the other at the cemetery. Lots of dignitaries. Police escort, that kind of thing. I'll have to ask my mom if there was gossip at the time."

"Yeah, do that," Tony said. "Still, from what I found out, the only one to profit after their father died was Abigail. Adam and Aaron got nothing."

"You know Abigail didn't write these letters," Jenny said. "Nothing points to her."

"Still," Zoe said, "if Abigail did write these letters, maybe her brothers were trying to blackmail her with something and she wanted it back. I'm still thinking there's a later will."

"Then took Fida with her?" Jenny snorted. "Rushed out to kill Aaron? You see Abigail doing something like that?"

"Why would anyone take Fida?" Zoe was almost moaning. "Except to make me look guilty."

"Because she barks?" Jenny said.

Tony nodded. "Could be. Grab her first. Put her in your car. Then you're stuck with her, so why not take her with you? Maybe Fida was what got him into Aaron's house. Who knows?"

"Ed doesn't really like thinking you're the one who did it," Jenny said. "He's not a bad guy."

"He's grasping at anything just to get this behind him," Tony said. "Kind of feel sorry for him."

"My head hurts," Zoe said and slid off her chair. "I'll tell Penelope six thirty at Myrtle's will be fine. I want her to know about the key and the box. She'll go right after it. Funny how some people start looking better to you all the time."

Chapter 35

"Aaron's lawyer didn't really have to tell me anything," Penelope said from her corner of the booth after digging into a small bowl of salad and drinking down her hot water and lemon. She sat back, her neck a stone column, hair like a wig plopped on her head and left uncombed. "But he figured since Aaron Cane was dead, there were no client privileges left. And anyway, he said he'd never dealt with him before getting that letter about an appointment."

They were huddled around a table set with a vase of fainting red tulips. Zoe kept trying to make the tulips stand up while Jenny and Tony went over and over the menu.

There were people Jenny knew at other tables. Mostly Dora's friends. Jenny spotted Millie Sheraton, whose daughter had needed a fairy tale book—she raised a hand and waved. There was Vera Wattles, a widowed neighbor on Elderberry who had a passion for romance novels; Pastor Everett Senise from the United Baptist Church, who loved a good mystery; and Priscilla Manus, who, as the president of the Bear Falls Historical Society, was always on the lookout for histories other than her own—be they historical romance or a history of a great war.

None of them came over to talk, which Jenny found odd with this voluble group.

Delaware came to take their orders and smiled appreciatively when Tony and Jenny ordered rare steak and fries. Delaware took Zoe's order for a burger, then leaned down close to say something in Zoe's ear. Delaware nodded her head fiercely, then looked up at the ceiling before she went off toward the kitchen.

"What'd Delaware say that was so important the rest of us couldn't hear?" Jenny leaned close to ask.

Zoe made a face. "Just said she doesn't believe a word of what folks are saying about me. Which only makes me wonder what the devil they are saying."

"She meant to be nice," Tony said. "This'll be over soon."

"Hope I'm still walking the streets when it is."

Penelope cleared her throat. "Are any of you interested in what I learned from the attorney?"

They looked guilty. The meeting had a purpose to it. Penelope had taken the letter from the Traverse City attorney, Justin Princely, and promised to follow up.

"Sorry. What did Justin say about Aaron Cane?" Tony leaned in close.

"Just that he wasn't really his attorney. He had a problem that he wanted to discuss, is what he wrote to Justin. And Justin—as you saw—wrote back to confirm the appointment Aaron wanted."

"Did he keep it?" Zoe asked.

Penelope nodded. "Aaron showed up right on time, but it seemed he'd changed his mind about whatever it was he came for. Justin said Aaron got more and more nervous as they talked until he was about ready to jump out of his chair."

Zoe was disappointed. "But Aaron must have said something—"

"He did. He did. He kept saying, 'I don't want this to trouble Abigail. I don't want Abigail troubled over this.'"

"Justin said that when he tried to pin Aaron down, he wouldn't give him any explanation. Finally, he handed him the letter—same one we've got. Justin read it and said it looked like blackmail to him. Justin said to take it to the police, but Aaron refused. Said he didn't need trouble like that. Just as long as Abigail was all right.

"Justin asked him if he was a wealthy man, and Aaron Cane shook his head and said, 'Nope. All I've got is my social security and that's all I need.'"

Zoe was sitting on the edge of her seat but had to sit back when their food came. They went through the "Pass the mustard and ketchup, please" and "Is this your knife or mine?" and other such dinner trivialities until Zoe gave a huge groan and demanded to know what else Aaron said to the attorney.

"What was the purpose of the whole thing?" she asked.

Penelope shrugged. "Who knows?" She looked across the table, snaked her arm around her dish, snapped up one of Jenny's French fries, and popped it into her mouth. "Zoe said Abigail is coming to your house tonight. I'd like to be there. Maybe we can get this blackmail business cleared up. I've been asking around town and everybody who would talk to me seems to think Abigail's been heartless with her brothers. She got all the money and wouldn't share it. Doesn't sound that way, though. From what Aaron said to Justin, he was protective of her."

Penelope reached out again and took two more French fries this time, eating them slowly, one by one.

"I don't see why you can't be there." Jenny eyed her. "We're all working to clear Zoe. I'm sure Abigail wants to find the truth as much as we do."

Penelope's hand started to slide across the table one more time when Jenny tapped it with her fork.

"If you're hungry, I'll order you your own fries," Jenny snapped at her.

"No thank you." Penelope sat back, looking over Jenny's head. "I don't eat much. That's why I'm so thin. You should try it."

"You better not be charging me for these dinners," Jenny sniped back at her.

Tony and Zoe looked as if they were about to burst into laughter.

Penelope ignored them all. "I'd like to meet this Abigail, make up my own mind about the woman."

She reached into her purse and drew out copies of the two letters. "She's got to know something about these. After all, the writer speaks of 'you three' and 'what he did' and being 'cheated' out of something. Must be the father they're talking about, don't you think? Who else could they be covering for? When you've got old money like the Canes, there are always secrets and vicious hatreds buried somewhere near the roots of the family tree. Maybe Abigail will tell us what it's all about tonight."

The bell over the door tinkled. Two couples Jenny knew slightly walked in and stood looking around for a table. One of the women saw Jenny. Jenny waved, but the woman turned away, putting her head down and speaking to the other three. One by one they looked over at Jenny's table. None of them waved. One of the men made a face and nudged the other guy.

Delaware hurried out from the kitchen, stopping at the cash register counter to pick up four menus, then scurried to the waiting people. Jenny couldn't help but watch, having an idea what was coming. In a minute, one of the men nodded in the direction of the booth where Jenny and her friends sat. The two couples turned and left the restaurant.

Delaware stood where she was, her back to them. She set the menus carefully beside the register. She glanced over at Jenny, who still watched. Delaware shook her head almost angrily and went off to check on another table.

"That was about me," Zoe said. "Guess people don't like to eat with killers."

"Don't be silly." Jenny turned offended eyes on Zoe. "Everything's not always about you, you know."

Chapter 36

They got brittle with each other. All of them on edge. The couples, who'd smugly judged Zoe, left a trail of toxins behind them.

They settled for coffee, no dessert, and then sat without talking, glancing at each other from time to time and frowning or wincing or just pretending not to see each other.

Finally Jenny, unable to tolerate the silence, looked over at Zoe. "Weren't you going to tell Penelope about the key and the box?"

Penelope arched back to look at Zoe. "Key and a box? What'd you get me in, some pirate show?"

Zoe told her how she got the key. Tony showed her the key and the type of box it went to on his cell phone. Again she leaned back and looked from one to the other, skeptical, until Zoe told her the story and how they were almost sure the key and the box were at the heart of what happened to the Canes. Penelope looked at Tony. "You going to keep on it?" she asked, and he said that's exactly what he was doing.

She sipped at her lemon water and looked over the cup, first at Zoe and then at Jenny. "Think we should go a little deeper here." She sniffed as she spoke.

"Deeper? Into what?" Tony asked.

"Into murder. I thought we might have a serious conversation about the subject."

"Like what?" Jenny asked, although she made it clear she'd lost interest.

Penelope moved around on the hard bench. "Well, most murders happen because of money."

"Don't forget jealousy. Or insanity. Or sex. Or a couple of other things that don't count here," Tony said.

"Rule out sex." Zoe dabbed daintily at her mouth with a paper napkin.

"That leaves jealousy or insanity. But I'm betting on money. Abigail's got it. The brothers didn't," Penelope said.

"Or it could be one of those 'other things.'" Jenny glanced down at her watch. Time for her to get going home.

"Big help," Zoe groused and kept her head turned from the others.

Penelope smirked. "Well, at least I've whittled the causes down."

There was silence as everybody thought about the reasons one human being murders another.

"Don't you want to order more hot water and lemon?" Jenny frowned maliciously at Penelope.

Penelope turned cold eyes on her. "Is that meant to be funny?"

"Hmm. 'Even a cat may question a queen.'" Jenny was tired and felt like being ornery.

"That's not right," Zoe argued. "It's 'Even a cat may look at a king.'"

"But Penelope's not a king," Jenny said, pleased with herself.

"And you're not a cat," Penelope argued back, the pair of them into deep and nervous disagreement over nothing.

"Can we stop now?" Jenny felt as if she was trapped at a very strange party. Very strange indeed.

"I've been to see your police chief." Penelope got loud enough to shut the others out. "Seems he's changing his mind a bit."

"Is that a good thing?" Zoe asked quietly, almost as if afraid to hope.

"I think so. He's finally coming to his senses. He said he's got a new suspect. The man, I understand, who destroyed your mom's library."

"Not Johnny. Johnny wouldn't hurt—" Jenny stopped herself abruptly.

Penelope turned toward her. "Zoe is my client." Her words came quick and clipped. "Whatever helps her, I'm taking a look at, Jenny. I welcomed the news, myself. I hope we're not running into divided loyalties here."

Tony stared hard at his knuckles.

Penelope waited, eyes trained on Jenny.

"What time's Abigail coming?" she asked when Jenny didn't answer her other question.

"Eight o'clock." Jenny, face burning, checked her watch. "I'd better get back, in case she's early."

"From what I've heard of the woman, she won't be early, or late, she'll be right on time. Who else will be there when you talk to her?"

"Just me and Mom."

"Not Zoe?"

"If she wants." Jenny glanced over at her.

Zoe shook her head, saying nothing.

"So maybe just you and me." Penelope's eyebrows rose pretty high. "Think she'll bring that Alfred Rudkers with her? You know I checked him out. I can't find where he's licensed to practice in Michigan. Could be I spelled his name wrong. I'll look deeper. Something about that man I dislike."

"She didn't mention bringing him. Not even her secretary. Seemed she felt a need to get away from both."

"You'd think he'd want to be there. From what I saw of him at the funeral, he seems very attentive. Must be on retainer. A pretty high one. Honestly, I can't imagine he'd want her running around spilling family secrets to just anybody."

"You mean like me?" Jenny said.

"No, I mean like anybody. I tried to make an appointment to see her. That secretary of hers wouldn't put me through. I'm eager to hear what she's got to tell you. She could be a witness for our side, in case we need one."

"Witness!" Zoe sat up straight. "For what?"

"Trial. In case Ed changes his mind again and comes after you. He does have some strong circumstantial evidence, you know. We have to be prepared."

Zoe fell back in her seat, her face pale. "I thought you said . . ."

Jenny pushed her plate away and reached for her bill. "I've got to get going."

"I'll drive you." Penelope laid her twenty-dollar bill beside her plate and pushed at Tony to let her out.

"Zoe and I came with Tony," Jenny objected.

Penelope turned to Tony. "Would you take Zoe home? I don't think she should be with us if Abigail's there already." Tony agreed, but only after checking Jenny's face.

"And I don't want you there when Abigail arrives. I want some time with her first," Jenny said.

Penelope shrugged. "We don't always get want we want, do we, Jenny?"

Jenny fumed, knowing she'd been outmaneuvered.

She drove home with Penelope, the girl who'd peed her pants in third grade. She almost laughed, thinking how far they'd both come to sit together now.

Chapter 37

"Ronald called this morning. I forgot to tell you." Dora filled the teakettle at the sink.

Jenny looked over her shoulder at Dora, dressed in her best pantsuit, hair freshly cut and curled. Penny sat across from her, rejecting coffee and requesting hot tea.

"Beauty parlor?" Jenny gestured toward Dora's hair.

"I wasn't going to let Abigail Cane catch me looking frumpy. I'll bring in the cookies and tea when she gets here and then go someplace else so you three can talk." Dora hesitated. "Did you hear what I said? Ronald called."

Jenny's smile came out as a grimace.

Penny raised her eyebrows. "Ex?" she whispered toward Jenny. "Want me to talk to him for you?"

Jenny shook her head. "What'd he want?"

"Goodness, Jenny. He's your husband. Said to tell you to call him back when you can manage it. He left a number. I tried to talk to him. I mean, it's been a while, you know. Guess he was in a hurry. Cut me short . . ."

"You know what he's like." Jenny truly was sorry, especially sorry that Mom had to talk to him at all. She'd have to break down and tell her about the divorce soon. "Not much I can do."

"Oh, I know that. I've been telling myself what a lucky woman I am." Dora smiled and reached out to touch Jenny's cheek.

"Lucky?"

"Lucky that his child will never be my grandchild."

"What do you mean?" Jenny thought she knew what was coming.

"To tell the truth, I never liked Ronald much, dear. Not half good enough for you. You don't have to worry. I know about the divorce. Now don't look like that! No big secret anyway, and I say what you should be doing is thanking that woman for stealing him away from you. It's like finding a brand-new TV out by the garbage. Attractive thing to take until you get it home and plug it in. Doesn't work. Doesn't do anything. Can't trust it when a good game show's on. That's him. Not much of a friend."

Jenny, relieved, laughed. "How long have you known?"

"Your sister mentioned it."

"I swear that Lisa's got the biggest mouth."

"Lisa doesn't have a big mouth. She's got a big heart and you should thank her. Not telling would have come too close to not caring. Someday you will be a mother and you'll understand that every mother wants to help when her child is suffering."

Dora hugged her daughter. "Mistakes don't have to be wounds, Jenny. A mistake can sometimes be the best thing that can happen to a person. Just imagine if you'd married Johnny Arlen? Now that's a mistake for you. Poor Angel got her wish. Broke the two of you up. She's on child number three—with a damaged husband." Dora looked sad, downward wrinkles at the edges of her mouth.

She pushed Jenny's long hair away from her face and patted it into place. "Now I've set out my best cups for Abigail. We'll show her that Westons are every bit as good as Canes. Wait until you taste the walnut cookies I made this morning. Don't care who she is; Abigail's never tasted anything like them." She meant the last for both Jenny and Penny. The women smiled and agreed they might as well taste one of those cookies ahead of time. Just making sure they were as good as Dora claimed.

* * *

Eight o'clock came and went. The women moved to the living room with little left to talk about.

Eight thirty.

No phone call.

Nothing.

"What happened to her?" Penclope was very close to anger.

At nine Dora put her extra teacup away. She poured the last of the fancy Earl Grey down the sink and rinsed out the pretty, fluted pot with rosebuds on it.

At nine thirty-five, Dora asked Jenny if she should call and ask Zoe to stay the night. "I know she'll be eager to hear what happened with Abigail and surprised she never showed up. But that burglary disturbed her. I could tell. She's been upset all day. Don't you think it would be best to have both of them here for the night?"

"'Both of them'?" Penelope stood to leave, mistaking the phrase for Zoe and her.

"Why, Zoe and Fida, of course." Dora's cool answer signaled that she'd come close to Jenny's opinion of Zoe's attorney.

Penelope sat back down. "I think I'll wait then. I'd like to talk to her. I might have bullied her—"

"Might?" Jenny asked. "And after what those awful people did, right there in the diner . . ."

Dora went to call and came back to say Zoe and Fida were on their way. "She seemed relieved that I called. That little woman can seem more alone than any person should ever be. For all her talent . . ."

Jenny, disappointed that Abigail hadn't shown up, still half-expected a sturdy knock at the outside door. She had so many questions for her. Odd that a woman like Abigail hadn't kept her word. It couldn't be because she forgot. Who would forget the deaths of two brothers?

Jenny was in the kitchen—anywhere to get away from Penel-ope. She supposed she should call Ronald back. He'd probably had a change of heart and wanted to weasel her down on the alimony. Charity or Sybil or whoever was probably higher maintenance than Ronald had imagined. He didn't have imagination enough to think that Jenny might not give a rat's behind about his problems anymore.

Still . . .

He didn't answer his phone and she didn't leave a message. After all, the worst thing that could happen was that he *would* return her call. She went back to sit across from Penelope in the living room, vowing not to say a single word to the woman.

* * *

The screaming came from somewhere outside the house. Jenny heard but didn't move. She told herself it wasn't more trouble for them, only teenagers giving a party in one of the houses along the street. Or a drunk . . .

It came again. The voice was familiar. Still, she waited.

Dora rushed in breathlessly, stopping under the arch leading back to her bedroom. "Didn't you hear that?" she demanded first of Jenny and then of Penelope, who sat at the edge of her chair, blinking fast and seeming to be holding her breath.

Another high yell, this time for help. A dog yipped again and again.

"What on earth . . . ?"

They ran to the porch. Dora snapped on the light. A few yards in front of them, a figure was bent over: It was Zoe. She yelled out, "Call an ambulance. She's been hurt."

"It's Abigail," Zoe screamed even louder. "I fell over her. Oh, go call for help! Get some towels for the blood. Her head! Hurry!"

Chapter 38

"It's that damned box," Zoe said from the car seat beside Jenny. "We've got to find it. I'll bet anything that's what Abigail was coming over to talk about. Had to be. Somebody doesn't want us, or Abigail, to find it. And is willing to kill for it."

Jenny couldn't think of a thing to add. A box. The key. People dying. She hated to say it to Zoe, but she didn't have a clue to any of it.

Flashing red lights led them all the way to Munson Medical Center in Traverse City. Dark roads and strobing lights stretched ahead; taillights pulled over here and there to let them pass.

No moon. No stars. Just darkness and the ambulance. It was Jenny, Dora, and Zoe in Jenny's car, and everyone was silent, having nothing more to say after they'd stood in shock as Abigail was hurriedly bandaged, wrapped in white cotton blankets, and taken off on a stretcher.

Penelope didn't join them, not explaining, only leaving to go in another direction.

Jenny couldn't let herself think—as she walked in the emergency entrance behind the EMTs and the stretcher—of another time she'd walked into this hospital. Dora was holding her hand.

Lisa was ahead of them. That same sense of horror was trying to bring her to her knees.

Abigail was taken away as soon as they got into emergency. They were sent to the waiting room, then called to the front desk for information on the patient—though they could give nothing beyond her name and address. No hospitalization information. Nothing on allergies to drugs.

"We'll need a relative here as soon as possible." The small, middle-aged woman behind the desk wasn't cold, only attempting to handle the business of tragedy.

Jenny gave her Abigail's phone number and Carmen Volker's name.

"Her secretary and a good friend. If you call her . . ."

The words were hardly out of Jenny's mouth when Carmen Volker, hair wild, a black sweater hanging crookedly across her shoulders, hurried in, low black heels clicking atonally on the white tiles as she ran toward them. Her voice neared hysteria when she got to the desk.

"Where is she? Where's Abigail?" Her voice broke. Her eyes were wild, searching from one side of the room to the other. "She's not dead, is she?"

She saw the gathered women and ran to them. "What did you do to Abigail?" she demanded. Strands of hair stuck up from the bun at the back of her head. Her chest was heaving. She laid a flat hand there. "She's not dead. No! No! She can't be dead. You didn't do this, too," she implored Zoe, who sat very still, her eyes leveled on the woman, little hands crossed delicately in her lap.

A nurse hurried over to take Carmen by the arm and direct her through a doorway to an interior office, all the while trying to quiet her.

Dora reached out to pat Zoe's arm a few times. "She must care for Abigail. She's terribly upset."

Zoe said nothing. She was frozen, staring nowhere.

Ed Warner came through the emergency doors, straight to where they sat. "Any word on Ms. Cane yet?"

Dora shook her head.

"In surgery," Jenny said.

He walked toward the office where the nurse had taken Carmen, and disappeared.

After a while, Zoe whispered, "That's what *everybody* will think, what Carmen said."

There was a ripple of despair in her voice.

"No," Dora shook her head. "This is only more of some big, awful thing we're caught up in."

Tony walked in and searched the room. The sweater, tossed over his shoulder, was wrinkled, as if thrown on hurriedly. He ran to where the women sat and took the chair next to Jenny, hands gripped between his knees, head as close to hers as he could get.

He didn't say anything at first, then whispered, "Heard on my scanner. What happened?"

Jenny shivered. "Zoe found Abigail lying in front of our house. She must've tripped."

"Accident?"

Jenny looked directly into his dark eyes, reading the question. "There was a lot of blood . . ."

"She fall over something?" He looked at the others, his dark eyes going to Zoe.

"I found her," Zoe said.

There didn't seem to be a right question to ask—for any of them. A nurse came over to say that Abigail had been taken to recovery and would then go to ICU for the rest of the night.

She couldn't have visitors. Her secretary was going to stay in the waiting room outside the ICU, but there wasn't space for anyone else.

"What about her attorney?" Tony asked. "Isn't that guy here?"

"Only one person will be allowed."

Jenny and the others were deciding what to do when Ed returned, nodding and bobbing toward Tony.

"'Nother one," he said mostly to Tony. "Severe concussion. Her head's stitched up. Hit pretty hard. Somebody tried to kill her, far as I can make out. Doctor says she took a couple of hard blows—head and back. Not from falling down either."

He turned to face the women. "I've got questions . . ."

"We were expecting her at eight o'clock. When she didn't arrive, we just thought she'd forgotten . . . or changed her mind." Jenny took a deep breath. She had the awful feeling she'd done this before, maybe said these same words.

"Who found her?"

Nobody spoke until Zoe said, "I did. I was going over to spend the night with Dora and Jenny. Since the break-in, I've been nervous. You know, that man might come back."

"If you don't mind my saying . . ." he started.

"Don't bother," Zoe interrupted. "I know what you're thinking, but all I did was walk over to the Westons' house."

"What business did you have with Abigail Cane?"

"Nothing. I wasn't going there to see her. Under the circumstances, it didn't seem right. But Dora called. She said Abigail never showed up and that I should come on over."

"You said 'under the circumstances.' Mind telling me what circumstances those were?" Ed's manner was almost lackadaisical, as if her answers barely interested him.

"I'd say you know pretty well." Zoe slid forward and planted her feet fast to the floor. She looked Ed straight in the eye. "And

I'm telling you a couple of things right out. Number one, I did not sneak over to the Westons' and bash Abigail in the head. Even if I was running around killing people, willy-nilly, how dumb do you think I am?"

She stopped to look at her circle of friends. Nobody looked back. She drew in a long breath. "Number two, I'm not dumb enough to dump bodies around me like banana peels. And now I will not say another word without Penelope, my attorney, here to advise me."

Ed looked hard into her set face. "Better call her," he warned. "I've been over to the Westons'. My men are there now. We found the weapon used on Ms. Cane. Turns out it was a fairy."

"Fairy?" everyone asked at the same time.

Ed almost smiled. "One of your statues, Ms. Zola. From that garden of yours. Heavy thing with a daisy on its head. Broke in a thousand pieces. Call that lawyer of yours. Then maybe we should go over to the station and have a little talk."

"I don't believe this." Jenny had nothing better to offer.

Dora said, "Why, Ed, this is intolerable. You know as well—"

"Sorry, Ms. Weston. I can't ignore what's right in front of me anymore. I know this woman's your friend, but I can't turn a blind eye to what she been doing. I feel bad. Been trying to tell myself nothing that was going on had anything to do with Ms. Zola." He shook his head and didn't look at Dora. "Can't anymore. She'll be at the jail until I call the district attorney. 'Fraid I'm turning everything I've got over to her."

"What'd she do, Ed?" Jenny kept her voice under control, though she wanted to bark at the man. "Jump up and down to hit her? All the while swinging that statue? This is totally crazy. Somebody's trying to frame Zoe. Even you have to see it."

"Then give me somebody else. You don't think I like this, do you?" He shook his head as if sincerely wishing for a different answer.

"Wait a minute here." Tony put a hand out to stop Ed Warner before he got out of his chair.

"You were a cop," Ed said. "You know I've got a job to do."

"But . . ." Even Tony didn't have an answer to that one.

For a moment, Zoe's spirit seemed to be back. She pulled in a long breath, put her fists at her waist, and leaned away as if about to spout what Jenny imagined could be the quote of all quotes. Her mouth was open. Her eyes were huge.

Nothing came out. Slowly she deflated.

Zoe walked out beside Ed. She was so tiny next to the tall chief, walking with her head bowed, her feet moving fast as she tried to keep up. She looked like a child.

Watching her broke Jenny's heart.

Chapter 39

They stood outside on the steps of the hospital when Johnny Arlen came out behind them. His hair was uncombed, his jeans dirty. The checkered flannel shirt he wore over a T-shirt hung open. Beside him, deep in conversation until he saw the group gathered on the steps, was his brother, Gerry. Jenny hadn't seen Gerry in years. She was as surprised to see him there as she was to see Johnny.

Gerry was much older than Jenny remembered, scruffier. When he turned to look at her, his eyes were half-focused and then startled.

He gave her a brief nod. Jenny felt the blood drain from her face at the sight of both men. Besides all their history, the fact that Johnny had destroyed the Little Library made her stomach churn.

"Angel just had the baby." Johnny wiped a hand over his mouth, avoiding everyone's eyes. He gave an embarrassed laugh. "No waiting this time. Gerry picked me up and the baby was born about the time we got here. Got to go tell the girls. They're with my mom."

"What did she have?" Dora's lips were dry, though her voice was steady and polite. Jenny watched her mom struggle with her feelings and was proud of her.

"Another girl." No excitement. Just the statement. He didn't look at Dora, only down at his feet. "Three girls now."

Tony introduced himself, sticking out a hand to shake Johnny's, and congratulated him. He took Gerry's hand, though it was offered halfheartedly.

"I've seen you around town," Johnny said. "Ex-cop, right?"

"Ex-cop. Carpenter now."

"In case I ever need something built, I'll give you a call. Hope you're cheap."

Tony ignored the remark and the laugh that followed. "You hear about the Cane woman?"

Johnny shook his head. "Abigail Cane?"

"She was attacked tonight. A few hours ago. On her way to Mrs. Weston's house."

Johnny turned a reluctant and uncomprehending look on Dora. "What was that lady doing at your house, Mrs. Weston?"

Dora didn't answer, so Johnny moved down a step behind his brother. "As I said, got to go tell the girls about the baby. Nice seeing you." He nodded to Dora, and then to Jenny, his face blank, eyes looking beyond her.

He loped down the hospital steps, shirt flapping around him. At the bottom of the steps, he turned to give Jenny a questioning look, then, shoulders hunched up to his ears, he fell in beside his brother, hurrying off toward the parking lot.

"Guess that lets him out on this one," Jenny said.

"Don't be so fast," Tony said. "Abigail was attacked almost three hours ago. You heard what he said: Angel *just* had the baby. This looks serious for Zoe. I'm going to take a closer look at this guy."

Tony ran down the steps ahead of her. Jenny watched him go and told herself what she needed was one of Zoe's turrets.

A big tower to hide in. Where none of the knaves and rogues could reach her.

* * *

Jenny and Dora, with nothing left that they could do, went home. Penelope called as they pulled into the driveway, asking Jenny to come to the station.

"Zoe needs you. She's really unhappy. I think a friend here with her would help keep her spirits up."

Jenny didn't want to be needed. For just a minute, walking up to the house behind Dora, she thought about leaving town. There was no rest here in Bear Falls. No time to think about the things sitting on her own plate. All she'd found was trouble on top of trouble, people caught up in old feuds, a Little Person who shouted "Off with her head" when it pleased her, a man she'd felt comfortable with until he'd turned on her, dead bodies . . .

"Is she in a cell?" she asked.

"I'm afraid so."

"Then what can I do?"

"The chief said he didn't mind if you stayed the night with her."

"Come on, Penny. Really? Share a cell with Zoe?"

"At least come and tell her Fida's okay. Read her bedtime stories for all I care. Just talk to her. That's all I'm asking."

* * *

When Jenny got to the police station, Penny was standing at the door.

"Don't act nice to the chief," she whispered near her ear while giving Jenny a surprise hug. "This is getting out of hand," Penelope growled as loud as she could. "I'm thinking maybe I'll file a civil rights action against this guy. He wants to charge her with assault now. Easier to prove than murder. It's a trick, Jenny. That's what it is. A lesser charge to hold her on until he scares up some evidence. I'll have her out of here by tomorrow. This is close to harassment, you ask me." She aimed her voice at Ed Warner, doing paperwork behind a desk and ignoring them.

Penelope took Jenny by the arm and led her to chairs in the farthest corner of the waiting room. Even there she looked around her before whispering in a voice so low, Jenny could barely hear her.

"Anything new with that box and key?" Penny asked, head bent so her hair masked most of her face. "I'm sure that's at the heart of all this. Nothing to do with Zoe in the least, this attack on Abigail. Came out of nowhere. If her brothers weren't both dead, I'd swear one of them was after her. Gotta be something with that box. That's what the killer wants."

She stopped talking when the chief got up and ambled out of the room, down a long side hall.

"I brought up Johnny Arlen," Penelope whispered, watching Ed Warner's skinny back disappear. "He's the only bone I've got to throw to the dogs."

Jenny shook her head. "Johnny didn't do this to Abigail. He barely knows her."

Penny leaned in closer. "Don't tell the chief that. We've got to hurl as much doubt his way as we can come up with."

The chief was back, a dejected Zoe walking behind him, her orange suit too long, the rolled-up legs hanging and tripping her. Her little arms hung from the wide sleeves like sticks on a snowman.

Ed Warner walked her to them.

"I'm letting her go," he said. "Don't know what'll happen tomorrow, but right now I've got a couple of other people to look at."

"Which means you don't have anything against her." Penny gave a snort and got up to put her arm around Zoe.

"Don't push it, Penny," Jenny warned, almost hissing.

"You can take her home," Ed said. "All she needs is her clothes. I've got her papers made out and signed. You can pick 'em up over there." He indicated the desk where he'd been sitting.

"Remember," Ed Warner called after them as two men with bloody noses made a noisy entrance. "No leaving town for any reason."

Chapter 40

It was morning after a long sleepless night. Dreams of Aaron Cane's house and the smell had haunted Jenny throughout the night. Something was there, in those shadowed corners where things lived a life of their own. The key came from there. She'd dreamed it was right in front of her, but every time she tried to pick it up, the key moved out of reach.

Then she was in Adam's yard and the hatchet came to life and chased her.

Jenny was grateful for morning.

She was on her second cup of coffee, still in her pajamas and trying to shock herself awake with caffeine. There was a knock at the door and Tony walked in with a brightly painted library house in his arms. He set it on the table with a mumbled "Good Morning" and went back out. "I've got the other house," he said over his shoulder.

The house in front of her sparkled: white walls, bright-green roof, and a red chimney. "Adults" was emblazoned on the green-and-white flag attached to the roof.

Tony was back with the other house, showing it off, proud as a kid of what he'd made. He pushed the sleeves of his work shirt up his arms. She could see his arms were damp with heat and exertion. She looked back at the house and grudgingly told him he'd done a great job.

He said he was glad she liked them.

They didn't look at each other. Didn't speak. They concentrated on the library houses, looking at them one way and then the other.

"See the space I was able to get?" he pointed to how the adults box was constructed: deep but with slots for books to sit in a double tier. "Hold at least two dozen books at a time. Got a sign-up sheet in the top—see the brackets? Should be good for years."

He cleared his throat and turned to the other house. "And see here? Kids' box opens right up." He lifted the front of the house to show her how easy it was for kids to pull out their books, the top settling back in place by itself.

"Mom will love them." She brought him coffee. "Are they going in today?"

"Whatever your mom wants. She was talking about waiting until a better time."

He looked at her, tipping his head just enough to see her. He pulled out a chair and sat, taking up the large cup she'd given him in both his hands.

Jenny wanted to laugh. What a game they were playing. A children's game. Whoever spoke sincerely first was the loser.

He went on about installing the houses. "I think she meant, with what's going on in town, maybe it isn't a good time for a celebration."

He drained his cup then turned to look out the window at the sunny morning.

"Are you waiting for Mom? I'll go see if I can find her."

She hesitated next to where he sat. She felt the heat coming from his body and wondered what would happen if she ran a finger down his bare arm.

He'd probably shake her off.

The eight-hundred-pound gorilla in the room gained another eight hundred pounds when he didn't answer.

Maybe she'd ask him what in hell was wrong with him. Or say she was leaving Bear Falls. Anything to force the empty space hanging in the room between them.

She watched the side of his face and longed to run her finger over that scar—just once.

He turned to look up at her. His large hands were braced on the table, ready to push him up. When he looked at her, the excitement over the houses was gone.

"Want to go over to the lake with me? Take a walk?"

"Now?"

She got an unexpected smile. Or a need for reassurance. Something.

"I'd like to talk to you."

"I can't. Zoe and I are meeting this morning. Penny's coming. She was hoping you could—"

"I want to talk to you about Johnny."

She stiffened.

"I know there was trouble. You left town over him."

"I went to college. Who have you been talking to? I'd love to know who makes *me* the topic of conversation around here."

"Actually, it was Ed Warner who brought it up, but I already knew. Not a well-kept secret in Bear Falls. Ed told me a shoe print on one of the books matched the shoes Johnny had on. They've got him on that one. Then he started telling me about the raw deal Johnny gave you and why you left town. I guess what I want to know is if you've still got feelings for him. Seems as if you might."

"If you're asking if I think he committed the murders, no, I don't. I can't see Johnny killing anybody. Before the booze, Johnny wouldn't have hurt a flea. But even now I doubt it. As for the library, yes, he did that. There's no question about that crime. It seems Johnny was getting even with me for coming back to town. Maybe he's mad about the way he turned out. As if I could have saved him."

"Are you okay with that?"

"With what? That he hurt my mother the way he did? No, not at all. That some people think he's a murderer? No, can't stand it. Would I throw him to Ed to get Zoe off? No, I wouldn't do that either."

"Do you still love him?"

She reached out to set her finger on the green door of the adult's house. The small screen door pushed in against a background of painted rocking chairs. Illusion.

Jenny squirmed. He'd asked the one question she couldn't answer.

"Am I pissing you off?" He leaned closer and put one of his hands on hers. She wanted to turn her hand and hold on tight.

"Can't answer?"

She said nothing.

Tony closed his eyes, then opened them and went to the door.

He looked back at her. "You know, Jenny. Lots of people are happy you're back."

"Really?" She couldn't look at him.

"Your mom, for one. Zoe—now that she knows you. Me. I'm glad you're here."

She prayed she wouldn't cry. His voice was soft. The words were kind. He confused her completely.

"I don't know why you got stuck with two bad ones, Jenny. I had one—she was no prize. But that's not all there is out here. Just wanted you to know." He tipped his head. The smile was teasing. "You're a beautiful woman. We've all got our scars. Real scars and the other kind."

"Sorry, I guess I'm not—"

"I'm not asking you for anything, just to be a friend."

She caught her breath. "Give me a while, Tony, okay?"

"How long?" he asked, his finger on her chin, tipping her head back so he could look into her eyes. "Ten years enough? I'll be fifty-four in ten years."

"And I'll be forty-six."

"Think we can still have babies?" His smile was wicked.

She thought awhile. "Okay," she said. "Let's make it five years."

Chapter *41*

"It's just terrible, what they're saying about you."

Delaware Hardy stood, coffee pot in one hand, beside the table where Jenny, Zoe, and Penelope sat waiting for their breakfast. She leaned toward Zoe. "Poor thing. You'd think you've got enough on your hands without being accused of murder. Why, I just tell all those people with their tongues flapping to hold their judgment until the real killer's caught."

Delaware shook her head and looked around the restaurant to make sure people were listening. "Me and the other waitresses have been going over things. Myrtle's even got a chart on the wall in the kitchen—where the bodies were found, where the little dog was found. Just added in that fairy statue somebody clobbered Abigail with. We're making a list of all the people Adam didn't get along with and nothing in our work points to you, Zoe. Except, maybe, that Adam was found in your backyard and your dog was found out in poor Aaron's house, and you had a beef with Adam Cane, and we hear Ms. Cane was hit with one of your . . ."

She hesitated, pushing the creamer absent-mindedly toward Jenny. She seemed to be thinking hard. "Anyway, we don't care what it looks like, we know it wasn't you who did that to those two men and their sister. Why, that's like saying a mouse could bring down an elephant."

* * *

Delaware wandered off, filling coffee cups along her way back to the kitchen.

"Help like that," said Penelope, leaning forward in her seat, "and you'll be in the electric chair before you know it."

Jenny wanted to change the subject—any other subject would do. She was thinking about Tony but kept him to herself.

"Mom called the hospital this morning. They said Abigail's resting comfortably. Think we can go over there in an hour or so."

Penelope nodded. "As far as I can see, she's the only one who can help us. Maybe she knows something about that box. And somehow we've got to get into Adam's house—Aaron's, too. See if we can find something the key fits." She shook her head. "Without a warrant, we're breaking the law. But they're both empty houses. I think we can work it out. Bet anything Ed'll be glad for some help."

"Does Ed know about the key?" Jenny asked.

Penelope nodded. "I think Zoe finally mentioned it, but Ed didn't think too much about it. He's got two murders. A broken library. A woman attacked. The man's doing his best, but with his limitations here—two deputies—well, I don't think we need to worry if we want to take a look at those houses. Maybe not Zoe, though. Don't think he'd understand."

"Abigail has to know something," Jenny said. "I can't see her protecting whoever killed her brothers. She had to be coming to my house for a reason."

"And somebody wanted to stop her."

"Let's pick up Zoe and get over to the hospital."

Penelope got the check, giving Jenny a weighted look as she slapped a twenty-dollar tip on the table. She went to pay at the front counter where Delaware, once more, bent toward them to say how much she believed Zoe was innocent.

* * *

"Only two at a time," the nurse told the trio of women. "And fifteen minutes is all you get. Ms. Cane's having trouble . . . well, with her memory and all."

Penelope said she had things to take care of. "I'll be back," she said and left as Zoe and Jenny went down the hall to see Abigail.

Abigail was in a private room. She looked like a roll of bandages with her head wrapped and white sheets tucked around her.

Machines pulsed—long breaths with a steady rhythm.

Abigail was sleeping. Her face was pale.

Jenny and Zoe brought chairs to the bedside to sit and wait. They only had fifteen minutes.

At five minutes, Jenny cleared her throat.

At ten minutes, Zoe scraped her chair across the floor.

Abigail stirred and made a little humming sound, then stretched and turned her head, wincing. She tried to raise a hand from the sheet, gave a startled sound and blinked, looking from Zoe to Jenny.

"Oh, yes." she said. "What was I saying?" She tried to sit up but couldn't.

"I need to talk to you both," she said before the women could say a word. Instead of talking, she lay back and closed her eyes.

A loud voice boomed from the doorway: "What are you doing in here? Time's up on that. You will leave my client alone or I will get a court order against you."

Alfred Rudkers, Abigail's attorney. He stood with his hands on his hips, eyes wide with anger. "You have a lot of nerve, Ms. Weston, forcing your way in here like this. And bringing this . . . this suspect with you. I, for one, think you both have a large role in what's happened here. A very large role. You have to leave this minute."

Abigail's eyes fluttered, then opened at the noise in the room.

"Out! Out!" the man demanded when they didn't move fast enough. His outrage settling into a firmer order.

"Alfred?" Abigail's voice was weak. "Alfred," she said again, searching from Jenny to the end of the bed where Alfred stood. "Who are you yelling at?"

"You see? You see?" He lowered his voice, hissing at Jenny and then moving around the bed to bend over Abigail.

"Nobody, Abigail. I'm so sorry you were disturbed. I shouldn't have left. Go back to sleep. Don't worry about a thing. I'm here and will stay to protect you. A terrible outrage's been done . . ."

Abigail's eyes were puzzled. "I know . . . something. I just don't remember."

"Your mind will clear when you've healed. You have a concussion. No one expects you to remember, Abigail. Carmen and I will take you home to rest."

She lifted her head from the pillow, searching out her visitors' faces, then settled back to the pillow.

"I'll clear the room," Alfred said. He turned a smug look on Jenny as he lifted his hands in a shooing motion.

"Thank you, Alfred." The faint words came from Abigail. "I need to sleep."

Chapter 42

"I'm afraid for her," Jenny said as she and Zoe drove home.

"Why isn't there a police guard outside her door?" Zoe asked. "She was attacked, for goodness sakes. He could come back at any minute."

"You're right. Let's go talk to Ed," Jenny suggested, ready to turn the wheel in the other direction.

Zoe hesitated. "I promised Penelope I'd come to her motel so we can talk about the new book contract Christopher e-mailed me. He wants it back pretty fast. Do you mind seeing Ed alone?"

"Penelope's your new arts attorney?"

Zoe shrugged. "Guess she's my attorney for life. Can't look a gift lawyer in the mouth, can I?"

"Not exactly a gift."

Jenny dropped Zoe off at her house and then drove to the police station where she found Tony with the chief. They turned when she came through the door.

"Telling Tony here that he's right about getting somebody over there to watch outside Abigail's room. Zoe's attorney, that Penelope, came in earlier, saying the same thing."

Jenny laughed. "That's what I'm here for, too."

Tony smiled at her and she felt shy, even tingly: a milkmaid out in a farmer's field, flirting with the goat boy.

Ed looked from face to face and shook his head. He scratched his nose. "I'm waiting to hear from my off-duty deputy now. If he doesn't call in soon, I'll get over there myself. Want her covered when she leaves ICU."

The phone rang on Ed's desk. When he was through talking, he gave them a thumbs up. "Officer Millard's on his way to the hospital now."

He chuckled. "My men don't get much overtime. Seemed awfully eager to me."

Business accomplished, Jenny and Tony left.

"Drive you home?" he asked, head tipped to look sideways at her.

"I've got my car."

"Want to talk a minute?" he asked as he opened her door for her.

She hesitated. "I'm tired." She thought of Dora home alone, fretting over Abigail.

He touched her arm. "It's just . . . I want to talk. Not about babies, I promise."

She took a deep breath before nodding. She'd regretted the baby talk of the day before, feeling she'd taken a steam shovel and started digging herself a hole that might cave in on her. "Just a few minutes, Tony. I should get home."

He went around to the passenger side of her car and got in, pulling the door closed behind him. She rolled down the windows and looked out at the little town with tidy little streets radiating off from the front of the hospital. Lawns neat. Lives neat.

"Somebody doesn't want Abigail talking to you or your mother. I wonder why." Tony cleared his throat.

He nodded at nothing. "Let me bounce a couple of things off you."

He leaned forward, hands together between his knees. "Must be something important somebody doesn't want her talking to you about. Gotta be that box, don't you think? I mean, Aaron hid that key on Fida before the killer shot him. Worried enough to tape it to her collar. So the key and the box are at the center of all of this. And that's what the killer's hunting for."

Jenny listened, thought hard, then turned to him and almost laughed. "You know what, Tony? I feel like a puppet. Somebody's pulling my strings and laughing. It's got to be somebody here in town. Somebody who's known the family a long time. Somebody who knows the rest of us. Don't you think?"

"I'm stumped, and you'd think I could figure this thing out. Fifteen years on the force."

Jenny's cell rang. She dug it out of her bag and checked the caller ID. An Illinois call. Might be Ronald's attorney. Or hers. Or somebody she used to know in Chicago. Or some Chicago charity that wouldn't let her go.

She let it ring. Who it was felt insignificant. Too much old stuff hiding in the ring of a phone. It went to voice mail. Too curious, she pressed the button and listened.

"It's Ronald, Jen. When you get this, call me back. We desperately need to talk."

From Chicago, not Guatemala. "Desperately need to talk" meant something he was desperate about, not her. She wouldn't call him back. There'd been too many times she'd fallen for his neediness. He was out of her life. Gone. Sailed off to greener pastures—a lot greener than her pastures at the moment. She stuck the phone back in her purse.

"The ex?" Tony looked at her.

She rolled her eyes.

"Figured, from your reaction, it wasn't your mother."

She didn't say anything.

"Maybe you stole his favorite shot glass. I covered a case where a husband shot his wife over a set of souvenir shot glasses she broke deliberately. I think the glasses were from the Olympics or some wrestling match."

"No shot glasses." She had to smile. "I got an extra twenty dollars a month out of him in alimony. He probably wants it back."

Tony laughed. "Then I'm on his side. My ex got the house, the car, and about as much of everything else as she could think to ask for."

"Probably deserved every cent."

Laughing cleared away the stuff in her head, all those spider webs of shame and anger and disgust.

Tony touched the door handle. "I'd better get going. Let's talk later, okay? Between us, I know we can figure out who's doing this."

She nodded, then wanted to kick herself for letting him go.

* * *

Zoe was working in her front yard, cleaning out a garden, when Jenny drove in.

Her jeans were damp at the baggy knees. Her Spider-Man shirt was stained with dirt. Sweat circles ringed her underarms. The children's gardening gloves she wore were long past pink. Fida, asleep on the grass, lifted her head, opened her blind eye, gave up, and took no further notice of Jenny.

"I was cleaning out Eugenia's bed. Poor Eugenia. That was her name. A wonderful fairy who looked after all the others. Now she's gone, like Liliana, the fairy who was smashed beneath Adam Cane's head. She's charged with attempted murder and sitting in pieces on a shelf in the police department. The other fairies are inconsolable." Her eyes glazed with tears.

Jenny gave a sound of halfhearted sympathy.

Zoe bent to pull a weed. "Remember that the Duchess said to Alice, 'Everything's got a moral, if only you can find it.'" Zoe was clearly downhearted.

Jenny pricked up her ears. The very chapter she'd been reading. She smiled her Cheshire Cat smile. "'I quite agree with you and the moral of that is, "Be what you would seem to be"—or if you'd like it put more simply—"Never imagine yourself not to be otherwise than what it might appear to others that what you were or might have been was not otherwise than what you had been would have appeared to them to be otherwise."'"

Zoe tipped her head and gave Jenny a one-eyed look. "'I think I should understand that better. If I had it written down: but I can't quite follow it as you say it.'"

They gave a happy hoot, even though Jenny couldn't come up with the next line of the story.

"You are improving," Zoe congratulated her. "But you will never be me"

"How could I hope for such heights?" Jenny teased.

Zoe's face soon fell again. "How can I possibly find the moral here? The sweetest of the fairies taken up as a weapon. There's not one good thing to say about an act like that."

Jenny thought that Lilliana wasn't the only thing at stake here and not the only being whose pieces might have to sit in the police station.

"We've got to talk about the key." Jenny's voice was firm.

"You must find me a very unpleasant character. I mean, I don't seem to lay out the facts of life in rows as neat at carrots."

"Don't worry, I know the facts of life." Jenny was impatient.

"Well then, I'll change it to the facts of my own world."

"Let me tell you the facts of your world as of right now," Jenny said, taking a deep breath. "You're in big trouble, Zoe. You know it as well as I do. You're lucky that Johnny's thrown Ed off the scent for a while."

Zoe stared at her dirty tennis shoes. She toed the ground. "If there's anything you can think of . . . any reason someone would want to put this all on you, please tell me now."

"I have my thoughts."

"Like what?"

"Because I'm here. Because I lived next door to Adam. Because I didn't get along with him and somebody heard of our trouble and his or her brain went, 'Bam, now that's who I'll blame for the murders I'm about to commit.' Then when Abigail said she was coming to talk to you, the killer then thought, 'Why, what a great opportunity to get Zoe Zola, too. Just use one of those silly fairies to break Abigail's skull.' Presto! Zoe Zola's guilty. How could she not be? But incredibly stupid, of course, killing people in her own yard the way she did, and with her own little friends."

"Then whoever it is doesn't know you, Zoe. And maybe that's a good thing. If he doesn't know what that brain of yours is capable of, maybe we can get ahead of him."

Zoe peeled the small gloves from her hands. "I've been thinking that maybe the key goes to a box that holds documents. What kind of document would have stirred up all this trouble? I went back to imagining there has to be another will, but now that Abigail's a victim too, I've pretty much ruled that one out."

"Let's go back to all that stuff in the letter." Jenny pulled out one of the copies she'd brought with her and read through it. "'You boys can't cheat us anymore. I hear you've got what I'm after but you're hiding it. All three of you are cheating us, just like him. A pack of cheaters. Time's up on that. You cheated her way too long, and now you're cheating me.'"

"I've been thinking about that." Zoe stopped to yell at Fida, who, awake now, was making her way over to Adam's front grass.

"Isn't that closing the barn door after the horse is gone?" Jenny couldn't help asking as Zoe hauled Fida back to her own property. "You might as well let her pee there now. Nobody's going to come after her."

Zoe shrugged. "It's the principle of the matter."

"And what principle is that?"

Zoe thought hard, then sighed. "I don't have a single principle in my head at the moment to fit this particular occasion." She flicked her hand at Fida, sending her over to Adam's house. "No principle, Fida. Go do as you please."

She turned back to Jenny. "What was I saying?"

"You were thinking about the box and the key."

"Oh, yes. The brothers had the key and so probably had the box, too. They stole it or paid someone to get it for them. Maybe someone like Johnny." She took a quick look at Jenny. "Maybe that's what the 'you didn't get it fairly' means."

"The letter said there were three of them. We figured Abigail was in on it but I don't think so now."

"And that lets Johnny out of trying to get it back for her since she wasn't in on it to begin with. Abigail being the only one who benefited from the old man's will to begin with." Zoe pushed her headband back.

Jenny thought as Zoe called to Fida, making her way back from Adam's house, nose to the ground.

"We've got to get that key to a place safer than your house," Jenny said. "You've already had one break-in."

Zoe lifted her head. "It's all I've got. I can't let it go."

She lifted the shirt she wore and showed Jenny the small key, taped just beneath her bra, again with duct tape. "Do you think this is safe enough"

Jenny's eyes were huge. "Unless Christopher Morley ravishes you in New York."

"Sure you don't want Tony to keep it? After all, an ex-cop."

Zoe frowned hard. Her eyes narrowed. "Right now, I don't trust a soul on this earth. It's the tale of three, you see. 'Ah, cruel Three! In such an hour, / Beneath such dreamy weather, / To beg a tale of breath too weak / To stir the tiniest feather! / Yet what can one poor voice avail / Against three tongues together?' So you see? We're up against the 'cruel three,' who aren't the 'cruel three' at all. Victims. None of them the murderer. There they go!" She made a swishing movement with her hand. "Right out the window."

"You scare me, Zoe." Jenny said. "And even worse, I'm beginning to understand how you think."

As an afterthought, Jenny threw in, "You're coming to stay with us tonight?"

Zoe frowned, "And Fida, too?"

"And Fida, too," Jenny nodded, heading back through the pines out of Oz, or Wonderland, or wherever this place was she'd landed.

Chapter 43

In the morning, they all visited Abigail at the hospital: Jenny, Zoe, Penelope, and Tony, since Penelope believed there was strength in numbers and at least one of them might get in to see her.

"There are already two people with her," said a plump and tough-looking nurse seated behind the floor desk. "Sorry. You'll have to wait."

"Is one of the people with her a policeman?" Tony asked.

She shook her head. "The policeman's in the hall. There's one woman and one man with her. That's all I can say."

"Could you go back and ask Ms. Cane if she'll see us?" Tony leaned heavily against the desk, taking the weight off his bad leg. Jenny noticed him wince and hurt for him. Too much going on. Of course he would be hurting.

The nurse reluctantly agreed and left them behind to wait.

When she came back, Rudkers was with her, walking fast, arms swinging beside him. His face was anything but friendly.

"Mr. Rudkers is Ms. Cane's attorney," the flustered nurse tried to say.

"We know who Mr. Rudkers is." Jenny stepped up to meet him.

"You certainly do," Alfred sputtered. "And you've been told to leave Abigail alone. My next step is to have you barred from bothering her, if I have to obtain a restraining order. No visits. No phone calls. There have been two murders in her family. Now an attempt on her life. Personally, I think the whole group of you should be jailed."

Tony's face was the best cop face Jenny had seen on him when he stepped up nose to nose with Alfred. "Abigail was on her way to see Jenny, here, about something important. It wasn't Jenny or her mother who attacked her. And not Zoe Zola."

"We don't know that." Alfred leaned back and shook his head. "The killer used one of her fairies to knock her down with. Zoe'd never hurt one of those little people."

Tony turned to the nurse. "Did you ask Ms. Cane if she will see us?"

The nurse was flustered, caught in the middle of a dogfight. "I was asking when he interrupted."

Alfred narrowed his eyes. "Ms. Cane has a concussion. She is not aware enough to know the danger she is in. These people are not her friends. They may be involved in her brothers' murders. As her attorney—" He reared back and frowned as Carmen Volker came hurrying down the hall, shoes half-tripping her. The woman's eyes bulged when she saw who stood with Alfred.

"They won't allow them in with Abigail, will they?" Carmen demanded of Alfred, her eyes going from face to face.

Something very odd about those eyes, Jenny thought. *More intrigue than worry.*

Carmen's face wrinkled. "Abigail's in pain, you know. This isn't right. You people shouldn't be bothering her."

Carmen turned to Jenny. "Not right at all. Why do you want to torture poor Abigail this way? She's lost both her brothers."

Alfred left them, but only for a few minutes. He was back with a new nurse. A male nurse. A burly nurse.

"We want these people to go. They're bothering Ms. Cane. I'm her guardian now."

"Show me the guardianship papers," Penelope demanded, standing in Alfred's face. He backed away. His thin eyebrows shot up.

"Don't have them? Okay, show me your power of attorney."

Alfred frowned as the burly nurse shook his head. "I have to check with the patient anyway. Rules are rules."

"But you don't know—"

The nurse was on his way back down the hall.

When he returned, he said, "Ms. Cane would like to see her visitors. Two of them can go on back."

Alfred sputtered, but Tony and Jenny were off to Abigail's room, with Zoe and Penelope waiting behind.

*   *   *

Her head was still wrapped in bandages, but her face had color today. She sat up to greet her guests, though the welcome look quickly turned to confusion. Like the good hostess she'd been taught to be, she covered her dismay with a warm welcome.

At first there was the usual hospital talk: she was doing fine and no, she didn't need anything. Then Jenny asked when she would be getting out, and she answered, "Oh, not long. Not long. I'm hoping to go home today. I'm fine, you know. Completely fine. Except for this . . ." She touched the bandage on her head. "I suppose I've been hurt. But I don't remember a thing. Can you imagine . . . eh, you are?"

"Jenny Weston. Dora Weston's daughter."

Abigail smiled but couldn't cover that the name meant nothing to her.

"Well, you're all my guests, so please sit down. And please, what is the weather like today? Hot yet? Soon enough it will be fall, then winter, and we'll all dream of these warm and sunny days, won't we? And dream of things that used to be."

Alfred and Carmen stood in the hall, listening near the door. Abigail leaned around Tony and waved at them. "My good friends," she beamed, then looked puzzled. "Now what was I talking about? Oh yes, about things that used to be . . ."

She leaned back on the pillows, her eyes drooped then flew open.

"What was I saying? Oh, yes—things that used to be. A sin. A terrible vision."

She lowered her voice to near a whisper, then looked hard at Jenny. "Have you ever done something so terrible it cost you everything?"

Jenny didn't answer.

Abigail fixed her eyes on Tony. She let her eyelids drift slowly closed.

They waited. It was a few minutes until she opened her eyes and motioned them as close as they could get.

"I saw it all so clearly," she said with effort. "Just the way it was. I don't understand how a brain can get so twisted. I was in my thirties; I should have been onto him by then. So much a dream now. More than thirty years."

"I spied on my father one day." She glanced at them coquettishly; in her eyes Jenny could see the little girl. She put her fingers to her lips. "I often did, you know. I never married. All my curiosity was focused on an aging man who never loved me."

"Abigail! You should be resting," Carmen called from the hall.

Abigail shook her head, which made her wince and put a hand up to the bandages.

She put a finger to her lips and motioned Tony and Jenny even closer, so she could whisper.

"He didn't love my brothers, either. Nor my poor mother. My father hated and distrusted the world around him. Sad, don't you think, that he had children who wanted to love him and he couldn't stand the sight of us?"

She drew a few deep breaths.

"I dislike telling this to anyone. Now there's something . . . my brothers are dead. But let me go on. I need you to understand. People shouldn't do the things my father did."

She rested another minute, tuning out the voices calling to her from the hall.

"I filled my life with good works and tried to stay out of Father's way." She tried to lean up to be closer to her listeners. "But as I said, I spied on him. As often as I could. Especially when he was in his den. My little game. Often, when he came out he would be smiling. A thing so rare, it made me uncontrollably inquisitive."

She exhaled slowly. "One afternoon, he was sitting at his desk, but he'd left the door open, so I could see through the crack. A small wooden box, I'd seen it long before when I was spying. He sat at his desk with the box in front of him. He unlocked it with a small key on a chain he wore. He took out a sheaf of papers and read them one by one. He smiled. The papers gave him pleasure. When he was finished, he bundled the papers together, put them back into the box, and locked it with that little key. He took the box to the closet, climbed up on a chair, and set it on the shelf. When he was finished, he locked the closet. I scurried away before he came out of the room, but what had surprised me was that there were four papers this time, where I'd only seen three when I'd spied on him before. For weeks I couldn't get it out of my mind. I was so curious as to what could possibly give my father so much pleasure and be such a welcomed addition to his file.

"I would never have looked, not really, but I found that little key on the foyer floor one day. It must have dropped off his chain. I picked it up and held it in my palm. What a conflict in my nine-year-old soul."

She closed her eyes at the rising commotion near the door. A nurse had come to quiet Carmen and Alfred.

Abigail cleared her throat.

"Where was I?"

"You found the key to the box."

"Yes. Sneaky, I know. Reprehensible. Father was to be out all that morning. I couldn't help myself. I put a chair in the open closet and climbed up. I took the box down and sat on the chair. I opened the box and found many papers, not just the four I'd recently seen him gloating over. There were deeds to forest land we still own—which made me dream of being free to run through the trees. There were signed agreements and contracts I didn't understand. On top of the others were the folded sheets of paper that gave him so much pleasure.

"In my heart, I think I'd hoped they were our birth certificates—his three children. And maybe his wedding license. That would have been nice. He would have seemed to be a caring man even though he never showed his feelings for us. How I wished that I'd find something that made him human, something exposing a heart."

"What were those papers, Abigail? Did you find what you were looking for?"

She lay back and closed her eyes again. Jenny and Tony exchanged a look across the bed. They wondered if she was asleep, if they should wake her. Their fifteen minutes with her were almost up.

It was a few minutes more until her lips moved.

"I didn't read them, only unfolded them. I looked up, and he was standing in the doorway, watching. I had no place to hide. No place to quickly stash the papers and the box. I've often wondered . . ." She looked above their heads, back into a place no one should ever go. "I've often wondered if he left the key behind to test me."

She closed her eyes and this time dropped into a deep and soundless sleep.

Chapter 44

Zoe's little head was bent down into her hands. She sat atop a stack of thin phonebooks at Dora's table, surrounded by her friends. "Terrible. Awful. 'Oh what a tangled web we weave.'"

"Stick to *Alice*," Jenny complained. "I have enough trouble with one writer."

"I wonder if she suspects we have the key." Zoe looked around the table at the others who shrugged.

"We didn't get to ask her where the box was," Tony said. "She fell asleep and our time was up."

"Maybe tomorrow. If she goes home." Dora filled iced tea glasses around the table. "You have to ask her."

"My head hurts," Zoe said. "There's a gong inside my skull, swinging back and forth. Suitcase words: Key—a hard metal object. Key—a code to a secret. Key—the most important part of the problem."

"No." Jenny put up a hand. "Box. Box. Box. A receptacle for many things. A sparring match. A special place in a theatre. A small space with sides on it. A place for terrible secrets." Zoe nodded to herself.

"Now, let me think." Zoe screwed her face into a tortured grimace. "I think . . . I think . . . I think . . . it was about 'time.' Not really 'about time,' but it was a relative of time."

The others thought along, though Penelope checked her watch.

"'Time' as days and hours," Zoe said. "It's about 'time.' I don't have 'time.' I'm doing 'time.' Or . . ." She put a finger to the end of her nose and pushed hard. "It's a suitcase word, all right. When I try to recall why, the words wrinkle up and slide behind the Cheshire Cat, because I worked on him today. If only . . ."

She leaned forward over the table and put her head in her hands.

Fida snored under the table. A teapot whistled on the stove. White plates and polished silverware were set awaiting goulash and other wonders Dora promised to spring on them for lunch.

"You ask me, I think the poor woman suffered horribly at his hands," Dora said. "Maybe not because of the box and key, but because he was a terrible father. Go back to what she said, that he held it against her the rest of her life."

Tony stared into space before asking, "But what did she really say? Maybe it wasn't real. Maybe she made it up for some reason of her own. Her brain's pretty messed up."

"Pretty clear, if you ask me," Penelope snapped. "Joshua Cane laid a trap and punished her forever for falling into it."

She looked around the table, daring anyone to say any different.

"There was talk," Dora said. "There always is in small towns. Village sport, you know."

"What did people say?" Penelope pushed.

Dora leaned back and sighed. "It wasn't very nice."

"Mom!" Jenny said. "We are *so* beyond that!"

Dora took a deep breath. "None of this is decent to talk about."

Zoe touched the woman's nervous hand on the table. "Murder's not decent either."

Dora nodded. "Well, this is what I've heard over the years. First there was Joshua's wife. Her name was Abby. Abigail was named after her. She died in a . . . well . . . mental facility. People said Joshua put her there because she was depressed. But who could blame her? Talk was he had one mistress after another, sometimes invited them to the mansion. People said Joshua Cane was a cold man with a heart like Lake Michigan ice. The boys weren't quiet about how they felt. Despised their father. I never knew about Abigail though, that she had to live the way she did. After Joshua Cane died, people in town didn't like her much. They thought she kept the money from the boys somehow. Maybe talked the father into leaving it all to her."

She looked from face to face around the table. "We never know about people, do we? I mean, the whole family so superior. Maybe not the boys, but you wouldn't have called them the friendliest. Adam, mad at everybody all the time. And Aaron, a dear, sweet man, but so shy. Barely ever said a word, shuffling along in town, never looking up from his own feet. And that long hair of his. Couple of hippies, they were. That's what started the trouble with Joshua Cane. He was disappointed in his sons, is what I was told."

Jenny couldn't help but feel something monumental, almost biblical, had just been laid out. The family fighting each other and the father giving up the love of his daughter because she broke a rule. Was that it? *A rule?*

The room felt heavy, even dark. Jenny found herself wishing the facts behind the murders would just roll themselves out like a cleaned carpet and give them a road map leading from the past right up to the attack on Abigail.

Penelope pushed her chair back. "I've got to go. I'm out of time. No time for goulash. Thanks anyway."

Zoe sat up, eyes wide open. She bounced on her phone books. "That's it. Clang! Clang! Clang! Time. Time. Time. 'Time's up on that.' Where did I hear that before? 'Time's up on that.'"

For all her struggles, Zoe had brought forth only another riddle.

The unaccustomed ring of the doorbell broke the tension in the room.

Dora got up to answer, following Penny across the living room. When she came back, a man followed her into the kitchen.

At first Jenny didn't recognize him. Then she didn't want to recognize him, and when she did, she didn't want to introduce him to anyone: it was Ronald Korman.

She struggled up from her chair. "What in . . . ?"

He put his arms out to her, a look of joking sorrow spreading over his tanned face. "It's so good to see you," he said and tried to close his arms around Jenny, who pushed them forcefully away.

Ronald looked crushed.

He tipped his head and pursed his lips, letting his self-serving drama unfold as he stood in his patchwork Berluti shoes, his two-hundred-dollar jeans, and a blue Rag & Bone shirt, which was open at the throat.

Jenny ticked off the cost of his outfit in her head, well-schooled as she was in male couture. This wasn't a maximum effort. More something in the thousand-dollar range, which meant he was sorry but didn't want to overdo it.

Ronald's dark hair was freshly trimmed and combed. There was an outline of white around his Guatemalan tan. He put a pout in place—just for her because he thought it brought out the motherliness in every woman. He'd said as much once, not knowing that all she felt, the last few years, was a monumental disgust at his childish sulks. Now there was shame to go with the disgust—as he made it clear to everyone that she'd married a monumental ass.

"I forgot which house was yours." His arms were still out to Jenny. Disappointment crossed his face. "I went next door—what a strange place. All those fairies and houses. Must be quite the odd neighbor."

"You can say that again," Jenny answered, not daring to look at Zoe.

Not a man to grasp nuance, Ronald looked around the gathering, stopping briefly at Tony, his eyebrows going up, then moving on to Dora.

"Dora, dear. How good to see you."

He hurried to put his arms around a hunched-up turtle of a Dora, who buried her head and closed her eyes as Ronald kissed the rounded lump of her back.

He put his hands out to Jenny then dropped them when she didn't respond. "I've been calling. You haven't called back. I don't understand."

"Really?" Jenny lifted an eyebrow at him. "You don't understand why I don't call you back? Hmmm . . ."

No one offered him a chair. He leaned against Dora's range and crossed his arms over his chest. He glanced at Tony again, who was playing with a kitchen knife, testing it for sharpness in the palm of his hand.

Zoe sat straight up, smiling, waiting for a chance at him.

"Where's Chiquita? Or was it Tansy?" Jenny refused to introduce him and enjoyed the slight flush creeping up his cheeks. "I never can remember. Are you stopping on your way to Chicago? Or is this only a quick layover on the way back to Guatemala?"

Ronald threw his head back and laughed, not a hair on his head moving. "That madness is behind me. That's why I came looking for you." He gave a slowly circling look at the others. "But we have to talk. I mean alone. I think you've misunderstood . . ."

Tony leaned back and put his arms behind his head, one hand still holding the knife. He frowned as if an obnoxious car salesman had just dropped in.

"Really!" Jenny said. "Guess I misunderstood about the divorce?"

He laughed as if they shared a joke. "That's all in the past. I'm here now. And I have to get my practice up and running again. You understand. I could use your help, of course." He put a hand out to her. "Could we go somewhere, please, and talk? We can move beyond all this. We have before. And I'm sure these nice people would rather we air our laundry in private."

Zoe looked at Tony. Tony looked at Dora. Dora looked at Ronald.

"We're fine, dear," Dora said. "You're not bothering us."

Zoe said, "Air away."

Ronald hesitated, anger sparking briefly before he moved around to Jenny. With one hand on her bare knee, he squatted beside her. His voice fell to a whisper. "This is partially your fault. You know I always come back. You could've waited."

"Has Marmalade left you?"

He hesitated at the name, finally giving her his sweetest smile. "It was mutual. Guatemala was a terrible place. She had family there, but they didn't like me. And they were *poor*. Can you imagine? Lived with monkeys."

"Awful for you." Jenny smiled as she removed his hand from her bare knee. "But now you have to go."

She got up, took him by the arm, and pulled him awkwardly to his feet. With one hand on his back, causing rows of wrinkles across the expensive shirt, she prodded him toward the archway. They crossed the open rooms to the front door where he stopped to protest, asking if they could talk later. "I'm willing to hang around. Find a hotel . . ."

She smiled sincerely at the knowledge that she was free of him. There was a huge sense of kindness in her. "Oh no, Ronald. Go back to Chicago. The apartment's gone. The furniture's in storage—I forget where. Your office is closed. You'll have to begin again. But you're good at that."

"Why are you being so cruel?" He was genuinely hurt. His face showed pain. "I love you, Jenny. You knew that when I left."

She stopped for only a few brief seconds before shutting the door in his face.

He sang such a tired old song. The tune was fuzzy now, riddled with static. Jenny didn't think she'd ever be able to hear it again.

Chapter 45

She didn't wake up until the middle of the next day. She'd cried part of the night and wanted to laugh another part of the night. She finally fell asleep curled up with *Alice in Wonderland* tucked into the curve of her body.

Jenny slid her bare feet slowly to the wood floor, mouth open wide midyawn. It didn't seem real, Ronald showing up, with all the other things happening around her.

All she could hope was that he got the message and stayed away, though she doubted it. Ronald Korman might be her eternal penance. Nothing she couldn't handle and without a hair shirt. All that pain was gone, with only a minor hole in her psyche left behind.

"'You'll get over it.'" She laughed at herself, checking her bleary eyes in the dresser mirror. The voice was Zoe's. Pragmatic. Tough. Hardheaded.

The room was humid. It was a cloudy morning. Trees, beyond her windows, dripped from an early rain. Everything was so very green and polished. Mom was banging things in the kitchen—her idea of how to wake a slugabed.

Jenny smiled, then slowly unwound the sheet she was wrapped in and thought about a cup of hot tea and a muffin.

She could smell the muffins baking. Blueberry muffins were Mom's way of soothing a daughter's misery.

And it worked. Jenny felt better sitting at the table, bare knees drawn up in front of her, a large red mug of tea on the table, the half-eaten muffin leaving a trail of warm crumbs from the plate to her mouth.

"They say anything about Ronald?" she finally asked Dora, who was emptying the dishwasher.

"Who?"

"Tony. Zoe."

Mom shook her head, but said, "Didn't you think the man was a bit overdressed for Bear Falls? Zoe and Tony seemed . . . unimpressed."

"I bet." Jenny laughed, knowing she was being teased. "*Unimpressed.* I guess you could call it that. Or maybe *dumbfounded*'s a better word."

"Tony called an hour ago. He's coming at noon, after a meeting with a client. He said you've all got to get in Adam's house to search. Penelope and Zoe are joining in."

Jenny felt a sliver of ice run over her skin. Go to that house? Not what she wanted to face this morning, but there was no other place to turn. If anyone had that box, it would have been Adam or Aaron. Neither of the men knew he was about to die. Neither would have moved it.

"I'm glad Tony covered the Little Libraries with a tarp last night, before it started raining," Dora said. "He's going to leave it like that now until our party. People have been so kind. I'd like to repay everyone. But not yet." She sighed. "Not yet. Abigail will want to be there."

Jenny glanced toward the living room where some of the books were sorted, lodged in brimming crates and boxes, ready to go out when the time came.

"A party sounds like a great idea. Maybe Lisa would come home."

Dora waved an impatient hand. "I'd love to have her, but she's so busy. She'll come when she can." Dora heaved another sigh. "I hope it's soon, though. Things do go so much more smoothly when she's home."

Jenny felt the old catch at her throat. Just the teeniest touch of jealousy. She got up and put one arm briefly around Dora's waist. "I know they do, Mom. We'll make sure she's here."

*　*　*

Jenny was nearest to the phone and answered when it rang just before noon. The voice on the other end whispered something.

"I can't hear you," Jenny said.

"It's Abigail." The voice was still low, but huskier, solid.

"Oh, Abigail. I'm so happy to hear from you. How are you feeling?"

"I don't have time for that, Jenny. I'm still at the hospital. The doctor says I can go home tomorrow." There was a pause. "I'm afraid to go home, Jenny. But I'm also afraid to stay here."

"What can I do?"

"Find the box. Your little friend has the key. We need the box. I think I know everything but . . ."

There was a voice behind Abigail. She must have turned away to speak to someone.

When she came back, she said only, "I'm at the nurses' station. This is their phone. I'm not supposed to use it, the nurse said. I guess . . ." There was a long pause. "I'll call you when I get out of here. Don't come until I call."

"But Abigail, do you know where the box is?"

The phone was dead.

Chapter 46

The air was hot and stagnant in Adam's house with a faint whiff of rotting potatoes to it. The living room was small and spare, except that the chairs were knocked over and the cushions torn apart. The old sofa threw up stuffing. A mirror had been torn from the wall and smashed to the floor.

"He's been here," Tony said between clenched lips.

"Before or after he hit my house?" Zoe asked. She was dressed in old gardening jeans with patches at the knees. "My breaking-into-houses suit," she'd told them when they met on Adam's porch.

"Probably this was before he—or they—tried your house," Jenny said.

"So he's getting desperate. Unless it was hidden at Aaron's and is gone by now."

"Should we split up and look around?" Jenny asked, feeling uncomfortable in the murdered man's house. "We might be better at hunting than the killer was, you know."

Zoe's looked bothered. "I hope Adam's ghost isn't hiding around a corner. He'd be roaring at the sight of me in here."

"He's in the cemetery, Zoe. Won't be chasing anybody today." Tony, having had about as much as he could take of fairies and ghosts for one day, spoke in a very coplike voice. "We'll each take a room. Check out what we can. Look for any place a wooden chest could be hidden. If Adam had it, and the killer's still hunting for it, it's got to be here."

With their orders set, Zoe took the kitchen where every drawer yawned open. The refrigerator—door ajar—was still running, food tossed out to the floor.

Jenny went into Adam's bedroom. Dingy sheets, a bare pillow, and a striped featherbed lay in a tumble on the floor.

A single bureau, the only piece of furniture other than the bed, stood against one wall with the drawers pulled out, the contents dumped into a haphazard pile of yellowed T-shirts and old boxer shorts. Jenny went through the man's belongings, hardly touching them, moving things aside with one finger to see if there was something hidden beneath.

In the closet, a white shirt lay among old flannel shirts and plaid cotton shirts on the floor. Under the shirts, there were a couple pairs of tired-looking dungarees and a single pair of ancient, almost colorless dress pants, all dotted with impressive dust bunnies.

Jenny brought a wooden chair in from the kitchen and stood on it to search the top of the closet where there was a tipped-out cardboard box. Old bills and receipts from town stores and utility companies were scattered along the shelf. A photo album lay open behind the box. She pulled the album down to look through it. Images of the boys—little tykes in short pants to pale men in their forties. There were photos of the brothers standing beside the wall of a house they were building. The wood behind them almost gleamed with newness. Both men held hammers in their hands. Adam was dressed in dungarees and one of the striped shirts from the closet. Both wore do-rags wrapped around their long, gray hair. Neither man smiled.

She turned the page. Old photos of Abigail. Nothing more. Not a graduation picture. Not a posed photo with their father. No family pictures at all—though there were many empty places where photos must have been. She closed the sad album and put it back where she found it.

Nothing under the bed but a few empty boxes.

A promising suitcase leaned in a corner, but it was empty.

She knocked along the walls, hoping for a secret compartment.

There was no wooden box needing a small brass key in this room. She joined Zoe in the kitchen.

Zoe, working the lower cabinets, was doing no better. Jenny got on the chair and searched the upper cabinets. They were all empty.

Together she and Zoe stood in the middle of the room, circling, looking around and around. There was a cubbyhole beside the refrigerator, closed off with a faded curtain. Zoe pulled the cloth aside and stuck her head in, reporting that spice cans and some Campbell's soup cans lay within. The shelves were empty and very dusty. There was no place to hide anything.

"Adam's not the kind to have trusted a safe deposit box." Zoe looked around again as if a wooden box could be right in view—if only they knew where to look. Or how to look. "Where would *you* put a box if you wanted to keep it hidden?"

Nothing came to either of them.

"I checked the shed," Tony said, coming back in the house from the yard. "Empty except for old tools and a broken mower. A lamp. Oh, and an inhabited mouse nest. Maybe Adam rented storage space in Traverse City."

"A whole storage area for a single wooden box?" Jenny scoffed. "It's somewhere in here or he destroyed it."

"Or Aaron had it," Zoe said. "That's where the key came from and where I found the letters." She put two fingers to her forehead and thought deeply. "His house must've been ransacked by now." She paused. "I can't think of an answer. 'I wish I hadn't gone down this rabbit hole.' I truly, truly wish."

"'A riddle with no answer,' right?" Jenny felt nothing at having answered with a quote. Zoe's world was a dream storm heading for some far horizon. Her joy in all their back and forth was gone.

"You've got to stop quoting things you know nothing about." Zoe, as if understanding, stood up as tall as she could reach.

"And you've got to stop pretending we don't have a real and enormous problem on our hands. One that if we don't fix will land you directly in jail, no passing Go."

Jenny stood tall too, in imitation of Zoe's high dudgeon.

Tony cleared his throat.

"I saw some photos." Jenny returned to the job they were supposed to be doing. "There's a photo album in Adam's closet. Most of it's empty, but there's a picture of Adam and Aaron building a house together. You think it was Aaron's house?"

"Gave them a chance to build in a hiding place. Into a wall. Into the foundation. Under the floor. A hole left behind a cupboard."

Tony headed back out. "I'll call Ed. Tell him we're going over there to take a look around. Don't want to mess with whatever he's got going."

"This is getting too weird." Jenny walked out behind Zoe. "An old chest. Letters from a blackmailer. A key on Fida. And none of it has anything to do with you, Zoe. So you probably aren't the killer."

"That's right, Jenny." Zoe turned to clap her hands. "You are such a sharp lady. I'm so terribly impressed. You have a useable organ up there after all." She pointed at Jenny's head.

"And where is that usable organ of yours when we need it?" Jenny asked "You haven't smelled anything worthwhile in days."

Chapter 47

All Jenny could imagine was being alone, going somewhere her thoughts wouldn't constantly be fragmented. She grabbed her bathing suit and drove out to the Lake Michigan beach where she'd lost her virginity—though she didn't miss it.

She laid a towel on the sand and sat down to watch the water. The breeze was chilly, the way it got on northern evenings. Jenny shivered, rubbed her hands along her arms, and then ran everything from the last week through her head.

Not at all what she'd come home for.

Something had changed in her. To be honest, she thought it might be the possibility of Tony, the man she'd just told to wait five years for her. Or maybe something inside herself. Maybe the bravery of Zoe. The kindness of her mom. Even the inflexibility of Penelope. Or the détente between her and her sister.

The thought of all of them made her smile. Friends. Friends who'd made faces when Ronald was there. Friends who gave her space to learn what she felt for Johnny.

Friends.

Friends like Tony.

The beach was empty. It wasn't a weekend, when sunbathers gathered. And it was almost dinnertime. Not dark enough for lovers.

She walked into the water, surprised how warm it was. A good swimmer, she swam straight out, then turned to swim parallel to the beach, stopping to look at the horizon, the shadowed hills, the white ribbon of sand.

She wiped hard at her skin when she got out and huddled in a towel on the beach to think.

Everything was coming together, though she hadn't quite figured out what "coming together" really meant. These murders had nothing to do with Zoe, that was obvious to her worst detractor by now. And they had nothing to do with Johnny. He was an alcoholic, a cheat, a philanderer, a user . . . but he wasn't a murderer.

She leaned back, hands in the soft sand behind her. Everything that had ever happened to her started with this lake, with looking out at spaces that went on forever, unlike all the good things in her life.

She and Johnny had made love on this beach. She still couldn't take that lightly. But the babies were Angel's. The grown man was Angel's. Her Johnny was lost behind drunken eyes. Her Johnny was tangled in anger and something deeper. Something so much worse.

A car pulling into the parking lot up the sand hill surprised her. She couldn't make out the person getting out but watched, worried because there was no one else on the beach—in either direction. A figure stood atop the hill looking down at her.

She put a hand up to see better. A woman picked her way down through grasses and deep sand. Halfway to Jenny, she lifted her hand to wave.

Cindy Arlen. Johnny's mother. A woman she barely saw anymore. She came down the hill with her arms waving, feet slipping in the sand.

"I was coming to see you," Cindy said when she reached Jenny. "You pulled out just as I got there. I was going to leave you alone . . . sorry to disturb—"

"Oh no. You want to sit down?"

The woman wasn't dressed for beach sitting. She wore a blue pantsuit. Maybe she'd just come from the nursing home where she worked.

"I . . . I . . ." Cindy looked around as if a rock or blanket might appear where she could sit but had to settle carefully beside Jenny, brushing at the pants she wore, pulling the pant legs up to keep the edges from the sand.

"I wanted to talk to you, and Dora, too. But Dora wasn't home."

"About Johnny?" Jenny stared out at the water where gulls rode small waves. Low sun blinded her.

Cindy tipped her head up and away from Jenny.

"I didn't know." Cindy's words were haunted. "I swear to you, Jenny. They never told me anything."

Startled, Jenny leaned away.

"What are you talking about? Do you know who killed Adam and Aaron? You should go talk to Ed, not me."

She shook her head. "Gerry came home. He said he wants it stopped."

Jenny left the words alone. Left them hanging in the air.

"I have to tell your mother. He said he can't do it."

"Are you talking about my father?" A shock ran through her. "Was it Gerry?"

Cindy couldn't answer. Jenny couldn't ask again.

Finally, Cindy nodded. "It was an accident." Cindy's voice broke. She hesitated over her words as if she could change them halfway out.

"He could have called someone."

Nothing came for long minutes.

"I wanted you to know mostly so you'd understand what happened to Johnny."

"What happened?" Jenny wanted to explode at this woman. "He barely spoke to me all that summer when my family was hurting so badly. Johnny'd been the rock of my life . . ."

Jenny couldn't say another word.

"Johnny wasn't there. He'd didn't have any part in it. Only, Gerry begged him to help. That's his brother, Jenny. What could he do?"

Jenny didn't answer.

"They got Gerry's car out of town and junked it. Johnny got him to Chicago. Left him there. When he came back, he couldn't face you, that's what he said. And you were suffering with your own pain. By the time you two met again, you were out of his life, and Angel was in it. I never understood what happened. If they'd only told me . . ." Cindy bowed her head. "I swear to you, Jenny. I never knew."

"Gerry won't talk to my mother? Give her that much satisfaction?"

"He can't. Just can't bring himself."

"What about Johnny?"

Cindy shrugged. "I hope there's that much good left in him. But I don't know."

"I'll tell her. I hope she calls the police and gets them put in jail."

"I hope she won't."

"That's why you're telling me? To get my mother to forget it happened?"

"Of course not. Whatever she has to do, she'll do. They both came to me. I don't know why now, but Gerry doesn't look well. There could be more he's got to tell me. I don't know. Johnny and I talked, too. He wanted you to understand what happened. He could never explain. Maybe if he hadn't gone with Angel . . . but who can tell? He drank heavily all that summer."

Jenny had trouble catching her breath.

Cindy, hands tight around her knees and staring out at the water, went on, "Angel's not a bad wife, and she loves her kids. I think she tries her best, but Johnny's not an easy man . . ."

"He was with Deanna Moon when he broke up my mother's library."

Cindy nodded. "I won't make excuses for him. He chose his own path. I think, though, it was because he heard you were coming home. He knew he couldn't see you or talk to you. He took his anger out on something else your mother loved."

Jenny took a deep breath. She wanted Cindy gone. She wanted Johnny gone.

"You know Johnny's not who he would have been with you."

Jenny said nothing. Waves, like old, ugly sins, ate the sand under her feet.

"I'll go back with you to tell Dora."

Jenny got up from the towel and brushed sand from her shorts and legs.

"No thanks. I think I want to talk to Lisa first. She was hurt as much as everybody else."

Cindy got up. "I lost both my boys," she said, palpable pain in her voice.

Jenny wanted to scream at her that she didn't care. Only the terrible fact that Gerry Arlen killed her father was important.

She couldn't.

She ran up the hill to her car and locked the doors as if Cindy Arlen might try to get in with her.

She drove home, parked, and sat still for the next hour. She had no tears left for any of them.

Johnny was finally gone, just like that—a dark hole where he used to be.

Chapter 48

Fida barked from Jenny's front porch. Zoe sat there alone, waiting in a rocking chair.

"Your mom went to bed."

"Anything wrong?" Jenny asked and fell into the chair beside her.

Zoe rocked. "Ed's questioning Johnny Arlen again. I think it's a last-ditch effort. He doesn't know who the real killer is."

"That's good. I mean about Johnny." She was too tired to care.

"You ever think that maybe it's not a man at all? Could be a woman. I would have thought Abigail for sure if somebody didn't attack her right out there." Zoe jabbed a stiff finger toward the street then turned to look at Jenny.

"You seem . . . funny tonight," Zoe said.

"I'm not *funny*."

"Anything happen you want to talk about?"

Jenny shook her head. "Nope."

"Suit yourself. I saw Tony and Penelope. We're going out to Aaron's house first thing. Ed actually said he was glad for our help. I can't get it out of my head why the killer didn't find the box. He must have searched Aaron's place by now."

"Maybe he found it after all."

"Doubt it," Zoe said.

"Then why hasn't Abigail's house been searched? Someone tried to kill her, same as they did the boys. Abigail might be in the hospital, but Carmen Volker lives there, along with a few servants. No break-in there."

They listened to June bugs crash against the screens. An occasional mosquito buzzed their heads and moved on. The pines, nothing but a line of ragged silhouettes, moved slightly in a warm, southern wind as they sat in the quiet of early night.

After a while, Jenny thought Zoe was asleep and got up slowly. She needed rest. And some real understanding of what makes a man a coward. What allows him to leave another man to die? She hated Gerry, but she couldn't remember the real Johnny well enough to hate him, too. Everything about him was gone.

In midtiptoe toward the house door, Zoe sat up and stopped her, "Something happened tonight, Jenny. Maybe I can help."

"You'll only quote nonsense at me."

"It's not always nonsense, you know," Zoe said after a while. "Sometimes the most magnificent sanity sounds illogical at first."

"I went to the beach." Jenny held on to the doorjamb, talking without turning. "Cindy Arlen found me there." She turned now. "Gerry Arlen killed my dad. He came back to Bear Falls to confess but can't face us. Johnny knew about it and covered for him."

Zoe had not a single word to say. Nothing came out of her—bright or dull.

"I have to tell Mom. But I want to talk to Lisa first. She's a part of this, too."

"There are no 'parts,' Jenny," Zoe finally said. "There's only one ugly secret to tell."

Jenny took a deep breath that was half a moan. "I don't want to hurt her all over again."

And then she sat down and told Zoe about the phone call from Abigail.

Chapter 49

The weeds in the clearing were taller and drier, the sun was hotter than it had been the day they found Aaron's body.

Zoe, in the backseat of Jenny's car, next to Penelope, shivered. "Wish we didn't have to go in there again."

"But we do." Tony got out of the car. The others followed.

Jenny hesitated. She needed to tell her mother about Gerry but couldn't yet. There was too much going on. Dora had been hurt from so many directions over the last few months. Nothing felt secure around them anymore. Attacks were coming from all sides. She didn't want to hurt her mother any more than she had been. But she had to know. Sometime soon, when her cowardly daughter got up the nerve.

Penelope was looking around the clearing when Jenny joined the others. Penny had dressed for the outing in old jeans and a white T-shirt. She'd braided her lank hair and wrapped a red scarf around her forehead. She looked ready for scrambling in dirt or for a fight with a killer—or for anything that came her way: stiff, know-it-all Penelope.

"Think this is worth our time?" Zoe asked, a little of everybody's nervousness rubbing off on her.

Nobody answered, all intent on the house and what might be in it.

"Looks like a sarcophagus, you ask me," Zoe said, hanging back behind the others.

Tony pulled away the long, loose boards used to secure the house from the door, throwing them to the ground behind him. Jenny stepped easily through the open door into the long room where they'd found Fida alive and Aaron dead.

Zoe, behind Jenny, caught her breath. Penelope stepped in just as Tony swore. Nothing was in its place, or upright, or in cupboards where things belonged. The floor was littered with debris. The chair, where Aaron had been sitting when he died, was gutted, foam stuffing thrown around as if a storm had blown through.

"Would the police do this?" Jenny asked, looking around.

Penelope swallowed a comment and watched where she stepped.

"Look." Tony pointed to where the kitchen stove had been pulled from the wall and overturned. Behind the stove, a hole was cut in the wall. More holes were sawed in other walls. Holes in the floor were left gaping.

The searcher before them had done a good job.

"Bet this wasn't the police," Tony said. "Ed would have warned us."

Jenny couldn't concentrate; she could barely bring her mind back to murder or a mythical box.

She desperately wanted to call her mother, needing to hear her voice to make sure she was okay, wherever she was that morning. They'd hardly spoken ten words to each other at breakfast. It was as if Dora intuited something and had shifted back to that terrible place she retreated when Jim died. That was the place where she'd pulled away from the people who loved her and left her bewildered daughters to wonder if life would ever be the same again. Then the next summer came and the garden came alive and Dora thought about eternity. That summer, Dora dared to love life, and the people around her, again.

Jenny'd called Lisa first thing that morning and left a message for her to call back. She wasn't going to let it go on one more day. If Lisa called back or not, she would tell Dora who killed her husband by that evening.

But not now. Not this moment, she told herself, and fell in line behind the others, zigzagging through the mess and around the holes and into the bedroom.

Here the damage was even worse. Nothing of the mattress remained. The box spring was ripped open, bare springs poking out. The small closet was emptied of pants and shirts and the winter jacket, tossed back as if over a maniac's shoulder. Boxes were ripped apart and their contents of papers and old junk tossed everywhere. More holes had been cut into the walls and floor. There was hardly a square foot that hadn't been touched.

"He must have found it. This much damage . . ." Zoe whispered as she stood behind Tony and Penelope. "Or 'her.'"

"If the box was even here." Tony shook his head and looked around.

"Aaron had the key and taped it to Fida's collar," Penelope said. "I can't get that out of my head. We've got to keep looking."

"There's probably nothing." Jenny stood behind them in the middle of the main room, hands at her hips. "Maybe it was all a terrible joke Joshua Cane set in motion. A promise to someone. A hint at riches to come. A lie to ruin his children's lives from beyond the grave."

Zoe, standing in front of the blackened woodstove, wasn't listening. She opened the squeaking door to nothing but dead ashes. The black pipe snaking to a hole in the wall had been pulled away and left to dangle, ashes trickling out when the floor and walls shook.

Zoe bent to run her hands over the base—three bricks high, built of pink and white reclaimed bricks. With her fingernails, she picked at the mortar holding the bricks in place. It came away easily. She scraped some more.

Without a word, Jenny joined her, kneeling and picking at the mortar until large pieces fell from between the front bricks. Tony joined them—using a knife he found in the kitchen. Penelope stood behind them, watching closely.

No one said a word. They gouged and picked and brushed until the front four bricks were loosened, only bits of mortar holding them in place.

Zoe stuck her fingers under one of the bricks and worked at it until it came loose. She set it on the floor behind her.

She attacked the next brick. Jenny sat back to watch. Tony helped Zoe, poking with the knife until the next brick came loose, too. They pulled it away.

Penelope knelt on the floor to watch.

They pulled brick after brick away until there was a large opening. Zoe leaned forward to peer into the dark place beneath. She sat back and looked from Jenny to Tony, her eyes huge. "I think there's something in there," she said.

It was Jenny who stuck her bare hand into the hole they'd made—no thoughts of spiders or other crawling things. She felt around the hole until she found the smooth surface of what lay inside toward the back of the space. Wiggling her hand, she got ahold of the item and pulled it out.

A plain box, dust and mortar coating the wood surface except for where Jenny's fingers left clean places.

Jenny was disappointed. Nothing but a plain box, after all. Flat on top, not humpbacked. The wood was darkened with age and covered with scratches. A wooden handle was set in the flat top. On the front was a brass keyhole.

Jenny set the box on the floor and took in a long, strangled breath.

"My God," Penelope said. "What do you know? It's real."

Jenny couldn't turn her eyes away. "So ordinary . . ."

Tony looked at Zoe. "Did you bring the key?"

She nodded. She pulled her shirt up and pulled the duct tape away from her skin, tape and key falling into her hand.

Zoe was about to put the key in the lock when Jenny held up her hand, her body saying what she felt.

"No," Jenny said to Zoe. "It's not ours."

"We found it." Zoe was ready for battle.

There was something going on inside her that Jenny couldn't name. "Call Abigail."

Zoe opened her mouth to object, looked hard at Jenny's face—remembering—then pushed the key down into her pocket.

Chapter 50

Jenny called her mom from the car on the way back from Aaron's house.

The phone rang a long time. She expected the answering machine and had a new message ready. Dora answered on the fifth ring, out of breath.

"Mom?" Jenny demanded. "Oh, Mom. I'm so happy to hear your voice."

"Well, I'm happy to hear yours, too, Jenny. The trouble is, I can't talk right now. I have visitors."

"I didn't know you were expecting anyone."

"I wasn't. It's Johnny Arlen, of all people. He and his brother, Gerry, are here. They dropped over to see me."

"Oh, Mom. You have no idea . . ."

There was a long pause.

"I think I do, Jenny."

When Jenny said nothing back, Dora asked, "What do you want me to do, dear? They both have paid with their lives. What more can I get from them?"

Dora quietly hung up.

Jenny said nothing to the others.

When they were almost to town, Tony called the hospital and asked if he could talk to Abigail.

He looked over at Jenny as he said "Thank you" to the person on the phone.

"You okay?" he asked after he clicked off.

She said nothing. Any kindness right then could dissolve her. All of that would have to wait.

He turned to the others. "Abigail's not there," he said. "She went home."

"Let's go to her house," Zoe said. "Right?"

"I've got the feeling I should call Ed." Tony looked worried.

"And tell him exactly what?" Penelope asked from the backseat. "We've got nothing but the box. And that belongs to Abigail."

They agreed to get to Abigail's house and put an end to all of it.

Chapter 51

The Cane mansion stood high on its hill of grass and trees, a ship captain's house like so many in Northern Michigan towns: a widow's walk and turrets. Everything around the house was summer still: trees barely moving and geraniums blooming in perfect pots set in perfect places—all of it looking fake.

Three cars stood in Abigail's drive.

"She's not alone," Tony said.

"That's what I was afraid of." Zoe climbed out, stumbling over Penelope then hurrying toward the front door.

Tony pulled out a shopping bag he'd found in the trunk and handed it to Jenny.

Jenny couldn't move at first. Her instinct was to get home as soon as possible. Mom had nobody there with her. There was no knowing what Johnny and his brother would say. It felt like leaving Dora alone to drown.

Still, what was ahead of them here could clear up so much. And maybe put an end to what everyone was going through.

She took the bag and set the wooden box inside. She followed the others up the walk to the mansion door, stopping only when Zoe had an uncontrollable bout of sneezing and had to pinch her nose to stop it.

* * *

As they'd expected, Carmen Volker opened the front door. She peered out, holding the edge of the door with two hands. Her plain face showed alarm. "Ms. Cane is just out of the hospital. She can't see anyone."

The woman's voice was high and alarmed. Her eyes were slightly bugged. She started to close the door on them.

"We'd like to talk to her." Tony pushed back, taking Carmen by surprise.

Jenny, holding the precious bag, stepped back out of the way.

"How dare you? Ms. Cane says she doesn't want to see people."

Zoe stuck her head in as Tony pushed the door wider. "Ms. Cane!" she called. "Ms. Cane!"

"In here," a faraway voice called back. "In the library."

Tony gave Carmen a look that dared her to object.

"We're coming in," he said as Zoe, Penelope, and Jenny pushed around him and headed down the wide hall.

Carmen stumbled behind them, complaining as they called Abigail's name again and ran toward her voice.

They turned along another hall and then hesitated outside an ornately carved door. Tony put his ear to the door. He was about to knock when Zoe, after giving him a disgusted look, pushed him aside, opened the door, and hurried in.

"I'm calling Alfred," Carmen screamed behind them. "You aren't allowed . . ."

She pulled a cell phone from the pocket of her misshapen dress.

The four of them stepped into the shadowy, high-ceilinged room. Penelope, clearly awed, stopped to look nervously at the darkened bookshelves covering all four walls. Chairs and reading tables and unlighted lamps stood around the room as if a throng of readers might walk right in.

It was a dark, unwelcoming room. There was nothing of the cheerful sickroom to the place.

"Over here," Abigail said, her voice weak, one arm up, hand waving from an overstuffed chair drawn close to the cold fireplace.

Jenny was the first to reach her, to kneel beside the chair and swallow her shock at the woman's drawn face. Her eyes were barely focused.

"I thought you were going to call when you got out."

Abigail leaned forward, her hand trying to grasp Jenny's. "I remembered . . ."

"Alfred's coming," Carmen insisted behind them. "Abigail's not to be disturbed. Alfred said none of you have any business being here. The doctor has ordered that she be kept perfectly quiet."

They ignored her. "What's going on?" Jenny bent toward Abigail.

"I remembered . . ." She looked up with unfocused eyes.

"Remembered what?" Zoe asked.

"My next phone call will be to the police." Carmen got loud as she tried to thrust her body between the visitors and Abigail, knocking Zoe aside as she pushed through.

Zoe, expanding like a blowfish, pushed back, sending Carmen staggering away.

Jenny took that moment to put the package she carried under Abigail's chair, out of sight.

Penelope, her skinny body drawn up into a dart, bent over Carmen. "The police chief told us to check on her. You better stay out of our way."

Carmen scurried back, eyes wide open. She put a hand to her mouth and looked from face to face.

Jenny, ignoring Carmen and the others, took Abigail's hand in hers. "What do you remember, Abigail?"

The woman shook her head. "I . . . they've given me so many shots . . ."

"Try."

"I remembered why I was coming to your house." She looked into Jenny's face. "I think . . . it was about . . ." She stopped talking and shook her head. When she was in control again, she searched Jenny's face. "It was about my brothers' money."

"Money?" Jenny looked skeptical. "Your brothers didn't have any money."

Abigail almost smiled. Her mind was clearing. "Of course they did. They wouldn't take it . . . something they held against our father. Refused, even after his death. I never understood, but my brothers were very principled men, you know. Even if those principles were often misguided. They were obstinate while my father lived and worse after he died."

She stopped to gather strength. "I never understood their actions, so I put the money into bank accounts for them despite their refusals to take it. I always thought there might be a day when they would change their minds."

She lay back and rested. With one limp hand, she rubbed at her forehead.

"Do you want to get out of here?" Jenny asked.

Abigail smiled. "I can't. They won't let me . . . Alfred's too busy hunting for something. I hear him hour after hour . . ."

Carmen tried again to breach the wall Zoe, Jenny, Penelope, and Tony formed around the woman. "That's enough of that. Time for an injection, Abigail. You're rambling."

Carmen tried smiling as she spoke to Abigail.

No one paid her any attention.

"What was it that turned them against your father?" Jenny asked. "You said 'after his death.' What happened then?"

Abigail blinked, seeming to have forgotten what she was saying. After a short while, her eyes opened wide. "Nothing that I knew of. But there is something else. My reason for coming to your house, Jenny."

Jenny took her icy hand and held it tight.

"I went into the bank the other day. Before everything got so bad. It was about the boys' money. I was going to take it out, write a check to each, and have it over with. They lived like paupers for absolutely no good reason. They needed new cars. They needed better houses. I was sick and tired of their stubbornness."

"Did they take the checks?" Penelope asked.

Abigail blinked up at Penelope, trying to recall who she was. She shook her head. "There was almost nothing left in either bank account when I got there. Where there should have been at least a few million, there were only a few dollars."

"They must've changed their minds. They took it out themselves," Jenny suggested.

Abigail shook her head and closed her eyes at the pain. "When I got back home, I went through the books. I rarely looked at them. I didn't have to. Alfred had found me such competent people for things like that."

"What was in the books?" Zoe leaned close, then jumped back at the sound of a loud male voice behind them.

"What on earth do you four think you're doing in here? This woman's ill." Alfred, behind them, stood with his hands on his hips, shoulders pushed forward.

Abigail ignored the man and put a clawing hand out to Tony. "Stop him, please. I remembered something else," she said. "I remember who attacked me."

"You're all getting out of here," Alfred grabbed Tony by his arm, pulling him backward, off balance. He next grabbed Zoe, pushing her aside, and then reached for Penelope, who swatted back at him. He reached for Jenny. She struck the man's hand hard, forcing him to let go of her.

"Time's up on this nonsense! You're all nothing but a pack of lying, grasping cheaters. You've got to go. This in unconscionable. *This* is a very sick woman here."

Zoe let out a sudden whoosh of air and pointed a wildly shaking finger at Alfred. "There it is!" she cried.

She looked at the others. "He's fallen into my portmanteau! Time. Time. Time. It's him. Oh, it's him. He wrote the letters to the boys."

Blank faces met hers.

"Don't any of you get it? 'Time.' 'Time's up on this.' Am I the only one who pays attention? 'Time's up on that,' the letter says. And 'A pack of cheaters.' A suitcase word to pack a lot of people in." She pulled the letter from her jeans pocket and began to read.

"'You boys can't cheat us anymore. I hear you've got what I'm after but you're hiding it. All three of you *are* cheating us, just like him. A pack of cheaters. Time's up on that. You cheated her way too long, and now you're cheating me. I'll get it, you know. One way or the other . . .'"

Alfred screamed and pulled the letter from her hands. "Get out! All of you. You are doing damage to Miss Cane. There will be a lawsuit. I'll guarantee it."

Zoe hunched her shoulders, drew herself up as tall she could stretch, and went on talking to the others.

"You see? 'The three of you.' Three tongues together. I've told you this before. Abigail, Adam, and Aaron."

"I'd forgotten," Abigail stared at Alfred. "Adam brought the letter to show me, and then I didn't see it again."

"'*All three of you are cheating us, just like* him,'" Abigail repeated from memory. "Oh, but we weren't, you know. We never cheated anyone, if that's what this is all about. My father tried many times to get the boys and me to sign papers we knew were false. Once he demanded I change the name on a deed. I wouldn't and paid dearly for it—as I always did. He wasn't an honest man." She looked at the faces around her. "But my brothers and I cheated no one."

"This 'him' . . ." Zoe tapped the paper. "He's your father?"

"It has to be. He hurt so many."

"And this 'I'? That's you, Alfred?" Penelope turned slowly toward him.

Alfred's thick hair stood up on his head. He looked wild and dangerous. "Of all the preposterous . . ."

Tony watched Alfred closely. The man's eyes were crazed.

Tony turned away and signaled something to Jenny. "Maybe we better get out of here." His loud voice was toneless. "The man's right. We have no—"

Abigail gasped and put out a hand. "Don't leave me alone with . . ."

Tony snapped his head around at the women. "Let's go," he ordered.

"Are you crazy?" Penelope said, unwilling to move from Abigail's side.

Tony pulled Jenny by the arm and grabbed Zoe. He shot a look at Penelope, who sputtered but, seeming to read something in Tony's face, followed, not without protest.

At the door to the library, Tony turned back to Alfred, who followed close behind, smiling oddly.

"Could I talk to you for a minute? I'm an old cop, you know. Got a question."

Alfred made a face and seemed about to refuse. After a few thoughtful seconds, he nodded and stepped over to stand closer to Tony. He sniffed. "What is it now?"

Tony kept his smile until the man stood in front of him. He reached forward, as if about to shake Alfred's hand, but instead grabbed his arm and twisted it—bringing a pained howl from him.

"Take your hands off me," Alfred screamed. He kicked at Tony, who secured his arm tighter, then swiveled the man around, pushing the arm as far up Alfred's back as he could go.

At Alfred's high scream, Carmen scurried up behind Tony, beating at his back.

Zoe grabbed Carmen's dress, heard a satisfying rip, and pulled with all her might.

Jenny was about to dive in and grab anybody she could grab when Tony yelled to her.

"Get his gun! Holster. Left side."

Jenny did as she was told, moving around to reach inside the jacket of the writhing man. His free arm hit out at her with as much force as he could muster.

She got a hand inside his jacket and felt the holster.

"Get away from me!" Alfred screamed and squirmed. "You don't know who I am."

Jenny pushed Carmen off and pulled the gun from the holster. She stepped back, gun held in both her hands, and pointed it at the group centered around Alfred.

"Not at us," Tony yelled at her as surprised noises came from Abigail behind them and tortured screams came from Carmen.

"Please!" Carmen begged and tried to pull their hands off Alfred. "Don't hurt him. He has a right!"

Ed and his two deputies ran in with their guns drawn. It didn't take long for the group to fill Ed in, falling over each other to describe what took place, that Alfred was the killer with help from his mother, Carmen.

"Mother?" Ed stood back and looked from one harried face to the other.

Alfred, standing in handcuffs between the two officers, ranted at all of them, one direction to another. He spewed the worst of his venom on his cowering mother.

Abigail, a single hand in the air, struggled up from her chair and over to confront the man she'd made a trusted advisor on Carmen's recommendation. "What did you want, Alfred? Why couldn't you come to me and ask?"

Alfred's eyes had closed to slits. He licked at his lips.

"Tell her." He spat the words at Carmen, her arm held tight by Ed.

"Tell her who I am, Mother." Alfred snarled the word.

Carmen looked over at Abigail, a hand out, pleading. "I didn't mean . . ."

"What a liar!" Alfred laughed, then turned to the surrounding circle. "She's the one who found me. She called me to come here. Said I could get millions."

"But you did, Alfred. You did get millions, just as I promised. You got the boys' money." Carmen stood taller, her eyes only on Alfred. "That's what I meant. That's all I meant. Money that was doing no one any good. You shouldn't have wanted everything."

Alfred's voice bloated with anger. "*You* are irrevocably stupid. Joshua Cane walked all over you. I wish to heaven I'd known he was my father when he was still alive. Mean, sick bastard. I'd have fixed him."

Abigail, beginning to take in what they were saying, choked out a single word. "Father?"

Carmen folded in on herself as if she'd been kicked.

Alfred spit out, "You're pathetic. Ruined your own life. Now you've destroyed mine."

"I didn't mean . . ."

Jenny took Abigail's arm to help her back to her chair. Zoe took her other arm.

"Carmen?" Abigail looked at the woman who'd been her only friend. "Who are you?"

Chapter 52

When Ed and the others were gone, Abigail sat in the chair by the fireplace, where Tony built a small fire to warm the room.

Jenny set the wooden box in her lap.

Abigail's hands hovered above it as if she didn't dare touch the thing.

"I feel like Pandora. Should I open this box of evil?" She looked around, trying to smile but failing.

Jenny, worry crossing her face, leaned close to Tony. "Maybe it's too soon," she whispered.

"She won't be free until she knows," he whispered back.

"This is what it's come to." Abigail resolutely set both hands on the wooden lid. "Where did you find it?" she asked Jenny.

"Hidden in Aaron's house," Jenny said.

Abigail smiled. "Dear Aaron. He would have wanted to protect me. They opened it when he died, as Father knew they would, but refused me access, saying only that the man wasn't who we thought he was, meaning, I suppose, he was exactly who we thought he was. Adam wouldn't touch his money after that. Aaron wouldn't either. Didn't want anything to do with him.

Adam was going to change his last name—but for my sake, he didn't. People would be curious."

"When you open it, you're going to find things you might not want to know," Jenny warned.

"What could be worse than what he did to my mother? She was never mentally ill. She didn't have to die in a mental institution. She was depressed, for good reason." Abigail sat up straighter, some of the old Abigail coming back. "Alfred stole from us and murdered my brothers. He tried to kill me outside your house—I remembered seeing him. But more than that, he wanted this . . . thing. I have to finally know what's in here."

Jenny backed off.

"Do we also have the key?" She looked from face to face, a lot of the dowager running up her straight spine.

Zoe pulled the key from her pocket and set it into her hand.

"And which of my brothers had this?" She held the key up.

"Aaron," Jenny said.

"Of course. Adam couldn't be trusted not to blow up and give everything away. Poor Adam. How he hated Father. What a sweet brother Aaron was. He buried that hatchet in Adam's yard, you know, in the spirit you would imagine he'd bury a hatchet. To make peace with his brother."

She lowered her head and closed her eyes for a minute before turning the key and opening the box.

She reached inside and brought out four sheets of paper lying atop what looked to Jenny, standing behind her, like deeds and other documents—bits of a gold seal showing on one.

Abigail frowned at the folded papers in her hand.

"This is it?" she asked. "This is what Father hated me for? Why Alfred and Carmen killed my brothers?"

She unfolded the papers and slowly began to read. First the top sheet, which, from where Jenny stood, looked like a legal paper—signatures at the bottom, dated below that.

Abigail read slowly, set that one aside, and read the next.

And then the next.

And the last.

She put the papers in her lap. "My father was a monster." She could hardly speak.

No one else said a word.

Abigail took a deep breath.

"Alfred *is* my father's son. There are three others—a girl and two boys. My father gave their mothers money and made them sign these documents guaranteeing they would never contact him again and never ask for more money. Not for themselves or for their children." She took a deep breath. "These women must have been his mistresses, the women I only surmised he kept in Traverse City. My mother knew. She had to."

She handed the four contracts to Jenny, who shared them with the others.

Zoe read and looked up, asking, "Is this woman, this Carmen Fritchey, who signed the agreement in 1978, is this your secretary?"

She shrugged. "I'm assuming. Do you see the child's name?"

Tony looked over Zoe's shoulder, searching the paper. "Alfred," he said almost sadly.

Abigail nodded. "Poor Carmen. I suppose she married at one time and the boy took that man's name rather than her maiden name."

Abigail hunched her shoulders. "I wonder where my father's other victims are."

Penelope read another one of the contracts. "These things stink," she said, "Wish I'd represented one of these kids."

"He didn't take responsibility for anything." Tony shook his head and set the paper he'd been reading back into the box.

"He gave them each . . . what is it?" Abigail took the paper back. "A hundred thousand dollars to never ask for more, to never claim paternity, and to keep his name a secret from the children." Abigail sat quietly for a minute. "I was the one who told Carmen about the box. I trusted her." Abigail's voice caught in her throat. "I had no other friends.

"That must be when she contacted Alfred," she went on. "She knew the agreement had to be in that box. I remember her face when I told her how much he enjoyed reading those plain papers. He took pleasure in knowing he'd beaten the women. I thought her shock was at what he did to me. It wasn't."

"Alfred needed to find the box," Penelope said. "If he could destroy the agreement, he could claim an equal share of the money. DNA would prove his lineage. Carmen would testify for him. Maybe she even had letters from Joshua. If everybody else was dead, he'd get it all."

"Poor Carmen." Abigail's face was pained. "All she found was that her son was just like his father. She'd started a maelstrom she couldn't control."

There was silence until Zoe said, "Why'd Alfred blame me? I didn't even know him." She searched the faces around her.

"Because you were there," Jenny shrugged. "Maybe putting blame on you was Carmen's idea. She heard about you. An outsider."

"Or maybe just because you're odd, dear." Abigail patted Zoe on top of her head.

They remained still as Abigail fed the papers to the fire. No one spoke. It was too much to take in: the injustice, the cruelty—all beginning in this mausoleum.

In this house of ice.

Epilogue

June was hot and muggy the day of the grand opening. Eighty-five degrees in the morning. Threatening rain by party time. Dora worried that the paper tablecloths on the folding tables set up around the lawn would wilt in the dampness. Then she worried that the roses she'd picked and put into glass vases were spreading ants.

"They're beautiful." Jenny came up from behind her mother to hug her. "Everything okay?" Jenny asked, leaning around to check her mother's face. "I mean, are you all right?"

Dora nodded, though her eyes were still sad. "I'm doing what Jim would have wanted, don't you think? No retribution. No terrible secrets." Dora looked down into the roses. "Too many people are hurt, Jenny. Gerry's at a rehab place. That was all I asked for. He was drunk the night he hit Jim's car."

"What about Johnny?" Jenny asked.

Dora shrugged. "Community service will be enough. I hope Angel helps him after that. Alcohol seems to be the Arlens' sad drug of choice. He'll need her, and she loves him."

Jenny nodded.

"And if you think about it, Johnny was hurt the most of anyone. Except maybe you."

"And you."

Jenny didn't want to think about who got hurt the most. It seemed so long ago. Maybe only Fate, after all. Johnny didn't turn out to be who he was meant to be. But neither did she.

"What's going to happen to Minnie's daughter?" she asked.

"Deanna?" Dora rolled her eyes and hooted. "Minnie's taking care of that. Deanna's helping Minnie in the kitchen here today, whether she likes it or not. That's just the beginning. I have a feeling Deanna's going to get used to a lot of things foreign to her—like work."

Since Dora was doing fine, Jenny looked around the lawn to see where she was needed. She waved to Lisa, visiting to celebrate with her family.

Dora called after her. "Angel and her girls are coming. She wants to volunteer with the library, wants her girls to get to know books better than she ever did. I said that would be fine. You don't mind, do you?"

How could she? Jenny shook her head. She didn't mind anything right then.

Lisa wandered over to direct Dora out to the crates of books in front, the stacks growing as people dropped off more boxes for the new libraries.

"Why don't you go restore order out there?" Lisa hugged their mother. "That pile is going to fall and kill somebody."

"You're right. I should. I'll get one of the deputies to help."

"And don't accept any more copies of *Alice in Wonderland* if you can help it. It's Zoe and that mouth of hers. We're swamped with fairy tales," Lisa called after her.

Jenny followed Lisa to the cake table where Lisa set out the bookmarks she'd brought with her from Montana. She fanned the bookmarks, emblazoned with the name of her documentary, next to a memory book where people could sign their names and leave comments for Dora to look back on in later years.

Zoe laid out plastic silverware, paper coffee cups, and plain white paper plates for the celebratory cake and coffee. The paper plates and cups were Jenny's choice—always practical. The multicolor cake with fireworks shooting out at the corners was Zoe's contribution. It was a cake Jenny had taken exception to—preferring a simple cake, in good taste—which had started a contretemps until Dora judiciously decided that Zoe's cake on Jenny's plain paper plates was the perfect pairing.

Through all this, Fida hid under the table, paws over her head.

Zoe, on her stool and bored with guarding her cake, sang out to Jenny when she next came around, "The trap is sprung. / The killers hung. / There's nothing more to say on that particular subject."

"What subject?"

"The subject of Carmen Volker and her son."

"They're not hung."

"No, but they are hoist on their own gun."

"Meaning?"

"Ed Warner, who, by the way, is my new best friend, stopped by to tell me the gun Tony took from Alfred is the gun that killed Aaron Cane."

Zoe beamed with her news.

"So what's this big secret I've heard hinted at?" Zoe went on, narrowing her eyes. "Everybody's buzzing about it but me. I'm a bee without a buzzer. Will it make someone happy or disturbed, do you think? And more important than anything else I can think to ask, is the secret something wonderful for me?"

"What's your nose tell you?"

Zoe frowned hard. "That you're a terrible person."

"Who told you about the secret?"

Zoe made a face. "If you tell me, I'll tell you."

Jenny stuck her tongue out. Zoe rolled her eyes in return.

"I'll leave you to guard your cake." Jenny moved away to find Ed, who, along with Johnny Arlen—starting his community service—unloaded brown folding chairs borrowed from Tannin's Funeral Home.

Johnny nodded when he noticed her. She nodded back but turned away. Too early yet to greet Johnny as anything but an unhappy memory.

She showed the chief where to set the chairs, rearranging some into circles for convivial groups, where book talk could replace gossip about murder and old tragedies.

She looked around for Tony. The last week had been so hectic, she'd hardly seen him. There was the party to get ready for. Then Lisa flew in and they had their beach days. Tony was swamped with carpentry jobs. Dora needed her—long nights rocking on the porch and talking about Jim Weston.

Jenny found Tony touching up the paint on the children's house and then signing his name with a flourish on the back. He pulled down the cloth to cover it.

"Whew! Bit of an ego," she teased, looking directly into his eyes.

Tony grinned. "I've earned it. You Westons sure caused me enough trouble."

They stood close, Tony cleaning his paintbrush and Jenny looking up and down Elderberry Street where Saturday mowing was in full swing.

"I missed you," he said so low she almost didn't hear it.

"Me too," she said back.

Tony checked his watch. "I better get moving if I'm going to get to the airport on time."

He climbed into his truck and was gone without another word.

While Jenny waved after Tony, Minnie Moon and Deanna, in a magenta stretch top and short shorts, strolled up the walk. They were there to take over whatever had to be done in the kitchen, though from the look on Deanna's face, this wasn't a party she looked forward to.

* * *

Penelope's Porsche pulled in soon afterward, followed by a bakery truck. There were loud words between the baker— supervising the delivery of his special Stack of Jam Tarts cake— and Penelope, who, it turned out, was donating the cake out of the kindness of her heart, though she'd already bruised the poor baker's ego.

The two continued to argue as four helpers rushed to get the cake from the truck and carry it to the waiting table. Penelope warned the baker that the cake better not tip and ruin the party, and the baker warned back, "Madam, you know nothing about baking."

Penelope, never to be outdone, looked down her nose, gave a queenly sniff, and declaimed, "And you, dear sir, know nothing of jurisprudence."

Then there was trouble at the cake table with Zoe up in arms over Penelope's intrusive, though kindly meant, cake. A war over cake space ensued.

* * *

Dora's friends drove in with boxes of plain, ceramic coffee cups, clucking and dismissing the thought of Jenny's paper cups.

Jenny let it all go. Nothing would spoil this perfect day. Penny and Zoe would work out their dispute, the coffee would soon be flowing, and the women would stay to clean up afterward, doing much to erase the perpetual scowl on Deanna Moon's face.

They would wash and repack their cups. People did that in Northern Michigan. They called it "looking out for each other."

Later, at the ceremony, there would be a short speech from Dora, thanking everyone for their donations and all their good wishes. Then would come a *very* short speech from Tony, who'd fought saying anything at all until Abigail, in charge of the programming, hinted that if their plan to spread Little Libraries across all of Michigan came about, as they hoped, he would be very busy making houses of all sorts. Little ones, but houses nonetheless. New business was, after all, new business.

Tony had written his speech about the design and the execution of miniaturization and made Jenny listen to it over and over until she balked and refused to listen one more time.

After the speeches would come the grand unveiling, then bookmarks, a mass checking-out of books, and finally the casseroles everyone had dropped off, followed by the cakes and coffee and plenty of genteel discussion of the higher (and lower) forms of literature.

Jenny greeted the people who gathered early. She checked her watch. Four thirty.

Tony was due back any minute. She was nervous. Maybe she'd had no right to invite their guest. Maybe she was wrong about Christopher Morley's feelings toward Zoe. All her life, she'd avoided interfering, until these last weeks, when she'd interfered in every life around her.

The clouds rolled off to the east precisely at five o'clock, when the party officially began. The sun came out. The humidity fell. The day turned late-June-in-Michigan perfect.

Neighbors greeted each other, twittered over the new libraries, and looked over the books, laughing as they made their choices and argued the merits of an Elizabeth George over a Louise Penny.

Jenny stayed away from the cake table, watched over fiercely by both Penelope and Zoe, with Fida barking at Penelope from time to time.

Abigail arrived and explained the sign-out sheets to Vera Owen.

A strange woman in a green hat with a feather on it clutched a stack of books to her chest.

Priscilla Manus waved her history of Bear Falls in Cassandra Hatch's face.

Angel sat in the shade of a pine tree with her new baby. Her married daughter, Margo, breastfed her own baby while sitting on the ground, skirt up, top down, bare legs crossed in front of her on the grass.

Tony was back at five minutes after five. He pulled to the curb, turned off the motor, and hopped out. From the passenger's side, the stately gentleman pushed his door open, unfolded himself from the front seat, and slid to the pavement.

"Is that Christopher?" Zoe's voice went into her highest register as she ran up beside Jenny. "You invited Christopher? How did you ever know?"

"Know what? I thought it would be nice to have him back when you weren't in jail."

"And he's cancelled all his other plans and asked to be my escort to the award ceremony in New York. I truly think the man is smitten." Zoe's eyes were huge. "You've made magic, Jenny. Truly magic. I didn't think you had it in you."

Lisa was back, fuming behind them. "Minnie Moon's driving me crazy in the kitchen. Mom's sitting by the curb, reading a book she can't put down. How do you people ever get a party together?"

"'Patience, young grasshopper.'" Jenny said.

"Show off," Zoe huffed as the tall, thin man coming toward her stopped to squint down at his watch, shake it, then put his wrist to his ear.

"If you know so much about Alice," Zoe muttered toward Jenny while keeping her eyes on Christopher, "then tell me, 'Why is a raven like a writing desk?'"

"'I haven't the slightest idea, said the Hatter,'" Jenny shot back, smiling at her new best friend. She and Lisa leaned against each other, laughing at Zoe's outraged face.

"No! No! No! The answer is 'Because neither of them is *me*.'" Zoe smirked at the women, satisfied with herself.

"That's not fair." Jenny put fists at her waist. "You made that up. That was an unanswerable riddle."

"Says you, Jenny Weston. Says you."

In front of them, the two men put out their arms. Christopher, bent in half, got a hug from Zoe and a nip at his ankle from Fida. Jenny was soundly kissed by Tony.

Behind them, Minnie cried out, "Food's on!"

Dora instructed people to stand in a straight line to get their books.

Their neighbor, Warren Schuler, dressed in a clean, red-heart T-shirt, slugged down the beer he'd brought with him.

Penelope and Zoe pushed plates of their cake at people until Abigail cried out imperially that there would be no more food until after the speeches.

The new Little Library was open for business.